PRAISE FOR LISA GRAY

"Lisa Gray explodes onto the literary stage with this taut, edge-of-the-seat thriller, and her headstrong protagonist Jessica Shaw, reminiscent of Lee Child's Jack Reacher, delivers a serious punch."
—Robert Dugoni, *New York Times* bestselling author

"Mazey Los Angeles noir for fans of Sara Gran. I'm liking it a lot."
—Ian Rankin, bestselling author of the Inspector Rebus series

"*Thin Air* is an exciting whodunit that kept me guessing until the end. PI Jessica Shaw is so capable and strong, I couldn't get enough of her!"
—T. R. Ragan, bestselling author of the Lizzy Gardner series

"One of this year's best new thrillers . . ."
—*Evening Standard*

"You'll find this one hard to put down."
—*Daily Record*

"The very best sort of detective fiction: gritty, real, and gripping with a brilliantly realized main character."
—Cass Green, *Sunday Times* bestselling author

"A fast-paced, perfectly plotted killer of a thriller with a fantastic female lead and a cracking premise."
—Susi Holliday, author of *Substitute*

W9-CLA-506

"Gray writes with the confidence and appeal of Peter James and Lee Child. A blistering novel, deftly told."

—John Marrs, bestselling author of *The One*

"*Thin Air* is an assured and fast-paced debut with a compelling central character and plenty of twists to keep you guessing until the very end."

—Victoria Selman, author of *Blood for Blood*

"Lisa Gray weaves a clever and stunning tale like no other, a twisted and breathtaking thriller that I raced through in one sitting. You will too."

—Gregg Olsen, bestselling author of *If You Tell*

"Smart, sassy, and adrenaline-fueled, this kick-ass debut is a must-read for thriller fans."

—Steph Broadribb, author of *Death in the Sunshine*

"A deftly plotted slice of modern noir with a tough and likeable heroine . . . a proper thrill ride."

—*Best* magazine

THE
DARK
ROOM

ALSO BY LISA GRAY

THE

DARK

ROOM

LISA GRAY

THOMAS & MERCER

This is a work of fiction. Names, characters, organizations, places, events, and incidents are either products of the author's imagination or are used fictitiously. Any resemblance to actual persons, living or dead, or actual events is purely coincidental.

Text copyright © 2022 by Lisa Gray
All rights reserved.

No part of this book may be reproduced, or stored in a retrieval system, or transmitted in any form or by any means, electronic, mechanical, photocopying, recording, or otherwise, without express written permission of the publisher.

Published by Thomas & Mercer, Seattle

www.apub.com

Amazon, the Amazon logo, and Thomas & Mercer are trademarks of Amazon.com, Inc., or its affiliates.

ISBN-13: 9781542035354
ISBN-10: 154203535X

Cover design by Dominic Forbes

Printed in the United States of America

For Lorraine—best friends forever

1

LEONARD

They say you never forget your first, and that was definitely true for Leonard Blaylock.

Angela had brassy blond hair, blue eyes, and a wide smile that showed off the gap between her two front teeth. She wasn't a knockout in anyone's book, but she knocked the breath clean out of Leonard the first time he laid eyes on her.

She was wearing a white dress that complemented her deep summer tan, and there was a burst of freckles on each shoulder where the skin had been burned by the sun. She was holding a glass of white wine, and she had a tattoo on the inside of her wrist that looked like a swallow.

Leonard liked to think that it represented her love of travel, that it showed she was a free spirit. But it was so faded and blurred by the passage of time that it could have been Elvis for all he knew. He guessed her to be in her midthirties.

Later, he'd taped her photograph to his bedroom wall, smack-dab in the middle, so he had a perfect view of her as he lay in bed. He'd lost count of the number of times he'd stared at that picture since, wondering what she'd been thinking at the exact moment the shutter went off. Was she happy? Or was the gap-toothed smile only on display long enough for the click of the button?

The camera never lied, but it rarely told the truth either.

He'd committed every line and every curve to memory, but in technical terms, it wasn't a very good shot. The composition was poor, the focus wasn't sharp enough, and the flash had bounced off a shiny surface in the background, resulting in a yellow blob directly above Angela's head. It looked like a halo.

Angel Angela.

That's why he'd given her the name.

Angela wasn't her real name, of course. Or maybe it was. Leonard had no way of knowing. She wasn't his first kiss or first lay or first love. She was a complete stranger. Just as the fifty-eight other people whose images were taped to his wall were complete strangers. But she was the first, and that made her special.

Leonard Blaylock wasn't a photographer. He never took any of the photos in his collection himself.

He was a memory collector, a rescuer of lost moments. At least, that's how he'd described the mystery-film enthusiasts—those who got a kick out of buying and developing other peoples' old, discarded, and forgotten camera film—in a newspaper feature he'd written a couple of years back.

A bunch of loons was how Leonard had initially thought of them when he'd first been commissioned to write the piece for a Sunday paper.

He couldn't, for the life of him, understand the appeal. He didn't have many friends left by then, not since the night his life had gone to shit, and they'd gradually melted away one by one. But he remembered all too well being subjected to their vacation photos or pictures of their kids back in the day. Smiling politely and pretending to be interested. That was bad enough. To actually seek out and then spend money on old rolls of film belonging to people you didn't even know? That was just crazy.

Even so, Leonard had decided to give it a go himself. It would add a nice, personal touch to the article. Provide an easy intro. Maybe even result in some decent images they could print along with the words.

So he'd logged on to eBay and made an offer on two used rolls of Kodak Gold 35 mm film from a seller in Knoxville, Tennessee. Twenty-five bucks plus another $5.25 for the shipping that he'd claim back on expenses from the newspaper on top of his fee. What did he have to lose?

A week later, he'd found a bubble envelope with a Tennessee postmark on it stuffed inside his mailbox, and Leonard realized he was intrigued by what he might discover. Maybe even a little excited. That was the start of it.

He should have called in a favor from one of the photographers at the *New York Reporter* and gotten them to develop the film for him. Leonard had spent twenty years at the paper, working his way up from intern to senior crime reporter. He had been the guy who broke the stories, the one who could always be relied upon for a front-page splash.

But that was then. Everything had changed thanks to the events of a single night. There was Leonard's life before, and there was Leonard's life after.

After, he was a freelancer, working for himself, finding excuses not to leave his apartment most days, barely scraping together enough cash to pay the rent. He'd quickly dismissed the idea of contacting any of his former coworkers. Decided he'd be better off going old school and having the photographs developed the old-fashioned way.

Rookie mistake.

That first time he'd had mystery film developed was two and a half years ago, but Leonard remembered the day like it was yesterday.

◆　◆　◆

The photo-printing place was a family-owned business that shared its premises with a dry cleaner's, which struck Leonard as an odd combination. Did their customers usually get a comforter or a suit cleaned while picking up the vacation pics, seeing as they were in there anyway? It was like those people who put slices of pineapple on their pizzas. They were both foodstuffs, but that didn't make it right. He dropped off the two film rolls and ordered the one-hour service. Then he went around the corner to a coffee shop where he was interviewing an actress from a daytime soap opera.

The interview dragged on forever. The only thing the actress loved more than herself was the opportunity to talk about herself. Her plumped-up lips moved and her hands gesticulated, and Leonard tried to nod in all the right places like he used to do with his buddies' boring photos. He couldn't focus on a single word she was saying. He didn't give a rat's ass about her exciting new storyline or that she would be appearing in an off-Broadway production later in the year. His head was full of what might be on those rolls of film.

Ninety minutes later—with two double-shot lattes churning in his gut—Leonard practically ran the three blocks to the store, pushing his way past passersby, nerves jangling from the caffeine and the anticipation. It was a pleasantly warm day, early summer, the temperature hovering around the low seventies. Blue skies and lots of flesh on show. By the time he reached the photo place, he was sweating like a criminal in a church.

Leonard finally understood, in that moment, the appeal of the mystery film. It was all about the gamble. The element of risk. The not knowing what the outcome would be but hoping for the best anyway. Like those people who religiously played the lottery twice a week, or the gamblers who kept the slot machines fed in the casinos, or the seniors who visited the bingo halls in Queens and Brooklyn on the weekend.

Anything could be on those rolls, and that was the thrill of it.

Leonard pushed open the door with eager anticipation, the electronic beep announcing his arrival as he stepped inside. He already had the ticket in his hand. Then he stopped dead, sneakers rooted to the carpet. He felt as if his heart had just stopped.

Anything could be on those rolls.

Why hadn't he thought of that before? Idiot. Half a dozen terrible possibilities crashed through his brain in quick succession, each one worse than the last. Nudie pics. Hardcore porn. Up-the-skirt shots. A long lens trained on a teenager's bedroom window. Oh God. Something awful happening to little kids.

The woman behind the counter, who had been all smiles earlier, frowned at him. Her lips were a thin pink line of disapproval. He glanced around anxiously, expecting a burly security guard to appear at any second. Did photo-stores-slash-dry-cleaners have security guards? Did they need them? They did if perverts and weirdos wanted their sick photos developed there.

Maybe the counter assistant had called the cops already. Maybe they were on their way while Leonard stood there giving the statues in Central Park a run for their money. He considered turning around and getting the hell out of there, but he'd paid by credit card, hadn't he? It wouldn't take the NYPD's finest too long to track him down. What if he was arrested? What if they fingerprinted him? Once they had his prints, he was finished. Life over. They would find a match in their system, and they would know what he had done.

Then the woman asked, "Are you okay, hon?" And Leonard realized, with a flood of relief, that the frown and the grim expression were out of concern, rather than disgust.

He mumbled something about the warm weather making him feel woozy for a moment before thrusting the ticket at her. He shoved his quarry into his backpack, next to his notepad and voice recorder. One of the envelopes was depressingly thin, the other enticingly thick. As he made his way toward the nearest subway station, Leonard told himself he'd wait until he got back to the apartment before looking at the photographs. Just in case there was something bad on them.

The train car was stuffy and busy. The sweat from his back stuck his shirt to the plastic seat and made his skin itch. His beard was damp. As the train picked up speed, the distinct, dirty-warm smell of the subway became even more pungent in the humidity.

Leonard removed the envelopes from his bag, his fingers leaving damp marks on the glossy paper. He wouldn't look just yet. Best to wait. He tried to distract himself by reading the overhead ads for an energy drink and the perfect mattress and a new Don Winslow novel he'd already purchased. He idly wondered if he needed a new mattress. A handful of passengers disembarked at the next station. He heard the safety announcement and the doors sucking shut. The train was on the move again, accelerating fast through a tunnel, screeching and shaking. Leonard opened the fattest envelope.

The first three prints had been spoiled by the flash. The next was a photo of a tiled floor, the one after that a ceiling. Then two almost identical images of a glistening turquoise swimming pool, someone's foot resting on an outdoor chaise just in shot.

The eighth photo was the winning lottery ticket, the coins dropping into the slot machine's tray, a full row on the bingo card.

Blond hair, blue eyes, gap-toothed smile. White dress, white wine, swallow tattoo. Little yellow-blob halo.

Angel Angela.

Leonard stared at the photo for a long time. When he finally looked up, he realized he had missed his stop.

Leonard never did give Angela to the newspaper. He'd known immediately he would be keeping her for himself.

The other envelope had contained a half-dozen prints of someone's backyard. Downy woodpeckers and a small dog snoozing on a parched lawn. He'd scanned and emailed those along with his copy. Earned himself an extra fifty bucks for the photography.

Leonard had realized two things the day he first saw Angela. One: he was now completely hooked on the buzz of the mystery film. Two: he'd have to learn how to develop the film himself. The photo-store experience had been just a bit *too* adrenalized for his liking.

So, he'd turned his spare room into a dark room. Bought a red safelight, an enlarger, trays, printing easel, tongs, multigrade filters, resin-coated paper, developer, stop bath, and fixer. Watched a bunch of YouTube videos. Gradually added more images to his DIY gallery.

In the more than two years since Angela, his finds had ranged from complete garbage to pretty fascinating. The latter were the ones that made it onto the bedroom wall. There had never once been anything even close to illegal in what he'd picked up from eBay, estate sales, and flea markets.

Anything could be on those rolls.

Even so, Leonard knew he was wise to take precautions; that there was a chance he could come across a roll of film one day that contained something so damaging, so shocking and horrifying, that the police would be called, no doubt about it, if anyone other than Leonard was responsible for developing it.

Today was that day.

Leonard measured out the chemicals for each of the three trays, then placed a negative in the enlarger carrier and adjusted the height. He turned on the enlarger. Adjusted the aperture ring of the lens as the image was projected onto the baseboard. Even though he was looking at a negative, he could make out the shape of a woman lying on a bed. There was something dark on her clothing and the bedsheet.

Leonard's heart thudded hard. He licked dry lips. Wiped perspiration from his brow.

He went through the test-strip steps, then placed the exposed paper into the tray of developer. His hands trembled as he gently rocked the solution back and forth. Then, under the bordello glow of the safelight, the image gradually began to appear on the paper.

The woman's eyes were open but lifeless. It was clear that the stains on her clothing and the bedsheet were blood, even though the print was black and white. There was blood spatter on her face too. A knife was on the bed beside her. It had blood on it. There was a hell of a lot of blood in that room.

As he went to remove the print from the developer, Leonard's shaking hand knocked the flimsy plastic tray to the floor.

The woman was nothing like the fifty-nine portraits taped to his bedroom wall. For a start, she was dead. Not just dead. Murdered. She also wasn't a complete stranger. Leonard had known her. Had spent a night with her once, five years ago.

A different night from the one when this photograph of her murdered body was taken.

The night that ruined his life.

The night he thought he'd killed her.

2

LEONARD

FIVE YEARS AGO

"Don't look now, but the redhead at the bar is totally checking you out," Bobby Khan said.

Leonard turned around. "No, she's not. She's on her cell phone." He placed two draft beers onto the table and sat down.

"Jeez, Lenny. Did I not just tell you not to look?" Bobby took a sip of his Captain Lawrence and sucked foam off his top lip. "And she definitely was. Watching you the whole time you were waiting for the drinks, then all the way back to the table. I think she's into you, bud."

Leonard laughed. From the glimpse he'd gotten—and it wasn't much more than a glimpse—the woman was stunning. "Out of my league," he said. "Probably waiting for her boyfriend to show. In any case, I'm on my best behavior these days."

Bobby snorted. "If you say so."

They'd started off at the Long Acre Tavern for hamburgers and beers after their respective shifts at the *Reporter* finished. Like Leonard, Bobby worked at the news desk, covering the crime beat. Then they'd walked a few blocks south to Jimmy's Corner, a boxing-themed dive bar half a block east—and a million miles away—from the tourists and fizzing neon and animated billboards of Times Square. In a town that was constantly changing and evolving, there wasn't a whole lot that stayed the same. The timeless hole in the wall, with its fight posters and memorabilia and jukebox loaded with classics, was one of the few exceptions.

The bar was usually their last stop, but Caroline was away for the weekend, and Leonard was hoping he'd be able to convince Bobby to make a night of it. Maybe even head to a club later. He'd meant what he said about being on his best behavior. He'd only slipped once since popping the question to Caroline in the spring (okay, twice, but the second time was just a kiss, so it didn't really count). But now that he was on his fourth drink, he had a taste for it, as well as some coke in his back pocket if the night did look like it would be a late one.

"Still getting fan mail from your old pal, Walter Shankland?" Bobby asked, his voice raised over the jukebox tunes and chatter.

"It's the highlight of my day." Leonard rolled his eyes. "Apparently, I'm no longer just doing the devil's work, now I *am* the devil himself. At least the crazy ramblings he mails to me at the office aren't as bad as the creepy love letters he sends to the women he stalks."

"The joys of the crime beat." Bobby laughed.

"And don't even get me started on Remy Sullivan's nutso supporters."

"What're they up to now?"

"Just the usual online abuse," Leonard said. "Different day, same old crap."

"Block and ignore, my friend. Best thing to do."

Bobby's phone lit up on the table, and he groaned when he saw the name on the screen. "Ah, shit. It's Amina." He pointed to his ear and then the door, indicating he was heading outside to the street, where it was quieter, to take the call.

Leonard nodded as his heart sank. So much for making a night of it. He knew what was coming before Bobby even had the chance to swipe to answer. Bobby's wife had given birth to their first child seven months ago, and Leonard was surprised Amina hadn't already put a stop to her husband's occasional nights out. He took a big swallow of beer, then glanced casually over his shoulder and saw the redhead was staring straight at him. She smiled. She really was stunning. Leonard turned away.

Bobby returned and pulled on his coat. "Sorry, Lenny. The baby's teething, and Amina can't get him to settle. He's driving her nuts. I'd better head on home and help out, otherwise I'll be spending the next week sleeping on the sofa. And let me tell you, that sucker ain't comfortable."

Leonard forced a smile. "No worries, bud. Hope little Zain is okay."

"He's great when he's sleeping. The rest of the time, he's a pain in the ass." Bobby drained his glass. "You leaving too?"

"Nah," Leonard said. "The night is still young. Would be rude not to have another drink or two, what with Caroline being away."

Bobby grinned. "Nothing to do with the redhead, huh?" He slapped Leonard on the back. "Make the most of it while you still can, Lenny. Give it a couple of years, and you'll be the one with the sleepless nights and dirty diapers to deal with. In the meantime, enjoy. I'm not jealous at all, you lucky bastard."

Once Bobby was gone, Leonard was left alone with half a drink and a head full of thoughts. The truth was, he was jealous of Bobby. Despite the jokes and the fact that he looked exhausted most of the time, Bobby was crazy about Amina and the baby. Leonard wanted that for himself. A wife and kids and the kind of family life he'd never had growing up, after his mom had walked out on him and his dad not long after Leonard's tenth birthday.

He tapped the screen on his cell phone and saw that Caroline hadn't responded to any of his texts. She was staying at a luxury spa resort in Montauk with her mom and sister, scoping out the place as a potential venue for her bachelorette party ahead of the wedding next summer. It was supposed to be the maid of honor's job to plan the festivities, but Caroline had insisted on micromanaging everything as usual. She wanted something classy—spas and massages and fluffy bathrobes and matching slippers and expensive champagne. She didn't want to risk ending up on a tacky bar tour wearing a tiara, dancing on tables, and slamming back tequila shots until she threw up.

Leonard knew the Hamptons' biggest selling point was all the rich and famous folks who flocked there in the summer months. He was just glad she was only talking about the affluent seaside resort for the bachelorette party, rather than the wedding itself. Her dad was paying for most of it, but Leonard knew he'd be expected to cover part of the final bill, and as much as Caroline was special, she wasn't a celebrity.

Meanwhile, a tacky tequila-soaked bar tour—minus the tiara— sounded perfect for the bachelor party, but Leonard still hadn't decided whom to ask to be his best man. Either Bobby or Drew, his best friend from high school. But Drew lived in Seattle, and even though they spoke regularly via FaceTime, Leonard hadn't actually seen him in over a decade. He'd probably ask Bobby, but Bobby had sold him out more than once over a story, which reminded Leonard that they were coworkers first and foremost, and their friendship came second to a byline on the front page of the *Reporter*. In short, he liked Bobby a lot, but he didn't entirely trust him.

Leonard's thoughts were interrupted by someone hovering over him. It was the woman from the bar. She carefully placed a fresh beer in front of him. It was another Rolling Rock, like she knew his order.

"Mind if I join you?" She didn't wait for an answer. Just slipped into the seat Bobby had vacated and held Leonard's gaze. Sucked an orange-red cocktail through a tiny black straw.

He swallowed hard. "Um, sure. I guess."

"Don't worry, I'm not trying to hit on you." Her voice was low and sexy. "My friend has been held up at work, and the longer I sit at the bar on my own waiting for him, the more I look like a hooker scouting for business."

"Is he your boyfriend? This guy you're waiting for?"

Why was he asking? What did it even matter?

The woman arched an eyebrow. "He's not my boyfriend. He's a friend who just happens to be a boy. What's your name?"

"Leonard."

"Nice to meet you, Leonard. I'm Red."

"Red? So, it's like that, huh?"

She gave him a quizzical look. "Like what?"

"You don't want to tell me your real name?"

"All my friends call me Red, so why would you be any different?"

He shrugged with his mouth. "Fair enough."

She wasn't a natural redhead, but she wasn't trying to fool anyone into thinking that she was. Her hair was hibiscus red, and her lipstick was the same color. Even though it was November, she wore a short dress with bare legs that were longer than a ten-year stretch in Sing Sing. Black suede ankle boots and a leather biker jacket completed the look.

The title of one of Leonard's all-time favorite books popped into his head. *Devil in a Blue Dress*. Red's dress wasn't blue, it was red. But that's the image that sprung to mind all the same. The devil disguised as a gorgeous woman. Leonard trying to resist temptation.

Devil in a red dress.

The narrow room was starting to fill up. Every time the door opened, a chill wind and the smell of damp cigarettes from the street outside snuck into the warm bar. A ceiling fan whirred overhead. Colorful Christmas lights strung along framed posters illuminated the faces of Muhammad Ali, Floyd Mayweather, and Lew Jenkins. The lights cast Red in a flattering glow, not that she needed it. She leaned in closer to be heard over the music. "Whatcha See Is Whatcha Get" by the Dramatics played on the jukebox.

"What do you do for a living, Leonard?" Red asked.

"I'm a journalist."

"Sounds interesting. Have you ever interviewed anyone famous?"

"Not really. I mostly write about crime. Robberies, drugs, homicide. You know, all the fun stuff. What do you do?"

"I'm an actress and a model." Red finished the cocktail, then sighed. "But mostly I'm a bartender."

"A model, huh? Can't say I'm surprised. And an actress too? That's pretty cool." He thought it best not to dwell on the bar work. "What have you been in?"

Red mentioned some TV shows, and Leonard shrugged apologetically. He'd never heard of any of them.

She said, "I was also in an episode of *Rizzoli & Isles*."

Leonard was impressed. "Really? I love that show. What part did you play?"

"A corpse."

He laughed, then realized she was being serious.

"It's a lot harder than you'd think." She bristled. "Pretending to be dead takes a lot of skill."

He was worried he'd offended her. "I'm sure it does. Look, can I buy you another drink?"

Red pulled her cell phone from her purse and made a face. Her shoulders slumped. "Yeah, I guess so. My friend just messaged. He's not going to make it tonight."

Leonard said, "That's too bad." He didn't mean it.

"Yeah," she said sadly. "I'm only in town for a few days for some auditions. I'm so disappointed. I haven't seen him in months, and I was really looking forward to catching up."

"You don't live in Manhattan? Where are you from?"

"You ask a lot of questions."

Leonard grinned. "And you don't give much away, including your name." He stood up. "What're you having?"

"Negroni, thanks."

"I'll get us some shots too. Try to lift the mood, seeing as we've both been let down tonight."

Leonard made a detour to the men's room first. He used the urinal, washed his hands, and splashed cold water onto his face. What was he doing? He was thirty-seven years old and had a lovely young fiancée, who was far too good for him. Yet here he was, up to his old tricks again, buying drinks for another woman. Hoping to get lucky, while trying to convince himself that he wasn't. He dried his face and hands and trashed the paper towel. He guessed Red would be gone when he returned to the bar, that the table would be empty, and he could stop beating himself up about something that hadn't even happened.

He was wrong. She was still there. She caught him staring and smiled.

Leonard ordered the drinks. He decided to ditch the beer and join Red in a Negroni. They both drank quickly, and he bought another round. More cocktails and shots. By the time they moved outside a while later, he was intoxicated by the booze and by her.

It was raining hard. The street was crammed with folks with hoods up or huddling under umbrellas. Leonard and Red sheltered under the awning that stretched from the doorway to the edge of the sidewalk. She was shivering in her short dress and leather jacket. He held open his overcoat for her, and she quickly obliged, snuggling up against him, stealing his body heat. Their eyes met and then their lips did the same. She tasted like a sweet mix of Campari and tequila and lipstick. She was a great kisser.

When they finally pulled apart, Leonard spotted a hazy glow in the distance. He disentangled himself from Red and stepped off the curb, then whistled and stuck out his hand. The yellow taxi slowed and pulled up in front of them.

"You take this," Leonard said, moving back under the awning. "I can walk home from here."

She gave him a look that he couldn't interpret, then got into the cab. She left the door wide open. Leonard stood there, the rain battering the canvas above him, his heart thundering every bit as loudly in his ears.

The driver lowered his window. "You gettin' in or not?"

Leonard knew he should say no. Knew he should head off into the wet night, the downpour acting like a cold shower to douse his desire. He pulled his cell phone from his coat pocket. Still no response from Caroline.

"Hey, buddy," the driver shouted. "The engine's running and the meter will be too in a minute."

Leonard walked out into the rain and climbed into the taxi.

3
LEONARD

Two people lost their lives that night.

Leonard, in the sense that he stopped living and became a shell of the man he used to be.

Red, in the sense that, well, she stopped breathing. Ended up in a pool of blood, with her skull cracked open, and white foam drying on her lips.

Admittedly, she came out of it a whole lot worse than Leonard had. Or, at least, that's what he'd believed for a long time.

He had replayed the moment with the taxi in his head a million times. The scene playing out on a loop like an old 8 mm home movie.

What would his life look like now if he'd turned Red down and gone home alone like he should have done? If he'd let his brain—rather than his crotch—call the shots? Would he be married to Caroline, with a son or a daughter and a nice apartment on a nice street, still writing stories for the *Reporter*?

Leonard remembered when he was a teenager taking a girl to the movies to see *Sliding Doors*. It was their first date, and he'd been more interested in making out in the back row than what was happening on the big screen, but two things about that movie had stuck with him all these years. One: John Hannah's character was out of his league trying to hit on Gwyneth Paltrow. Two: the plot seemed to center around showing two different scenarios for Paltrow's character depending on whether she missed a train or caught it. The idea was that a seemingly inconsequential event could have a huge bearing on the rest of your life.

If someone had asked Leonard five years ago to name his own sliding-doors moment, he might have said applying for a newspaper internship straight out of high school instead of going to college. Or agreeing to have a drink with a young radio reporter by the name of Caroline Cooper after they got talking at a press conference. Or nervously producing a diamond ring from his pocket at the top of the Empire State Building and dropping down onto one knee while random tourists cheered and applauded.

Nope. None of those things.

It turned out the biggest sliding-doors moment in Leonard Blaylock's life was getting into a taxi with a stranger on a cold November night.

The photograph of Red had ended up on the dark room's linoleum floor, along with the developer tray and its contents. Leonard reached down and picked it up. The exposure and contrast were both off. Under normal circumstances, he would make the necessary adjustments and keep trying until he ended up with a perfect print. These were far from normal circumstances. Leonard placed the image into the stop bath tray, then the fixer. He washed it and hung it to dry, and then he left the room.

Dusk had stolen the last of the day while he'd been in there, and the rest of the apartment was almost as dark now. He went into the master bedroom and swapped the jeans that had been splashed with the spilled developer for a pair of gray sweatpants. Leonard had become one of those people who owned a lot of athletic wear despite never exercising. He padded down the dim hallway to the kitchen and flipped the wall switch. The fluorescent light hummed and buzzed before bursting into life, and Leonard blinked in the sudden glare. He wet a dishcloth under the cold faucet and returned to the dark room, where he mopped up the spill.

He didn't look at the print hanging on the clothesline.

Back in the kitchen, he threw the cloth into the trash and washed his hands. Then he pulled a tumbler from the cupboard and cracked the seal on a bottle of Laphroaig. Whenever Leonard restocked at the liquor store, he told himself he'd only buy the expensive Scotch to keep for special occasions. Then he remembered he didn't have special occasions anymore and still bought the bottle anyway.

He poured a generous measure and drank it down in two thirsty gulps, barely registering the burn. Leonard's dad would be horrified if he could see him now, downing a fine single malt like a can of soda instead of treating it with the respect it deserved. He refilled the glass, another double, and took it into the living room.

The only light came from the street outside. Shadows hid like monsters in the far corners of the large room. Leonard went over to the window. The sky was a navy-and-purple bruise. Quite a few of the lights were on in the building across the street, peeking through tree branches that had been stripped bare by stiff autumn winds. Every one of those yellow squares represented a person or a family inside, each with their own stories to tell and secrets to keep. In the days and weeks after Red, Leonard had stood at this exact spot and envied the people in those apartments and their normal, boring lives.

At first, he'd expected the cops to come knocking at his door. When that didn't happen, the fear was replaced by guilt that ate away at him, day by day. He saw Red everywhere he went—in the grocery store when he was buying bread and milk; on the street laughing with friends; drinking an orange-red cocktail in one of his favorite bars.

Leonard took a sip of whisky before drawing the curtains and turning on a lamp. Caroline had hated the view from the window, namely the fact that there wasn't much of a view at all. Just ugly apartment blocks, rusted fire escapes, and modest stores and eateries. Truth be told, she hadn't liked much else about Leonard's place either, despite spending so much time there and leaving her stuff everywhere.

His building was old and dreary and creepy, she'd moaned. The lobby smelled bad, and the stairs were dusty, and the paintwork was chipped and peeling.

Even so, Leonard had assumed she would move in with him once they were married. After all, he already had his own place, while she still lived with her folks. Caroline had assumed they would lease a modern condo with at least three bedrooms and a working elevator. When Leonard told her that his spare room was the perfect size for a nursery, she had responded, "There's not a chance in hell of me dragging a stroller up and down those fucking stairs if we have a baby."

He'd pointed out that his building had an elevator. She'd pointed out that it was out of service more often than it was working.

Their future living arrangements had still been unresolved when Caroline dumped him six months before the wedding. Less than a year later, she was married to a hotelier by the name of Harry Belman, an older man who had less hair than Leonard but a lot more money. Caroline had inherited a couple of step kids, as well as a potential fortune, but there was still no sign of a baby.

Leonard didn't expect a pregnancy announcement any time soon, not with the way her career was going. She didn't live in a modern condo either. Funny how old houses were absolutely fine as long as they were worth a few million.

Caroline may have disliked his apartment, but Leonard loved it. It was on the top floor of a six-story brownstone built in the 1920s, west of Midtown, on the edge of Hell's Kitchen. It had a ton of character if not a lot of class. And it had a central laundry room to boot.

He went over to the corner of the living room that doubled as his study. Sat down at his desk and tapped the keyboard of his iMac to bring the computer to life. He logged on to the Found Film forum and saw that WVR-16 was one of the users currently online.

Leonard opened a new private chat message:

To: WVR-16

From: LAB123

Subject: Help

Message: Something very strange has happened . . .

The cursor blinked on the screen. He didn't know what else to write, how to explain what was going on. He didn't even know WVR-16. He had never met her. Didn't know if she was even a she. Not that it mattered, not really, other than she'd led him to believe that she was a woman. It was a site for mystery-film enthusiasts to share and discuss their finds, not a dating app, but still. They'd started off commenting publicly on each other's photos, then started messaging each other privately.

They had established that they both lived in Manhattan, but as far as personal details went, that was it. They chatted about their love of mystery film, and their favorite TV shows, films, and books, and so on. But they never spoke about their jobs or family or even told each other their real names. Leonard's messages were signed "L," while hers were signed "MW." What he did know about WVR-16 was that she seemed warm and smart and funny, and she was the closest thing he had to a friend these days. He continued typing:

Something very strange has happened . . . You know that stall you told me about at Chelsea Flea? Well, I went last Saturday and picked up the camera rolls you said would be there. Something really bad was on one of those rolls. L.

He hit "Send" and waited for a response. MW had told him there would be some good stuff at the market after a contact of hers had done some house clearances. She was working all weekend and wouldn't be able to make it herself, so she had tipped off Leonard so they both wouldn't miss out. He could see she was typing a response.

WVR-16: Really?! Bad, how???

LAB123: I don't want to say online . . . That contact of yours . . . is he on the up and up?

WVR-16: 100 percent. No doubt about it. How bad is bad?

LAB123: As bad as it gets.

WVR-16: I take it sending me the photos is out of the question??

LAB123: Absolutely.

WVR-16: So, what do you suggest?

Leonard's heart was pounding hard. Real-life hookups were off limits on the forum. Even so, MW had hinted more than once in the past about them meeting in person. Or at least he thought she had. Now he was doubting himself. Maybe he had read her all wrong.

LAB123: Can we meet up to talk about it?

His message immediately showed as read. Then—nothing. Leonard thought he'd blown it, had crossed a line, *had* read the signals all wrong.

Shit.

He really needed her on board. He had no one else. He hadn't been in contact with Caroline since she dumped him, and he had ignored Bobby's invitations to meet for a drink since the night, not long after the breakup, when he had taken a bit too much pleasure in telling Leonard about the rumors that Caroline had slept with news anchor Jim Sanders to land a job as a TV reporter. She was now one of the main hosts on the morning show *Rise & Shine* after replacing Sanders himself earlier this year.

After what felt like forever, the ellipsis started bouncing, indicating WVR-16 was typing a reply to him.

WVR-16: Okay. When?

LAB123: Tomorrow?

WVR-16: I can do around nine a.m. for coffee before work?

Leonard was about to agree, then reconsidered.

LAB123: Can we make it afternoon or evening instead? I have some stuff to take care of in the morning.

WVR-16: How about five thirty p.m.? I should be finished with my last job by then.

LAB123: Works for me.

WVR-16: See you then. MW.

She suggested a restaurant that was close to his apartment. Leonard took that as a good sign.

He wondered if he'd just walked through another sliding door.

4

LEONARD

Leonard was up and dressed and out the door by nine thirty the next morning, which was unusual for him because he rarely got out of bed before noon. Not unless he had a morning interview or Zoom call with an editor, both of which he tried to avoid like a bad case of herpes.

Most nights he'd stay awake until the early hours, bingeing shows on Netflix, before crawling off to bed as dawn was lighting the sky outside and the birds started chirping. Leonard couldn't sleep when it was pitch-black and he was alone with only his thoughts in the darkness.

It was mid-October, the day clear and bright and cold. A gorgeous morning. Leaves of brown and yellow and red were scattered across sidewalks and the hoods of cars like nature's confetti. A chill wind nipped at his cheeks and turned his nose pink. It was Leonard's favorite time of year, but he couldn't remember the last time he had enjoyed a crisp, autumnal day quite so much.

For the first time in a long time, he felt like he had a purpose.

First, Leonard got a haircut and a professional shave. Then he picked out some new clothes—good stuff from the places he used to shop in—and bought some men's grooming products and a bottle of cologne. It was more expensive than he would have liked, but he told the sales assistant in Bloomingdale's to make the choice for him after feeling overwhelmed by all the scented card strips she was bombarding him with.

Once laden down with shopping bags, he stopped off for lunch at an Italian restaurant before returning home. He transcribed an interview for a feature, then started getting ready for the meeting with WVR-16.

After showering, Leonard carefully selected what to wear from his new haul, settling on a smart navy shirt, dark jeans, and white sneakers fresh from the box. Despite the long shower and the designer deodorant (Dior Sauvage to match the cologne), he could feel sweat pooling beneath his armpits. The palms of his hands were damp too.

He wasn't going on a blind date, but that's what it felt like. After all, the dynamics were the same, weren't they? Spend a bit of time chatting online, hit it off, agree to meet in person, then open yourself up to the naked scrutiny of a complete stranger. First impressions, judgment calls, rejection or acceptance—all within those first few crucial moments.

Leonard stared at his reflection. With the Robinson Crusoe hair and beard gone, he felt several pounds lighter and looked five years younger. Now that he had the new threads on, he was almost like the old Leonard Blaylock again. Okay, there was the hint of a beer belly and the once gym-honed muscles had long since gone soft and there were a few more laugh lines that had nothing to do with laughter. But he didn't look too bad. Not bad at all. He was no Brad Pitt, but he was no Danny DeVito either.

He'd treated himself to a new overcoat too. Splurged on a quality one by Hugo Boss. He wasn't looking forward to seeing his next credit card bill, that was for sure. The last good coat Leonard had owned was dumped along with the rest of the clothing he was wearing the night he met Red. He shrugged on the new one—wool and cashmere classic fit—and swung his backpack over his shoulder and left the apartment. He would arrive right on time.

The restaurant was tucked between Eighth and Ninth Avenues and styled after a French bistro. It had a small red brick frontage below an apartment block with discreet signage on the outside. Polished parquet flooring, mustard-yellow walls, classic artwork, and starched white tablecloths inside. It was reasonably busy considering it was too early for dinner and well past the lunch rush. A popular spot with the locals, Leonard had passed it a number of times but had never dined there.

He glanced around, searching for someone who could be MW, and quickly discounted those in pairs and small groups. There were three diners sitting on their own. A middle-aged man reading a newspaper and sipping a glass of red wine. A slim lady in her seventies with silver hair tied up in a loose bun and wearing a silk scarf. A younger brunette, closer to Leonard's age, who looked like the classic girl next door all grown up.

He hoped MW wasn't the old woman. He wasn't ageist or anything, he liked the elderly, and his dad was his favorite person in the world, but he worried she might have a heart attack on the spot if he showed her the photograph in his bag. Or call the police. She also had the disapproving look of his fifth-grade teacher whom he had been terrified of.

The smiling maître d' approached him, and he knew she was going to ask if he'd reserved a table and what name the reservation was under. He realized he didn't know the answer to those questions. He doubted "MW" or "WVR-16" would be on their list. Then, from the corner of his eye, he saw the dark-haired woman half rise from her seat and give him a small wave. He nodded in her direction.

"I'm meeting a friend," he told the maître d'. "She's already here."

"Excellent." She handed him a menu. "Someone will be over shortly to take your order."

Leonard nervously approached the brunette's table. "Uh, MW?" he asked, feeling like an idiot.

"That's me," she said cheerfully. "Although you should probably just call me Martha from now on. Martha Weaver. You must be the mysterious L."

"Yes, Leonard Blaylock."

"Finally, we meet. Park your butt, Leonard."

He did as he was told, choosing the seat facing her, carefully placing his new coat and backpack onto the chair next to him. There was an empty coffee cup and a plate containing the remnants of a dessert in front of her.

She followed his gaze. "Yeah, sorry about that. I got here early and decided to go ahead and order. Absolutely starving. Hope you don't mind. By the way, the crème caramel is to die for."

Leonard ordered a latte and the crème caramel, even though he didn't have much of a sweet tooth. He was worried Martha might be offended if he ignored her recommendation, and he didn't want to get off on the wrong foot. She asked for another cappuccino and another portion of the caramel flan.

"When in Rome, huh?" She smiled. "Or Paris. Or Manhattan pretending to be Paris."

He guessed Martha Weaver to be mid-to-late thirties, like Angel Angela was in her photo. That's where the similarities ended, though. Martha had fair skin, very shiny shoulder-length hair, and brown eyes that seemed sad even when she was smiling. She wore a floral-patterned dress and black knee-high boots. A leather jacket, just like the one Red had worn, was slung over the back of her chair.

"Do you live nearby?" Leonard asked.

28

"Not really. Why?"

"I assumed that's why you suggested meeting here. My apartment is just a few blocks away."

"Really? That's convenient. I'm way downtown, but I had a job nearby. That's why I picked this place. I came here straight from work."

"What is it you do? If it's okay to ask?"

"Sure it is. I take photos of babies in baskets."

"Excuse me? You do what?"

Martha laughed. It was a nice laugh. "I'm a photographer. I specialize in family portraits and photos of babies. Mostly, I work out of my studio on the Lower East Side, but sometimes I'll shoot at a client's home. You'd be surprised how popular the basket shoots are. Here, take a look."

She picked up an iPhone from the table, tapped the screen, did some swiping, and then passed it to Leonard. Sure enough, there was a tiny baby sleeping on a pink blanket in a wicker basket, with some matching pink flowers on a wooden floor.

"Very cute," Leonard said, handing the cell phone back.

"What do you do for a living?" Martha said. "If it's okay to ask?"

"I'm a journalist."

"Who for?"

"I used to work for the *Reporter*. These days I freelance, work for myself. I mostly write lifestyle features."

"Sounds like fun." Martha leaned in closer and opened her mouth as though she was going to say something else. She sniffed the air instead. "I gotta say, Leonard, you smell amazing."

"Um, thank you."

"Dior Sauvage?"

Leonard nodded.

"I thought so." She lowered her voice. "So, this photo. I've been dying to know, what does it show?"

Leonard glanced around, making sure their conversation wasn't being overheard. He took a deep breath. "A dead body."

Martha frowned. "Dead how?"

"Dead as in not living anymore."

"Yeah, I understand the general concept of being dead. What I meant was, what kind of dead body are we talking about here? An old Victorian autopsy pic? Someone in a coffin lying in state? What?"

"Nope, none of those." Leonard paused. "A young woman. A murder victim. It looks like she's been stabbed. The knife is on the bed next to her."

"Wow," Martha whispered, her eyes wide. "You mean like a snuff pic?"

Leonard shrugged. "I guess so. Although I don't really know what a snuff pic looks like."

Martha considered for a moment. "Or it could be a crime-scene photo that got mixed up with some regular rolls of film by mistake."

"Wouldn't that all be digital now? This photo was taken recently according to the expiration date on the carton the film came in."

"I don't know. Probably. Maybe the police photographer took the photo for his personal collection, and he prefers those to be analog. Maybe he's into weird shit like that."

"Maybe," Leonard said doubtfully.

"Were there any other photos on the roll?" Martha asked.

"Some, but they were all pretty much identical to the first one, like the photographer kept clicking the same shot over and over. I only printed one of them."

The waitress returned with their desserts and coffees, and Leonard and Martha jumped apart like two kids caught making naughty plans. They ate and drank for a few minutes, with Leonard agreeing that the crème caramel was, indeed, to die for.

Martha finished her own, then said, "Well, show me."

"What?" Leonard asked.

"The photograph. I'm assuming you brought it with you. Let me see it."

"Are you sure? It's . . . not good."

Martha stuck her hand out in a "give it here" gesture.

"Okay," Leonard said. "Don't say I didn't warn you."

He lifted the flap of his bag, pulled out a brown envelope, and slid it across the table toward her.

Martha said, "This is exciting. Like being in a spy movie." She slipped the print out. "Holy shit!" she yelled. Several diners turned to stare at them. Martha shoved the photo back into the envelope. "Are you sure this came from Chelsea Flea?"

"No, I'm not sure," Leonard admitted. "I don't keep a record of where my film comes from. But I think it was from the market stall. That was my most recent haul."

"You don't keep records? Why not?"

Leonard shrugged. "It's all about the final image for me. I don't care where the photos were taken or where they came from."

"Really? That's the most interesting part." Martha picked up her cell again. "I'll see what my brother has to say."

"What? Why would you tell your brother?"

She met his panicked look with a calm smile. "Because his stall was the one you may or may not have purchased that film from. Don't worry, I won't tell him about the you-know-what."

To be fair, Martha didn't mention the dead body. After a lot of "uh-huhs" and "okays," she ended the call.

"What did he say?" Leonard asked.

"Michael—that's my brother—has a buddy who works for an auction house," she explained. "They're often called in by the next of kin of someone who's died, to clear their property. The good stuff goes to auction on behalf of the family; the garbage goes to

31

the dump. Well, it's supposed to anyway. That's where Michael comes in. His friend often passes the leftovers on for a few dollars, and Michael sells the stuff in his stall at the market. Now for the bad news."

"Which is?" Leonard prompted.

"Like you, Michael doesn't keep records. It's all off the books. All he knows from his buddy is that the most recent house clearances were a rich widow on the Upper East Side and an old hoarder in Queens. Neither sounds like the type to have photos of a homicide victim, but who knows? People are strange. Either way, Michael says there's no way this friend would be willing to hand over their addresses. That's never been part of the deal."

"Okay. A dead end, then. So to speak."

"Sounds like it. What are you going to do about the photo?"

"I have no idea," he said. "What do you think?"

"I think you either go to the cops or forget about it."

"No cops," Leonard said a bit too quickly.

"So, forget about it. Destroy it. Pretend you never saw it. What's it to you anyway? It might not even be real."

Leonard frowned. "How do you mean?"

"It could be from a Halloween photo shoot, a still from a low-budget movie, a shot from a makeup artist's portfolio, or a million other different things."

Leonard didn't say anything, just dropped his eyes to the table.

"What is it?" Martha asked. "What aren't you telling me?"

Leonard still didn't know if he could trust her, but he didn't see that he had much choice. He had no one else to turn to.

"I knew the woman in the photo. Well, I didn't really *know* her. I met her once, spent an evening in her company."

Martha said, "Who was she?"

"A model and actress."

"Well, there you go—"

Leonard cut her off. "She died. Five years ago. And it was my fault. Or that's what I always believed." He tapped the brown envelope. "Until this turned up. When I first developed the photograph, I felt like throwing up. Now I'm wondering how the hell the same woman can be dead twice."

Martha stared at him. "Okay, I think you'd better tell me everything."

He nodded, then caught the waitress's eye and ordered a glass of Bordeaux supérieur. Martha declined the offer of wine and asked for some tap water instead. They sat in silence until the waitress returned with the drinks and left again.

"Dutch courage." Leonard smiled wryly. "Even though we're supposed to be in Paris."

He drank down half of the Bordeaux. Then he told Martha what he did that night.

5

LEONARD

FIVE YEARS AGO

Leonard made his move as soon as he was in the taxi.

There was no uncertainty this time, not now that he knew he was getting a lot more than a good-night kiss outside a bar. He had his tongue in Red's mouth and one hand tangled in her hair, while the other hand reached into his coat pocket to flick the switch on the side of his cell phone to silent.

Multitasking.

Just in case Caroline called or texted.

He wasn't even aware that the cab had stopped until the driver cleared his throat theatrically. The engine rumbled loudly. The windows were all steamed up. The driver stared at him expectantly. Leonard had no idea where they were. He handed over ten dollars and told the driver to keep the change.

Leonard and Red stumbled out onto the street. It was still raining. He was surprised to see they were outside a hotel. It was far from fancy, budget lodgings in a residential neighborhood, squeezed between a vacant lot and a laundromat. He'd assumed they would be heading to Red's place, then he remembered she didn't live in the city, was only visiting for the weekend.

He took her face in both hands and kissed her again. There was something very sexy about kissing someone in the rain. It reminded him of a scene from a movie he'd watched as a kid, when he'd been far too young for such steamy viewing: *9½ Weeks*.

"You are so hot," he said, and his voice sounded very loud in the silent street.

A flash of irritation crossed Red's face. It was replaced so quickly by a smile that he thought he'd imagined it. She put a finger to her lips and nodded in the direction of the hotel. Leonard could see a faint yellow light spilling through the window of the front door.

"The hotel doesn't allow its guests to have guests?" he stage-whispered.

"No, it doesn't."

"What are we going to do?" He glanced up at the windows. The dirty-yellow building was five stories high. "I'm not exactly Spider-Man, you know."

Red laughed. "Don't worry. My room is on the first floor, right next to the rear fire door. I'll go in through the front entrance and pick up my key from reception. You go down there." She pointed to a dark alleyway. "I'll meet you at the back of the building and let you in."

"Won't the fire door set off an alarm?" Leonard asked.

"Nah, it's always being propped open by staff and guests who want to smoke out back."

Red headed inside, while Leonard staggered off down the alleyway. It was pitch-black and stank of urine. He was soaked to the skin and starting to wonder if it was worth all the hassle and guilt for a one-night stand. He found a tiny fenced-off courtyard with a table and two chairs and a drenched umbrella, as well as access to the fire door that Red had mentioned. He decided if the gate to the courtyard was locked, he'd call it a night. Leonard pushed it, and it creaked open.

He hesitated, just for a second, then made his way to the fire door. All the windows at the back of the hotel were in darkness, including the first-floor room with its barred window. Leonard blinked rainwater out of his eyes and shivered. After a few minutes, he started to think that he had been played. That Red had gone upstairs to a different room, that she was watching from behind a curtain and having a good laugh at him, wondering how long he'd stand out there like a fool.

He was just about to turn and leave when a light went on in the room. Then the fire door opened, and Red peeked out from behind it. "Get your ass in here." She grinned. "Unless you want to stand out there in the rain all night."

Leonard didn't need to be asked twice.

Once in the room, he dumped his wet coat on an easy chair and kicked off his shoes. Red had already ditched her jacket and boots. He dived onto a firm bed and landed among too many cushions and pillows. He pulled her on top of him, his lips quickly finding hers, softly at first and then with more urgency. His hands explored the curves of her body, and his breath quickened. He was just reaching for the buckle on his belt when she climbed off him and tugged her dress back down.

"What's wrong?"

"Nothing." She flopped down onto her side next to him and tucked a strand of red hair behind her ear. "There's no rush is there? We've got all night."

"Have you changed your mind?" he asked softly.

"Nope. I just want to take a breath for a moment."

He raised his eyebrows at her. "Is that your way of telling me you've changed your mind about us, uh, you know . . . ?"

"Having sex?" She laughed. "Of course not. I just thought we could chill. Maybe talk awhile."

Seriously? Leonard was in a hotel room with one of the hottest women he'd ever met, and all she wanted to do was *talk*?

"Um, okay," he said. "You have a minibar, right? Why don't we have a drink? I'll have a whisky if there's any."

He figured some more booze might get them both in the mood again. Leonard's spirit wasn't the only thing beginning to deflate.

"The minibar is empty," Red said.

"What? You've drunk it all already?"

She slapped him lightly on the arm. "Don't be silly. It was empty when I checked in. I think it's a dry hotel."

Leonard frowned. "Didn't the sign out front say there was an on-site bar?"

"Maybe it's a dry room, then. A family room or something. And the hotel bar's shut already. Which is a shame as I guess I'm losing that nice little booze buzz from the bar."

Leonard thought of the coke in his jeans pocket. "Hey, if it's a buzz you're after, I can help with that."

"Oh yeah?"

He reached into his back pocket and produced the little plastic bag with a grin.

Red raised an eyebrow. "Coke? I didn't realize the eighties were making a comeback. Next you'll be confessing to a love of double denim and offering to make a mixtape for me."

Leonard laughed and held out the bag of white powder. "Ladies first."

She hesitated.

"What's wrong?" he asked.

"I guess I don't really do drugs. Except for that one time in college when I smoked weed and then threw up."

Leonard was incredulous. "You've never done coke before? Seriously, you don't know what you're missing. The rush is amazing."

"I don't know, Leonard . . ."

"Trust me, you'll love it." He reached over and stroked her arm. "And sex on coke is incredible."

Red still didn't look convinced. Then she smiled and said, "Okay, why the hell not, huh? But you go first. I insist."

Leonard took out a credit card and a twenty from his wallet. He rolled the bill and cut the coke into a couple of neat lines under the glow of the lamp on the bedside table next to him. He leaned down and hoovered up the powder.

"Do you want to come around this side?" he asked, as the drug hit his bloodstream. There was no lamp on the bedside table next to her, just a telephone, a notepad, and a pencil.

"No, I'll manage fine over here."

Leonard handed her the baggie, the rolled twenty, and the credit card. He admired the slim shape of her back and shoulders as she hunched over and sniffed loudly. When she turned to face him, she had a tiny smudge of white powder on the side of her nostril. He laughed, wiped it with his finger, and tried to put it in her mouth, but she pushed it into his own mouth instead. He rubbed his fingertip against his gums, then pulled her toward him. Red straddled him, then reached over and turned off the lamp.

Leonard's mouth sought out hers in the darkness. He felt her undo the buttons on his shirt, then grip his hair hard as she gently bit his bottom lip. He moaned softly as his hands slid under her dress. Her thighs were as smooth and soft as butter. His fingers pulled at the lace of her panties. He was very hard now. Then he felt her tense up.

"Wait," she said.

"Are you okay?" he whispered.

"I don't suppose you have anything else in that magic pocket of yours?" Her breath was hot against his ear.

"What? More coke?"

"No. You know . . . protection."

Shit.

Of course he didn't. Why would he? He was engaged; he was supposed to have stopped all the screwing around. Leonard thought of his visit to the men's room in the bar earlier. It hadn't even occurred to him to check if they had a condom machine because he hadn't seriously thought he'd stood a chance with the gorgeous redhead.

Shit.

"Sorry, I don't. Do you?"

Leonard was starting to think the only ride he was getting tonight was another taxi home.

"Yeah, I think so. In my toiletry bag. I'll go look."

Red jumped off the bed, stumbling into the bedside table, and let out a little yelp.

"Whoa, steady there," Leonard said. "Are you all right?"

"I'm fine. Just a rush of blood to the head." She made her way unsteadily to the bathroom and hit the light switch. Closed the door behind her.

Leonard lay on the bed, his heart pounding from the coke and the—so far—unfulfilled desire. He heard the sound of a zipper being undone. He hoped it was good news, that Red would emerge with a foil square in her hand. Maybe two if he was really lucky. He unbuckled his belt, then undid his jeans and slipped them off.

He heard something smash in the bathroom.

Leonard sat bolt upright. "Red?" he called. "Is everything okay in there?"

Silence.

He sat still and listened in the darkness for any sound of movement. He heard nothing other than the wind and rain outside and his pulse throbbing in his ears.

"Red?" More loudly this time.

Still no answer.

Leonard slid off the bed and padded over to the bathroom in his boxers, open shirt, and socks. He tried the handle. The door was unlocked. He pushed it open.

Oh fuck.

Red was lying on the floor. Her body was convulsing. White froth spewed from her mouth and dribbled down her chin. Her eyes were weird. There was shattered glass everywhere. Probably a tumbler for a toothbrush. There was a smudge of blood on the edge of the sink. More blood pooled beneath her head and was rapidly spreading over the white tiles. A condom wrapper lay next to her in the scarlet puddle.

Leonard took a step toward her, then realized he didn't have the first clue what to do to help her. He stepped back into the bedroom. He should call an ambulance. He glanced around desperately for his cell phone. Didn't see it. Remembered it was in his overcoat pocket. Then his eyes fell on the hotel telephone next to the bed. He should call 911 and then leave. Get the hell out of there. Let the paramedics deal with it.

He peered into the bathroom again. Red was completely still now. Her eyes were open, but they weren't seeing anything.

"Red?" he whispered. There was a loud roaring in his ears. White spots danced in front of his vision. *"Red!"*

She didn't answer him. Of course she didn't. Leonard could tell from looking at her that she was dead.

He staggered into the bedroom and collapsed onto the bed. He dropped his head into his hands. Tears ran down his face. His heart was racing so fast he thought he might go into cardiac arrest.

He took a few deep breaths between the sobs. Then gulped some more air until the dizziness passed, his heart rate slowed, and his head began to clear.

He thought about Caroline. He thought about his career. He thought about his dad and his apartment and all the other good stuff in his life. And he thought about the woman lying on the bathroom floor.

A complete stranger.

There was nothing he could do for her now.

Leonard got dressed quickly, left the hotel room, and slipped out the fire door into the night.

6
LEONARD

Martha sat in silence after Leonard had finished speaking. She couldn't even look him in the eye.

The restaurant chatter carried on around them. The espresso machine rumbled and sputtered. Plates and cutlery and glasses clinked. The silence between them stretched to the point of being unbearable.

"Just say it," Leonard said. "You think I'm a terrible person."

Martha sighed. "I don't think you're a terrible person. I think you were stupid and selfish, but that doesn't make you a terrible person."

He flinched at her words as though she were throwing punches instead.

She went on. "When I say you were stupid and selfish, I was talking about the cheating on your fiancée, not . . . what happened afterward."

Leonard blinked. "But surely that's the worst part?"

"No. It isn't. You panicked. You weren't thinking straight. Who could honestly say they would have reacted any differently in the same situation?" The corners of her mouth tugged down into a sad half-moon. "But the infidelity—that was intentional. When you went back to that hotel, you knew exactly what you were doing. You were thinking only of yourself and your own needs. It seems to me like you didn't give a whole lot of thought to . . . what was her name again?"

"Caroline."

"Yes, Caroline. That's really shit, Leonard."

"You're right. And the worst part is, I'm being selfish again now. I shouldn't be dumping all of this on you. We don't even know each other."

To his surprise, Martha leaned over and placed a hand gently on his own. "That's where you're wrong. We've only just met, but it feels like we've known each other for a long time. I don't feel like we're strangers at all."

Leonard said, "I feel exactly the same way."

Martha withdrew her hand from his, and he wished she'd put it back where it had been. He liked the way her skin felt against his own. Leonard thought she was lovely. And possibly a bit crazy too. Anyone else would have run a mile by now.

"Tell me what happened after you left the hotel," she said.

"I wandered around in the rain for a while. Tried to get my bearings and figure out where the hell I was. Turned out, I was in Chelsea someplace. I got a cab back to my apartment. I must have passed out straightaway. I woke around five a.m. in a blind panic. Talk about the worst hangover ever."

"Yeah, I can imagine."

Leonard finished his wine and continued. "I realized I'd left the rest of the coke and—even worse—my credit card behind in the hotel room. I canceled all my cards and told the bank my wallet had been stolen. I figured, worst-case scenario, if the cops did fingerprint the plastic bag, I could admit that, yes, I'd had a small

43

quantity of drugs in my wallet when it was stolen. But, no, I was nowhere near a hotel room in Chelsea.

"I put everything I'd been wearing into a duffel bag, left the apartment before sunrise, and weighted down the duffel bag with some rocks. Then I tossed it into the Hudson. When Caroline texted me later that morning, I told her it had been a quiet night with Bobby. When Bobby messaged to find out if I'd gotten lucky, I said I'd left the bar not long after he did and claimed I never even spoke to the redhead. I assumed the cops wouldn't go to the trouble of fingerprinting a hotel room for an OD. At that point, I'd convinced myself I'd gotten away with it."

Martha took a drink of water and nodded. "Then what happened?"

Leonard said, "The more I thought about it, the more I started to think it was only a matter of time before the cops *did* come calling. No way would they let the credit card go unchecked. Maybe they *would* fingerprint the room and discover I'd been there. Maybe they'd track down the taxi driver or a witness from the bar who would confirm we'd left together. My brain started working overtime.

"I'd assumed Red had had a bad reaction to the drugs and hit her head against the sink while seizing. But what if the police didn't think it was an accident? What if they thought someone had smashed her skull in on purpose? I had no way of knowing if it was the drugs or the head wound that had killed her. What if the cops were treating it as manslaughter or homicide?"

Martha didn't appear convinced. "I doubt they would have suspected foul play. Surely they would have treated it as a straightforward OD? Just another sad drug statistic to add to all the others."

Leonard shook his head. "I reported on crime in this city for two decades. I saw people sent down for a whole lot less. So, I read every press release and every story that dropped on the news wires for any mention of Red or a drug death in a Manhattan hotel. I avoided going to crime scenes and press conferences and briefings with the NYPD. I convinced myself the cops would see the guilt written all over my face, that they were trained for that kind of stuff. It ruined my life. I lost Caroline, and my job, and I almost lost my home."

Martha was quiet for a few moments. Finally, she said, "Did you check for a pulse or attempt CPR on Red?"

"I didn't touch her," Leonard said. "It was pretty obvious to me that she was dead. Except she wasn't, was she? That's why the cops didn't come for me, despite the credit card being left behind. There was no dead body. I have to say, it feels like the biggest weight has been lifted off my shoulders after five long years, now that I've seen that photograph."

Martha appeared troubled.

"What is it?"

"Shit, Leonard. I don't know how to say this . . ."

"Say what?"

"You said Red was an actress and a model."

"Uh-huh. And?"

Martha placed her hand on the brown envelope. "What if this photo really was from a movie or a photo shoot? And it was taken *before* the night you met her? Maybe she did die in that hotel bathroom after all?"

"No, I already thought of that," Leonard said. "You know how I mentioned the expiration date on the film roll carton? Well, that date isn't up yet. Not even close. Which tells me the photo was taken a lot more recently than five years ago." He eyed the envelope on the table between them. "Whatever was captured on that print definitely took place after the night I spent with her."

Martha's smile was filled with relief. "In that case, it's finally over, Leonard. You don't have to beat yourself up anymore. No more guilt. No more regrets. This is good news. No, it's *fantastic* news. Red clearly managed to get help, and she survived. You can move on now."

Leonard held her gaze. "But that's the thing, Martha. I can't move on because this was no accident. I don't think anything that happened that night was how it seemed."

"What do you mean?"

"Someone wanted me to believe Red died in that hotel room," Leonard said. "And they went to a hell of a lot of trouble to make sure that I did."

7
LEONARD

FIVE YEARS AGO

"Afternoon, Lenny," Bobby said. "Late night, was it?"

It was ten past ten. Leonard was more than an hour late for the second time this week, and it was only Wednesday.

"Zip it, Bobby," he snapped. "Nobody likes a smart-ass."

"It was a joke, bud." Then Bobby said more quietly, "You okay? Seriously, you don't look so good."

Leonard logged on to his computer and pulled up the news wires. "I'm fine. What's happening?"

"Superman down on Canal Street."

"What?"

"Jumped out of a third-story window. Either that or he was pushed. He's at the emergency room, and so are the cops. You want it?"

"Nah," Leonard said. "You take it. I've got stuff to do."

"Seriously? Stuff like what? This could be an attempted murder we're talking about, Lenny. A big story."

"Just stuff, okay? I'm sure you can handle the Canal Street job yourself."

"Whatever," Bobby muttered. He picked up his coat and his car keys and threw a copy of the *Reporter* onto Leonard's desk. "Today's paper if you're interested. Catch you later."

Leonard spent the next half hour scrolling through the news wires to see if there was anything about Red. It had been more than four full days and, so far, nothing. His head was pounding thanks to the half-pint of Scotch from the night before. He had quickly come to the realization that the only way to quiet his brain and get some sleep was to knock himself out with hard liquor. He found a bottle of painkillers in his drawer and made two trips to the water cooler before picking up the paper Bobby had left for him. He flipped through the pages.

There was a story about a lawyer being arrested for fraud. A teenager convicted of murder. A basketball star being abused on social media. Leonard came to the lifestyle features, then the TV listings, then the classified ads. He licked a finger and turned the page.

The obituaries.

There she was.

Smiling back at him.

The photograph was small and grainy, and it was black and white, so you couldn't tell what color hair she had, but it was definitely her. The same beautiful face. Those big eyes with the long lashes, the slim nose, and the perfectly straight white teeth. She looked shier in the picture than she had in the bar.

Red.

Except that wasn't her real name.

It was Erin.

Erin Groves.

The gabble of the newsroom melted away. The sounds of phones ringing, keyboards clattering, chatter, and laughter were replaced by the same roaring in his ears that he'd experienced in the hotel when he'd seen her still body on the bathroom floor.

GROVES—Erin

Passed away unexpectedly. A beloved daughter, sister, aunt, and a great friend to many. Private Mass of Christian Burial to be held at St. Sebastian's RC Church, Woodside, Queens. Friday, November 17, at 3pm. Interment, Calvary Cemetery. Family flowers only.

Leonard got up and made his way quickly to the restroom, almost knocking over one of the secretaries who was carrying two mugs of coffee.

"Hey, where's the fire?" she yelled after him.

He ignored her. Just made it into a stall and locked the door behind him before the contents of his stomach—namely, last night's whisky—ended up in the toilet bowl. The stench of the booze made him heave again, as if he'd taken a punch to the gut.

A beloved daughter, sister, aunt, and a great friend to many.

Red—no, *Erin Groves*—had been a real person, with a family who loved her, and now she was dead.

Once he was sure he was done throwing up, Leonard wiped his mouth with toilet paper, flushed, and pushed himself to his feet. He slid back the lock and opened the stall door.

The paper's editor, Frank Fincher, was standing there.

Fuck.

Fincher was in his sixties. Silver hair and mustache, nose purple and bulbous like a plum. He always wore his shirt sleeves rolled up, as though he was ready for hard work or a brawl. The red elastic suspenders holding up his trousers strained over his gut. Leonard had

49

been shit-scared of the man for the first ten years he'd worked at the *Reporter*, before gradually coming to realize that Frank Fincher was hard but fair. If you did the job well, you had no reason to fear him. If you fucked up, well, it wasn't unusual for a dressing down in the editor's office to be heard from the other side of the newsroom.

"You okay, son?" Fincher asked. The words suggested concern; the expression on his face didn't.

Leonard swallowed. He could taste the vomit in his mouth. His teeth were coated with it. He suddenly felt like an eighteen-year-old intern again.

"Yeah, I'm good, Frank."

"Here's the thing, Leonard. You don't look good. You look like shit, and it sounded to me like you were doing a good impression of that dame from *The Exorcist* in there."

Leonard nodded. "You're right, Frank. I'm not feeling too great."

"Have you been on a bender, son? Believe me, I'm no stranger to a drink or two myself, but you haven't had a single byline in the paper this week, and it's not like you. When the booze starts affecting your work, that's a problem."

"No, no, nothing like that. I think I might be coming down with something, that's all. Flu bug probably."

"Is that so?" Fincher stared at him with narrow watery eyes for what felt like a long time. Finally, he said, "In that case, you'd better head on home—and don't come back until you're feeling better. We don't want this 'bug' spreading around the newsroom, do we?"

"No, Frank, we don't. Thanks, Frank."

Fincher nodded, turned on his heel, and left.

Leonard wet a paper towel with cold water and dabbed his face and the back of his neck with it. He cupped a hand under the faucet and tried to rinse the taste of sick from his mouth.

A beloved daughter, sister, aunt, and a great friend to many.

What had he done?

◆ ◆ ◆

Leonard took Fincher's advice and stayed home for the rest of the week.

He spent most of Thursday lounging around the apartment, self-medicating with whisky, staring at the TV without actually watching it. He ignored calls and texts from Caroline and Bobby and his dad.

On Friday, Leonard dragged himself out of bed at lunchtime, showered, and gargled with lots of mouthwash. He picked out a dark suit, white shirt, slim black tie, and black dress shoes. He didn't have an overcoat anymore after dumping it into the river with the rest of the clothing he was wearing the previous Friday, so he would just have to endure the biting cold.

It was raining again. The day was dark and gray and somber. Perfect funeral weather. It was the middle of the afternoon, but it felt like late evening. Leonard made a dash for his old Chevy Malibu. As he turned the key in the ignition, he briefly worried about being over the limit after last night's drinking session. The clock on the dashboard read 2:05. He decided he was probably okay to drive. He had to be. A taxi was out of the question, and so was not going at all. He'd take it easy, avoid giving the cops any reason to stop him. A DUI was the last thing he needed.

The wipers were on full speed by the time he reached the Ed Koch Queensboro Bridge. Once across the East River, he took Queens Boulevard, then Roosevelt Avenue. He cruised along the main thoroughfare, under the IRT Flushing Line tracks, hearing the rumble of the 7 train above him. St. Sebastian's was a grand Romanesque revival building on the corner of Fifty-Eighth Street. Mourners were huddled outside, smoking and hugging.

Leonard wouldn't be joining them.

His funeral attire was out of respect for the deceased, not because he planned on attending the service. Jeans and a sweater hadn't seemed appropriate somehow, even though he had no intention of setting foot inside the church.

He parked in front of a pharmacy across the street and turned off the engine. The wind howled and buffeted the car, but the rain had eased. He got out and found a vacant bench in Sohncke Square, which provided a good view of the place of worship. His thin suit was no match for the elements, and he tucked his hands underneath his armpits and tried to stop his teeth from chattering.

Just before three p.m., the hearse arrived. The coffin was light wood with brass fixtures. Pink and white flowers spelled out her name:

ERIN

Leonard thought about how he'd held open his coat for her to keep her warm against the wind and rain. Now she was lying cold and dead inside a box. A woman who didn't do drugs, who didn't want to do drugs that night either. But Leonard had convinced her, and she was dead because of him. He had killed her.

The limo with Erin's family pulled up behind the hearse. An elderly couple in their seventies—both gray-haired and gray-faced—got out. The woman was slim and frail under her black coat and leaned against her husband for support. The man was practically holding her up. They were followed out of the car by a younger man and woman in their thirties, each holding a little blond girl by the hand.

Leonard's eyes began to sting, and he quickly returned to his car and got out of there as fast as he could without drawing attention to himself. He drove aimlessly, taking random lefts and rights, with no clue as to where he was going. He came across a Walgreens and found a space at the far end of the lot, under the overhanging branches of a large tree in a neighboring yard.

Finally, he let the tears fall. He felt as if his heart were breaking. The last time he'd cried this hard was the day his mom walked out on him. He punched the steering wheel and slapped his face and wished it was him inside that coffin instead of Erin Groves.

◆　◆　◆

Twelve months later, Leonard stood on a street in Chelsea, outside a modest nicotine-colored brick building with rusted fire escapes that was squeezed between a still vacant lot and a laundromat.

It was another wet and miserable day. A small bunch of pink and white flowers had been placed outside the hotel entrance. The petals and clear cellophane wrapping were speckled with raindrops. The ink on the card had run, but Leonard could still read what had been written:

Our beloved Erin. A year gone but never forgotten. Always in our hearts xx

8

LEONARD

"Holy shit, Leonard," Martha whispered. "Did you go back to the hotel on each anniversary? Were there flowers every time?"

"I've been back every year. There were only flowers left there on the first anniversary."

"Even so, that's crazy. Why would someone go to so much trouble to make you think they were dead?"

"That's what I've been asking myself since I developed that photograph last night," Leonard said. "I was awake most of the night thinking about it. Now I'm questioning everything that happened when I was with Red and everything that happened afterward. I really don't think her interest in me in the bar was down to my rugged good looks and boyish charm. I think she targeted me."

"Why, though?"

"That's the sixty-four-thousand-dollar question. The only thing I do know for sure is that Red and Erin Groves were not the same person."

"You checked?"

"Yup, last night. An online search for *Erin Groves* produced quite a few hits, but none of them were models and actresses, and none of them looked like Red."

"Where and when did Erin Groves's funeral service take place?"

Leonard told her. Martha picked up her cell phone and tapped at the screen for a few minutes. She shook her head. "Nope. Can't find anything online about the death of an Erin Groves around that time." She tapped some more, then glanced up at Leonard. "Bull's-eye."

"What? You found Erin Groves?"

"No, not Erin Groves," Martha said. "But I think I've found the woman whose funeral you attended."

She gave him the phone. On the screen was information about a service for a woman by the name of Erin Hayward. Three p.m. at St. Sebastian's in Queens. November 17. Five years ago. She had apparently been "a beloved daughter, sister, aunt, and a great friend to many." Two things were different from the obituary for Erin Groves in the *Reporter*: Erin Hayward hadn't "passed away unexpectedly." She had died peacefully at home. And her family had requested any donations be sent to the American Cancer Society.

There was a photo of Erin Hayward too. She was in her late twenties or early thirties, and she had curly brown hair, wore tortoiseshell glasses, and had an endearing crooked smile. She definitely wasn't Red.

Leonard returned the cell phone. He had sat in a Walgreens parking lot grieving—destroying himself—over a woman he'd never even met.

"But why use the name Erin Groves? Why not Erin Hayward?"

Martha said, "I'm guessing in case someone who knew Erin Hayward spotted the obit in the *Reporter* with another woman's photo and complained to the newspaper? They'd be less likely to pay attention to the fact that the funeral details were the exact same if someone else's name was in bold type next to it. Or maybe whoever placed the obit in the *Reporter* didn't want you searching for Erin Hayward online and discovering she wasn't Red?"

"That all makes sense."

"Are you sure you didn't know Red before that night?" Martha asked.

"I'm sure."

"Are you really, though?" she persisted. "Maybe you wrote a story that upset her? Or didn't call her after a drunken kiss? Or yelled at her during a road-rage incident? Maybe you just forgot that you knew her from someplace?"

"I didn't forget," Leonard said. "The photo you had a brief glimpse of? Her lying dead on a bed? It doesn't do her justice. Not even close. Believe me when I say, you don't forget someone like her."

"I guess some women just have that effect on men," Martha snapped. She took a long drink of water, then appeared to regain her composure. "Now we have to establish who Red is—*was*—and find out if she really is dead this time."

"How do we do that?"

"By studying your photo of her." Martha glanced around the restaurant. It was starting to fill up with the evening crowd who had just finished work. "But not here. Somewhere more private."

"We could go to my place?" Leonard suggested. "If you're comfortable with that?"

"Good idea. But first, I have a confession of my own to make. And I don't want you to freak out."

◆ ◆ ◆

Night spread over the city fast, like ink spilled on a page. Streetlights blinked on, one by one, as Leonard and Martha made their way to his apartment.

He thought about what she'd just told him. "So, are you some kind of stalker or something?"

Martha hugged herself for warmth. Her breath formed little clouds in front of her face. "Of course not. I already told you, it's about finding out who they are. Not trying to get to know them or contact them."

She had revealed the reason behind her own interest in mystery film before they'd left the restaurant. For Leonard, it was the not knowing what he would discover. For Martha, it was using what she referred to as "the clues" from the photos she developed to track down the people who were featured on the camera rolls.

She stopped in the middle of the street and gave him a hard stare. "You do realize that what I do is nowhere near as bad as running away from a dead body in a hotel room in the middle of the night, don't you?"

Leonard stared back at her. She smiled at him. He started laughing and Martha joined in. They continued walking and were still laughing when they stopped outside his building.

"This is where I live."

Martha gazed up at the brownstone. "I like it. Seems familiar somehow. Maybe I have some pictures of this block somewhere."

Leonard unlocked the communal entrance door and ushered her inside, out of the cold. He pulled the old wrought-iron elevator gate shut behind them with a creak and a clatter, and they rode in silence to the top floor. Once inside the apartment, they headed straight for the kitchen, where Leonard removed the photo of Red from his backpack and placed it on the small drop-leaf dining table in front of Martha.

"Are you hungry?" he asked.

"Starving."

"Do you like Italian?"

"Love it."

"Wine?"

"I'd better not. I have my car. I left it near the restaurant."

"You could get a taxi home? Collect your car tomorrow?"

Martha considered. "I'm not working tomorrow, so I suppose I could. It is the weekend after all. I think it's allowed."

Leonard uncorked one of his nicer bottles of red and poured a glass for each of them. While he started making spaghetti Bolognese, Martha studied the print.

"Are you really able to find out who people are based purely on what's in their photographs?" Leonard asked. He thought of his DIY gallery and didn't think there were a whole lot of clues in those images. "I have to say, it seems a little unlikely."

"Not always," Martha admitted. "In fact, mostly I don't. I've probably tracked down thirty or forty percent out of all the film I've developed. The origin of the film helps too. For example, if I buy rolls or an old camera from Chelsea Flea or Grand Bazaar, there's a good chance the person who once owned it is from Manhattan. If I buy the film on eBay, they'll most likely come from the state where the seller is based. That's why it's important to keep detailed records."

He wiped his hands on a dish towel and went over to where Martha was sitting. "And the photo of Red?"

"There isn't a whole lot to go on, but there is some information. She's dressed casually in jeans and a T-shirt so likely hadn't been out on a date or trying to hook up with someone like the night she met you. In the reflection in the mirror, you can see a short jacket hanging up, which suggests spring or late summer. Cool enough for a jacket but not cold enough for a coat. Then there's the biggest clue of all."

"Which is?"

Martha tapped the print. "A telephone on the bedside table."

"Why's that important?"

"Because it's not 1989, Leonard. How many people do you know who still have a landline?"

"A few."

"How many have a landline next to their bed?"

"None."

"Exactly. She's in a hotel room."

Leonard leaned over Martha's shoulder for a closer look. "You're right. It does look like a hotel room rather than a regular bedroom."

"Is it the same hotel where your liaison with Red took place?"

"It's hard to say for sure. Maybe. From what I remember, it was pretty much like every other hotel I'd ever been in. White sheets, threadbare carpet, basic wooden furniture. I remember there was an easy chair too. It might've been green. That's about it."

"There's no chair in this photo. Doesn't mean it's not the same room, though."

"Now what do we do?" he asked.

"Now we eat. Then we get on your computer and search for a young woman who was stabbed to death in a hotel room between April and September."

After they'd finished dinner, Martha insisted on helping with the washing up. Leonard refilled their glasses, and they went into the living room.

Martha gasped when she spotted his collection of vintage cameras lined up on a shelf. She went up close for a better look. His finds included a Leica M3 double stroke, a Univex Mercury II, and a Kodak Happy Times instant camera. She carefully lifted a Rollei Rolleiflex and let out a low whistle as she studied it.

"That's my favorite," Leonard said proudly.

"It's a beauty."

Martha returned the old camera to the shelf, then took a seat at the desk in front of the computer, while Leonard pulled up a chair from the kitchen next to her.

She opened Google and searched for *woman murder hotel stabbing*. There were dozens of results from all over the country. She added *Manhattan* to the search term and found a result on the first page that looked promising. A newspaper report with the headline Homicide investigation launched after model found stabbed to death in Manhattan hotel.

Martha clicked on the link. There, at the top of the page, was a color photo of a beautiful redhead. Leonard's breath caught in his throat. The shot was professional, as though it had been taken from a talent agency website or model portfolio.

"Is that her?" Martha asked.

"That's her," Leonard confirmed.

The article was dated a month ago. They both read in silence, as Martha slowly scrolled down the page.

> The death of a beautiful model, whose body was found in a Manhattan hotel, is being treated as a homicide.
>
> Anna Bianco was discovered by a staff member at the Fairview Hotel, Chelsea, Wednesday morning.
>
> It is believed the 34-year-old had been stabbed a number of times, and police are still searching for the murder weapon.
>
> An NYPD spokesperson said: "The death of a woman in Chelsea, who was discovered on

Wednesday, September 14th, is being treated as a homicide.

"She has now been formally identified as 34-year-old Anna Bianco from Corona, Queens."

Dozens of tributes were posted on Anna's social media pages after news of her tragic death emerged.

A former beauty queen as a teenager, Anna was a part-time model and actress who had had a number of small roles in movies and television shows.

"Shit," Leonard whispered. He rubbed his eyes and shook his head. "So, she's really dead this time. That's just so . . . fucking sad."

Martha said, "We also know her name—Anna Bianco. Murdered one month ago. Is it the same hotel?"

"Yes," Leonard said. "I couldn't have told you it was called the Fairview Hotel that night, but I found out a couple of days later when I went looking for the place. I wanted to know if the name of the hotel came up on the news wires in relation to a drug death. Although why it's called the Fairview Hotel is beyond me. There's nothing fair about the view at all. It faces an ugly old seventies office block."

Martha was serious despite his weak attempt at humor. "As well as Red's real identity, we also know something else for sure now."

"Which is what?"

"According to the newspaper report, the murder weapon is still missing, but it's right there in your print—so this isn't a crime-scene photo that somehow made its way into the wrong hands. It was taken by the killer."

"Shit. You're right."

"There are also three other things to consider."

"Which are?"

"One—you likely didn't end up with the roll of film by accident. Someone probably planted it. Two—you now have what is effectively a very dangerous snuff pic in your possession."

"And three?"

Martha held his gaze. "Someone could be setting you up all over again. But this time for murder."

9
JIM

ONE MONTH AGO

Jim Sanders was sitting on a stool at the kitchen island, eating breakfast and watching *Rise & Shine* on the small TV, when the story broke on the top-of-the-hour news bulletin.

The dead woman who had been found in a hotel a couple of days ago had been named as Anna Bianco. Her photo flashed on the screen, while the somber voice of Sal Speirs informed viewers that the death was being treated as a homicide. The investigation was being headed up by Detective Jackie Rossi, who would be holding a press conference later in the day. Jim had known Jackie for years. They'd even had a short-lived fling once, a long time ago, before they'd both married other people. She'd been a useful contact throughout his career and was also a very good cop.

He pushed the plate of bacon and scrambled eggs to one side. He'd lost his appetite.

Debra breezed into the kitchen, smelling like a perfume counter, her high heels clacking on the tiles. She grabbed the cup of coffee that Jim had just poured for her.

"You look nice," he said. "I mean, you always look nice, but even more so today."

His wife smiled at him over the rim of the cup. "Big presentation at work this morning." Debra was creative director at a PR agency, having gone over to what Jim not-so-jokingly referred to as "the dark side" after a long career in journalism. "And don't forget, I'm meeting Maddie for dinner after work, so you'll have to fend for yourself."

Their youngest daughter was a sophomore at Columbia University. Despite the family's spacious, five-bedroom townhouse on the Upper East Side being within easy commuting distance, Maddie had chosen to live on campus, which meant they hardly ever saw her these days.

"Nice of her to make time for her old mom," Jim said. "And don't worry about me, I know which drawer the takeout menus are kept in."

"Hey, less of the 'old.'" Debra finished her coffee, her eyes on the television screen that Jim had muted. "No Caroline this morning?"

He followed her gaze. *Rise & Shine* had three hosts, which used to be Jim, Sal, and Darnell Morgan. Now it was Sal, Darnell, and Caroline Cooper. Only Sal and Darnell were on the couch just now. Thankfully, they appeared to have moved on from the story about Anna Bianco.

"Sick, apparently."

"Oh, that's too bad." Debra looked at the half-eaten breakfast now congealing on his plate, then back at her husband. "You don't look too good yourself, actually. I hope there isn't a bug going around."

"I'm fine."

She shrugged. "Okay. Anything fun planned for today?"

He took a drink of coffee. "Nope."

"Jim . . ."

"Probably golf, then the community garden. You know, the usual. If I can handle the excitement, that is."

"Well, it *was* your idea to take early retirement. Try to enjoy it." Debra kissed him lightly so as not to smudge her lipstick. "See you tonight, sweetheart."

Once she was gone, Jim turned his attention back to the television. It was still muted. Sal and Darnell were silently laughing about something now. He felt the usual resentment swell inside him. He should still be on that couch, breaking the big stories, sharing a joke with his cohosts. He was only fifty-five. He was in the prime of his life. He'd looked after himself. He still had the looks and the charisma. Was still being voted one of New York's most popular TV personalities right up until his surprise departure from the morning show earlier in the year.

Now what did he have to look forward to? Endless rounds of golf and volunteering at a community garden like he was a fucking senior, that's what. Debra was wrong. Early retirement had not been Jim Sanders's idea. But he could hardly tell her that, could he?

He got up and scraped the leftover bacon and eggs into the trash and dumped the dirty dishes into the dishwasher. Then he picked up the remote control and switched off the TV just as they were showing Anna Bianco's photo again.

The golf course was less than an hour's drive away in the North Bronx.

It was a public course—the oldest in America—but Jim liked the fact that he didn't have to leave the city to get there. Sure, he was well-known enough, and rich enough, to afford membership somewhere more exclusive in Westchester, but he really wasn't serious enough about the game to commit to a three-hour-plus round trip every time he wanted to play, even if it did come with a country-club experience. Here, despite being located between two subway lines, the parklike setting meant it was actually pretty easy to forget he was in the Bronx.

Jim had been a member for years but had been an infrequent golfer. Most of his appearances in the past were as part of celebrity tournaments for some charity or other and with a media presence there to capture the all-important publicity shots. Since his retirement, his handicap had gone from eighteen to eight.

He entered the clubhouse and made his way straight to the Edwardian locker room. Unlocked his own dark-wood locker and opened it. He was just reaching inside when he heard a booming voice behind him.

"Jim! Didn't know you were booked for a round this morning."

Jim snatched his hand back and turned to find Fred McClure standing there looking ridiculous in a pink Ralph Lauren sweater and black-and-white plaid pants. His spikeless shoes were the reason Jim hadn't heard his approach. McClure had been a prominent defense attorney in his day, making his fortune courtesy of the city's busy criminal fraternity for almost forty years. He now apparently had too much time and money on his hands. If he wasn't on the course, he was on the clubhouse deck overlooking the lake, sinking beers and whisky chasers.

"I'm not playing today," Jim said. "I left my cell phone in my locker yesterday. Just picking it up."

"Can't do without those damn things, can we? How're the wife and kids?"

"All good."

Jim glanced in the direction of his open locker, hoping the old bastard would take the hint and leave. He didn't.

"How's your game at the moment?"

"Not too bad, Fred. Improving all the time."

"What're you playing off these days?"

Jim wanted to scream. He had to try very hard not to punch McClure's craggy, weather-beaten face. He knew the whole point of the conversation was so that he would ask McClure what *his* handicap was, which would undoubtedly be more impressive. Jim couldn't care less about McClure's handicap. He didn't even care about his own. Okay, he did a bit. But he had more important business to deal with this morning, and Fred McClure was preventing him from doing it.

"I'm playing off eight," he said.

McClure raised bushy, unkempt eyebrows. "Impressive." He smiled expectantly.

Jim refused to bite. "Anyway, Fred. Don't let me hold you back."

McClure's face fell. "Oh. Right. Yes, I don't want to miss my tee time."

Jim waited until he heard the door click shut behind the other man, then turned back to the locker. He pushed aside boxes of balls, tees, gloves, and spare shoes until his fingers brushed an envelope tucked in the back. He pulled it out, folded it in half, and stuffed it into the inside pocket of his sports jacket. Locked up, then made his way quickly through the clubhouse and back outside to where his car was parked.

The early-morning mist was beginning to lift, and the sun was trying its best to force its way through the clouds. It was dry and cool, and there was barely a breeze.

A good day for a bonfire, Jim thought.

◆ ◆ ◆

When Jim had first told Debra that he'd decided to volunteer at a community garden, she'd assumed he was joking. When she realized he was being serious, she was . . . confused. Her confusion was justified seeing as Jim had never shown the slightest bit of interest in gardening or growing vegetables before. Or volunteering for that matter.

When Jim pointed out that he needed some new activities to fill his time, now that he no longer had a job, Debra had been satisfied by the explanation. She had even encouraged him until he had shown up with a wooden box containing some tomatoes, cucumbers, and eggplants from the little private plot he'd been allocated. Then she'd broken the news gently that she would continue to buy the organic stuff from the farmers' market instead.

Jim had actually been quite proud of his first crop, although he couldn't really take much credit seeing as the planting had already been done by the old boy who'd previously tended the plot. All Jim had done, really, was pull the vegetables out of the ground. Even so, the thought of reinventing himself as a celebrity gardener—kind of like America's answer to the famous British horticulturalist Monty Don—had briefly crossed his mind, before he remembered it was best to stay out of the public eye these days.

The real reason for his interest in the community garden was that Jim needed a place to escape to where he could be alone with his thoughts. Away from Debra and his friends and the neighbors. A place to mull over the chain of events that had led to his exit from *Rise & Shine* and to quietly seethe and think on what he might do about it all one day.

The group who ran the garden liked the idea of having a celebrity in their midst, which would have been fine in the past, but kind of defeated the purpose of his quest for solitude. Jim had quickly realized the likes of Fred McClure had nothing on the green-thumbed busybody brigade—but he had also figured out the days and times when the place was most likely to be quiet. Like now.

It was mid-September and chilly enough to keep the older gardeners and growers away; the ones who wore woolly sweaters and heavy coats in the middle of summer and who were the worst gossips. Jim figured another reason the group were so keen to have him on board was to bring down the average age by at least a decade.

Today, there were only a few others on site. They waved as he made his way to his plot but, thankfully, were content to carry on with their work rather than stop for a chat and a cup of coffee.

The garden, as a whole, was easy on the eye. It was the reason why he'd picked this particular one, even though it was way downtown. There were no weeds or overgrown bushes. Everything was well tended and neat and tidy. There was even a small firepit for burning twigs and leaves and grass cuttings.

Jim quickly got a fire going with the kindling that was already in the pit. He stepped back as he felt the heat hit his face. Glanced around to make sure no one was paying him any attention. No one was. He pulled the envelope from his inside pocket and removed a dozen eight-by-ten black-and-white prints and a typed note.

He had kept both the photographs and the letter all these months because he had thought, one day, he might take them to the cops. Show them to Jackie Rossi if his circumstances changed. He knew now that wasn't going to happen.

Jim threw the photos and the sheet of paper into the firepit. Watched as the flames popped and cracked and licked and curled the edges until there was nothing left but dust.

Images of Jim Sanders and a mysterious redhead.

He thought of the news bulletin he'd watched earlier that morning. Now he had a name for the woman who had destroyed his life.

Her name was Anna Bianco.

10

LEONARD

"You don't seriously think someone is trying to frame me for murder?" Leonard asked in disbelief. "That's crazy."

"And making you believe you were responsible for the death of someone for several years isn't?" Martha countered.

"True. But to actually kill someone . . ."

"I agree, it's extreme. But I don't think we can rule anything out right now."

"So, what do we do?"

"We find out all we can about Anna Bianco," Martha said. "That's what we do."

She turned her attention back to the computer, fingers flying over the keyboard. A list of website links filled the screen, as well as several photos of the woman Leonard had known as Red. Some were clearly professional shots, others appeared to be from her Instagram feed. All of them were carefully posed, expertly edited, and had an air of unreality about them. It was as though she had been afraid to let the world see the real Anna Bianco.

"She really was beautiful," Martha said softly.

"Even more so in the flesh." Leonard touched the black-and-white print on the desk in front of them. "It's sad that this is how she ended up."

Martha nodded. "The last photo."

"Let's have a look at her IMDb page," Leonard said, referring to the popular database for information about movies and TV shows.

Martha side-eyed him. "Why? Do you want to make a note of her movies so you can watch a couple later on?"

"No, of course not. I suppose I want to know if everything she told me that night was a lie or if any of it was the truth. That's all."

Martha moved the mouse over the link and clicked on it.

There were some stills at the top of the page, followed by a filmography that was hardly extensive. Anna Bianco may have had the looks, but she was clearly never going to be in the same league as the likes of Scarlett Johansson, Anne Hathaway, and Sarah Jessica Parker when it came to being part of New York's acting elite.

Leonard recognized some of the TV shows from their conversation in the bar, including *Rizzoli & Isles*, where she had been credited as playing "dead woman." There were a couple of other more recent additions, indicating that Anna Bianco had continued to pursue her acting career while Leonard had been grieving for her.

Martha said, "Do you think you fell for her that night you spent together? Before it all went wrong, I mean."

"Honestly? I don't think I did. Yes, she was gorgeous, and I was flattered—but that was all. It was only ever going to be a one-night thing. I had no intention of seeing her again. Something about her just felt . . . off. Now I know why. She was playing a role with me, the same as she was playing a role in those TV shows."

Martha navigated back to the results page and scrolled farther down. There were a bunch of newspaper reports naming her as the dead woman in a Manhattan hotel, similar to the article they had already read. Then she stopped scrolling.

"This one looks interesting," she said.

It was a story on the *New York Reporter* website. It had been written by their senior crime reporter, Bobby Khan. The headline read:

> EXCLUSIVE! Honeytrap homicide—the secret life of hotel murder victim Anna

The copyeditor's use of punchy alliteration—*Honeytrap homicide*—was kind of tacky, but Leonard had to admit it was a great story by his old buddy, Bobby. Exactly the kind of exclusives he used to come up with himself.

Anna Bianco had been supplementing the income from her acting and modeling career by working as a "honey" for an unnamed private investigation agency. The report explained that private investigators were often hired by suspicious spouses or partners to create a "honeytrap" or "honeypot," to discover if their significant other was being unfaithful or was capable of infidelity. If they were tempted to stray as a result of the honeytrap, incriminating photographs, videos, and/or texts would then be delivered to the client.

The idea of snooping private eyes sounded like something straight out of seventies and eighties TV shows, but Leonard knew hiring people to spy on cheating partners was something that happened in normal towns and cities all across the country.

The NYPD were apparently investigating this new line of inquiry and were in the process of tracking down Anna Bianco's honeytrap victims, according to an unnamed source. Leonard guessed the source was Detective Jackie Rossi. For years, Rossi had been Leonard's main contact at the NYPD. Back then, they'd spoken regularly on the phone, even had drinks together on occasion. It seemed that Bobby had taken over Leonard's old contacts book as well as his job.

The article ended by stating that a thirty-eight-year-old man had been questioned by police but had later been released without charge.

Leonard watched Martha as she read, her brown eyes fixed on the words, the glare from the screen lighting up her face in the gloom of the living room. The tip of her tongue was just visible through slightly parted lips. She turned to face him, and Leonard managed to avert his gaze just in time, before she realized he had been staring at her.

"Do you think the thirty-eight-year-old man was one of Anna's honeytrap victims?" she asked.

Leonard shook his head. "Probably her husband or an ex-partner. They're usually the first people the police speak to in a homicide investigation."

"Of course, I should know that from all those true-crime shows I watch. It's usually someone close to the victim, isn't it?"

"Yup. Or the person who finds the body."

"Here's another question," Martha said. "Now that we know what Anna was doing to earn some extra cash, do you think someone paid her to set you up, as opposed to Anna doing it herself?"

Leonard didn't need to think it over. "I'm sure of it. Like I said before, I'd never met Anna Bianco. She had no reason to hold a grudge against me."

"If she was paid to honeytrap you, can we assume that it was your ex-fiancée, Caroline, who hired her?"

"Not necessarily."

Martha frowned. "But it says right here in this article that it's usually suspicious spouses or partners who pay private investigators to set up these honeytraps."

"But this was a lot more than a simple honeytrap, with some incriminating photographs of me with another woman. I suspect what Anna Bianco did to me was very unusual. Not to mention batshit crazy."

"Unless Caroline was *really* pissed?"

"It's possible, I guess."

"Tell me about Caroline."

"She's smart, attractive, and very ambitious. She's seven years younger than me. We met through work. She was a news reporter with a local radio station at the time, and I covered crime for the *Reporter*. She's a TV host now and married to a rich, old guy."

"Wait, your ex is Caroline Cooper? From *Rise & Shine*?"

"The very same."

While Leonard's life was falling apart, Caroline's rise had been quite spectacular. Soon after their split, she'd landed a job with one of the big networks—either with or without Jim Sanders's help—and had been an instant hit with viewers as their entertainment reporter, hanging out with A-listers and becoming a social media star herself.

Earlier this year, she'd replaced Sanders on the couch at *Rise & Shine*. There had even been speculation that she was being lined up to appear on a popular celebrity reality TV show, although Leonard suspected those stories had been fabricated by Caroline's agent to garner even more interest in her. In fact, he wouldn't be surprised if the agent was the one who'd started the rumors about Caroline sleeping with Sanders. The only thing worse than people talking about you was no one talking about you.

Leonard never watched Caroline on TV—he was rarely awake that early for one thing—but he did occasionally check out her Twitter and Instagram feeds and then hate himself for it.

He had expected Martha to be impressed by who his glamorous ex-fiancée was. She didn't look impressed. She looked horrified.

"What's wrong?" he asked.

"I just didn't think she would be your type."

Was Martha *jealous*?

He smiled. "Pretty with blond hair and blue eyes, you mean?"

"No. Silly and ditzy and vacuous."

"Believe me, Caroline is none of those things. She may come across as bubbly and fun on TV, but she's sharp as a razor and very ruthless." Leonard drained his wineglass. "More wine?"

Martha's own glass was almost empty. "Sure," she said miserably.

He went into the kitchen and emptied what was left of the bottle into their glasses. He felt quite light-headed from the booze and the strangeness of having a woman in his home again. When he returned to the living room, Martha had moved over to the couch. She had taken off her boots and was sitting with her legs tucked beneath her. Leonard sat down next to her.

"So, who else is on our suspect list?" she asked, clearly keen to move on from the subject of Caroline.

Leonard laughed. "You make it sound like there were a whole bunch of people out to get me."

"Well, someone was. What about Bobby Khan?"

Leonard almost choked on his Châteauneuf-du-Pape. "Bobby? Seriously? He's one of my best buddies. Or at least he was back then."

"He also conveniently left you alone in the bar that night after pointing out Anna Bianco to you. He knew Caroline was away for the weekend, and to be blunt about it, he knew you'd be tempted by a pretty face."

Leonard didn't say anything. It was all true.

Martha drank some wine, then said, "Was Anna already at the bar when you both arrived?"

"I think so."

"Did you and Bobby plan in advance which bars you would visit?"

"Not exactly—but we pretty much always went to the same places."

"So, he knew you'd both wind up at Jimmy's Corner?"

"Yes."

"What did he have to gain from setting you up?"

Leonard thought about the honeytrap homicide article, with Bobby's smiling picture next to the byline and the job title that had once belonged to him.

"He got my job. Eventually, I mean. After I had my breakdown."

"Meaning a pay raise?"

"Of course."

Martha lifted her eyebrows at him. "I'm sure that extra money was very welcome with a new baby to take care of at the time."

"Jesus," Leonard said. "You're right."

Martha got up from the couch. "I need to go powder my nose before we move on to anyone else who might have had a grudge against you."

"You need to do what?"

"You know, visit the little girls' room."

"Oh, right. You mean you need to pee."

"I was trying to be ladylike."

Leonard chuckled. "The bathroom's straight down the hallway, next to the kitchen."

She headed into the hallway, and he shook his head with a smile. Why were women so embarrassed by their own bodily functions? Caroline had been the same. When they'd first started dating, she would run the faucet, so he wouldn't hear her pee. And she had never once farted in front of him in all the time they were together. Leonard wondered if Martha was sweet on him. Then he wondered if he was sweet on Martha.

He already knew from her messages that she had a great personality. Now he knew she was pretty too. Not in the same way that women like Caroline or Anna Bianco were pretty. Their beauty demanded your immediate attention, whereas Martha had a quiet allure about her. It wasn't something you really noticed at first and then—*bam!*—it suddenly hit you just how attractive she was.

Leonard heard the muted sound of the toilet flushing and then the faucet running. Then—nothing. Martha didn't return to the living room. He tried to call her name, but no words came out. His throat worked, and his mouth went dry. His mind flashed back to the scene at the Fairview Hotel. Even though he knew now that that had been staged, he felt panic explode inside him. He jumped up and darted into the hallway.

Martha was standing in the doorway to his bedroom. Not moving, not doing anything, just staring into the room.

Then Leonard realized what had caught her attention.

His gallery.

11

MARTHA

Martha counted fifty-nine photographs taped to the wall.

They were illuminated by a bright moon that cast a strange milky glow over the faces of dozens of men, women, and children. She stood there transfixed, until she became aware of movement behind her and felt warm breath on the back of her neck.

"You think it's weird," Leonard said.

Martha turned around. "No, I think it's beautiful."

The tension drained from Leonard's face, and his shoulders visibly dropped. He held her gaze, and for a split second she thought—*hoped*—that he was going to kiss her. Instead, he gently pushed past her into the bedroom and turned on a lamp.

"I was worried you'd think you'd stumbled upon a serial killer's lair. Especially with all those true-crime shows you watch."

"Not at all. I guessed they were your mystery-film successes. I recognized some of them from when you'd shared them on the forum."

"You don't think it's odd that I tape them to my bedroom wall?"

"No. It's better than the cold, exposed brick in the rest of the room. I don't hang my own prints, but I do keep them all in photo albums." She gestured toward the gallery. "The one in the middle is different. Why?"

"That's Angela. She was my first attempt at mystery film. It was developed at a photo-printing place, whereas the others I developed myself in my dark room. That's why hers is smaller than the others."

"Angela? Wait, I'm confused. I thought you didn't want to find out anything about the people in your photos? How do you know her name?"

Leonard hesitated, as though unsure how best to answer. Finally, he said, "When everything went to shit after Red, and I had no one, I suppose these people, these strangers, became my friends. I gave them names and made up stories about them. They felt safe, like they couldn't hurt me the way the outside world had."

Martha wanted to tell him that he had her now, that he didn't need these pretend friends anymore, but she thought it might be a bit much, seeing as they'd only just met for the first time a few hours earlier.

He seemed to misread her silence, and said, "Now you really do want to run for the hills."

"Nope. What I really want is to get back to our investigation."

They returned to the living room and settled on the couch again.

Martha cradled her wineglass. "Is there anyone else we should be considering for hiring Red to dupe you? What about stories you were working on back then? Someone you might've upset with something you wrote?"

"I can think of two people," Leonard replied after considering the question. "Remy Sullivan and Walter Shankland."

Martha's eyes went big. "Remy Sullivan? You mean the guy who murdered the college student?"

"Yes. Her name was Sophie Miller."

Martha vaguely remembered the case but not all of the details. "This must have been, what, ten years ago?"

"Even longer. He's been in prison for sixteen years."

"Wow. Time flies. Refresh my memory."

Leonard told Martha how Remy Sullivan had been convicted of the brutal murder of fellow student Sophie Miller after she was found stabbed to death in her student dorm. They were in a couple of classes together, but they hadn't been friends. Sophie was popular and sociable and had a wide circle of friends at the school. Remy was the opposite. He was a loner, someone who loitered on the fringes, the kind of person no one really noticed.

On the night she died, Sophie had been to a party and had walked back to her dorm with another student. Her roommate was spending the night with her boyfriend, so it wasn't until Sophie failed to show for class the next morning, and couldn't be contacted on her cell phone, that the alarm was raised.

She was found dead, fully clothed, on her bed. She'd been stabbed fourteen times. Campus CCTV placed Remy Sullivan near her dorm the night of the murder; his fingerprints were subsequently found in Sophie's room and his DNA was under her fingernails. A search of his own room uncovered covert photographs of Sophie and dozens of notebooks filled with poetry and stories about her.

"Remy," Martha said. "Interesting name, huh? You think his parents were fans of the French Renaissance poet, Rémy Belleau?"

"More likely the cognac," Leonard said.

"But why does Remy Sullivan have a problem with you?" she asked.

"It's not Remy who has a problem with me so much as his band of supporters led by his dad, Max Sullivan. He initially tried to alibi his son, only for a dozen people to place Max at a bar until the early hours on the night of the murder. Max didn't like the way I reported on the trial, and he *really* didn't like the opinion pieces I wrote over the years saying Remy should serve his full sentence and his supporters should stop the petitions, marches, and online campaigns protesting his innocence and allow Sophie's family to grieve in peace."

"What did Max Sullivan do to you?"

"Mostly online abuse. Some minor incidents, like my tires being slashed, that I couldn't prove were down to Max or Remy's other supporters. Remy lost an appeal not long before the night with Red at the Fairview Hotel."

"And Walter Shankland? Who's he? I'm not familiar with the name."

"A creepy oddball who stalked and harassed women."

"Sounds like a real charmer. Tell me more."

"He became infatuated with a young woman by the name of Gina Garcia who worked at his local grocery store. She was friendly with all the customers, would chat with the regulars, knew most of their names, and would ask after them and their families. You know the kind of thing."

"Sure. Sounds fairly standard for a local store."

"Exactly. Except Walter took Gina's friendliness as a sign that she was in love with him and that they were destined to be together. He'd go into the store several times a day. He'd invite her out for lunch or a drink, which she always politely declined. Then Gina started noticing Walter in places other than the store—in the park when she was there with her nephew or in a bar when she was out with friends. Soon, the flowers and love letters began to arrive at her home. He was banned from the store, and Gina contacted the cops, but they didn't do a whole lot to stop the harassment.

"Then he broke in to her apartment. Gina came home from work one evening, and there was Walter, sitting quite calmly at her kitchen table. The table was set for two, a bottle of wine was open, two glasses had been poured, and a lasagna was cooking in the oven."

"Poor Gina. That sounds absolutely terrifying."

Leonard said, "Walter did some jail time. When he got out, Gina started receiving letters from him again. I'd reported on the original case, so she contacted me, and I wrote a story about his ongoing harassment in the hope that the cops might actually do something this time. Then Walter started writing me at the *Reporter*, claiming I was doing the devil's work and trying to prevent two people who were destined to be together from being lovers. Other women came forward to claim they had also been stalked by Walter Shankland over the years."

"Did he go back to prison?"

"I don't know," Leonard admitted. "All that stuff at the Fairview Hotel happened, and I kind of lost interest in Shankland and everything else I was working on at the time."

Martha said, "Say Shankland or Sullivan—or someone else entirely—*is* trying to frame you for Anna Bianco's murder with that photograph. How would they even know about your interest in mystery film?"

"I wrote about it for a newspaper article a couple years ago. It's how I got started. I ended the feature by confessing I was hooked and would continue to seek out mystery film at flea markets and online and that I would learn to develop my own photographs."

"So, anyone could have followed you at Chelsea Flea and dropped the film into your backpack or even mailed the film to you, and you'd have assumed it was a purchase you'd made on eBay?" She gave him a reproachful look. "Because you don't keep records."

"Guilty as charged."

Martha went back to Leonard's computer. "I think we need to try to establish the whereabouts of both Walter Shankland and Max Sullivan when Anna Bianco was murdered."

She tried searching for Shankland, then Sullivan and the campaign group.

"Any luck?" Leonard asked.

"I can't find any news reports about Walter Shankland being sent back to prison, just some articles on the original case and your follow-ups about the letters he was sending to Gina after his release. I think we're going to have to dig a bit deeper on him. There's better news where Max Sullivan is concerned though."

"Oh?"

"The campaign group is holding a protest in Manhattan tomorrow. Can you believe it? What are the chances?"

Leonard didn't seem particularly excited by this revelation. "Does Remy have another appeal coming up?"

"Yes, he does actually. How did you know?"

"Because Sullivan's mob usually holds these protests whenever there's a sniff of a new appeal. There would have been one last weekend, there will be another one next weekend, and they will be taking place all over. The Sullivans are from New Jersey, so there will be one there tomorrow for sure. That's where Max will be."

"I still think we should go to the Manhattan protest. It's a great opportunity to ask around about Max and try to establish if he was anywhere near the city at the time of Anna Bianco's murder."

Leonard didn't look convinced.

"What's wrong?" she asked.

"I don't want you anywhere near those people."

"I can take care of myself."

"I'm being serious, Martha."

"And I thought you were being serious about trying to find out who made your life a living hell for five years? About trying to find out who murdered Anna Bianco? The very same person who could be trying to pin it on you, don't forget. Maybe it's just a coincidence that you wound up with a photo of a dead woman who ruined your life—a photo that shows the missing murder weapon—but I'm not so sure."

Leonard sighed. "Okay, I'll go to the protest. And I'll also check out the apartment where Walter Shankland used to live with his mother, see if he's still around. But I'm going on my own. No arguments. I definitely don't want you anywhere near Shankland. You can stick to the online sleuthing if that's okay with you, Jessica Fletcher?"

"I guess it'll have to be," Martha said. "And I guess I'd better order an Uber before I turn into a pumpkin. It's almost midnight."

"It is?" Leonard checked his watch for confirmation. "I didn't realize the time. Look, why don't you stay here tonight? It's kind of late to get a cab all the way across town, and it'll save you the fare too. You can walk over to the restaurant tomorrow and collect your car then."

Martha pretended to think it over. "Okay, that makes sense. If you're sure it's no trouble?"

"No trouble at all," Leonard said. "You can have my bed, and I'll take the couch. Let me go find something for you to sleep in."

Martha sat at the desk, her heart racing faster than a joyrider in a Porsche. It had been a long time since she'd last spent the night with a man. Not since she'd discovered David was cheating on her with another woman. This was different, of course, because she wouldn't be sharing a bed with Leonard, but her palms were sweating just the same.

Leonard returned a few minutes later with an oversized T-shirt for her and a pillow and spare sheets for himself. They said good night, and she retreated to his bedroom and closed the door behind her. She undressed and changed into the tee under the watchful eye of the fifty-nine mystery-film portraits.

Then she tiptoed over to the closet and quietly opened it. Ran her fingers lightly across the fabric of the clothes hanging there. Leonard Blaylock clearly favored dark jeans, dark shirts, gray sweatpants, and bright white sneakers. Martha closed the closet door, crossed the room, and sat on the bed. She opened the top drawer of the bedside table and found a paperback book, reading glasses, and an open packet of candy.

The contents of the bottom drawer were a little more interesting: a woman's pink tee with a faded Disney cartoon print on the front, a hairbrush, a cosmetics bag, a bottle of Marc Jacobs Daisy perfume, a framed photo.

She picked up the photo frame. Behind the smudged glass were the smiling faces of Leonard and Caroline Cooper. Caroline was holding her hand up to the camera, showing off a diamond ring on the third finger. His arms were wrapped protectively around her slim waist. The sprawling cityscape of New York was glittering and magnificent behind them.

Martha returned the photo to the drawer, facedown this time, and turned off the lamp.

12

LEONARD

If Friday's clear blue skies and exhilarating, crisp breeze had been nature's equivalent of happy hour, Saturday afternoon was the hangover. A black sky loomed over New York City like a threat, and a constant drizzle had turned yesterday's rustic leaves into sodden piles of muck.

Times Square was one of the world's most visited tourist attractions, even on drab days like this one. It was the home of Planet Hollywood, the Hard Rock Cafe, television studios, retail stores, and the theater district. It was the site of the annual New Year's Eve ball drop, and it attracted around fifty million visitors each year.

Today, it was also hosting around forty of Remy Sullivan's supporters, who stood around forlornly in drenched windbreakers, holding soggy homemade signs. The protest hadn't attracted much of a turnout. Whether that was down to the inclement weather or simple indifference, Leonard wasn't sure. Probably a bit of both.

A disheveled man in dirty, wet clothes sat on a granite bench nearby. He was cradling a bottle in a brown paper bag, even though it was barely lunchtime. His lips were moving, as though he was having a conversation with himself or maybe God, but he paid the protesters no attention. Hardy outdoor diners who were wrapped up against the cold in coats and scarves were similarly disinterested, their focus firmly on their meals or their cell phones rather than Remy Sullivan's guilt or innocence.

A handful of bemused tourists watched for a while before losing interest and moving on. A single photographer wove his way through the small throng, a Nikon slung over his shoulder. The guy was young and unfamiliar. Probably a freelancer hoping to make a few bucks. Leonard didn't like his chances. Most news outlets wouldn't run photos of the protest. The Free Remy Sullivan campaign was tired and no longer newsworthy, even with talk of a fresh appeal. There would have to be a new trial to spark any renewed interest. As expected, there was no sign of Max Sullivan.

Leonard had only bothered showing up himself to keep Martha happy. She'd already left by the time he woke, just before eleven, a crick in his neck and cramps in his legs after an uncomfortable night on the couch. There was a note on the dining table with her cell phone number and a request to text or call her after he'd been to the protest. She'd added a smiley face too, and that had made Leonard smile.

He'd been tempted to crawl into his vacated bed and give the protest a miss. He didn't expect to learn anything in the rain in Times Square, but Martha was clearly expecting a full report.

He sidled up to a woman now who was hovering on the fringes of the small crowd. She was around fifty, with wild purple hair and a green duffle coat that must have been twice its usual weight with rainwater. He chatted with her about Remy and the new appeal, while trying to gently pump her for information about Max Sullivan's recent whereabouts. It didn't take a whole lot of pumping to establish three things.

One: she didn't have a clue who Max Sullivan was. Two: she didn't know very much about Remy Sullivan either. Three: she was clearly a professional protester—one of those people who showed up to scream and shout and be outraged just so they could feel like they were a part of something, whether it was a protest about climate change, a new government bill, or the plight of a convicted killer.

A half-hearted chant of "Free Remy Sullivan" started up and fizzled out faster than a cigarette butt dropped in a puddle. Leonard searched for a better source of information. There were a few student types chatting and smoking hand-rolled cigarettes and a cluster of unfriendly-looking men around the same age as Max Sullivan. An older woman was pouring coffee into Styrofoam cups from two thermoses wrapped in blankets. Leonard joined the small line as she handed out the refreshments, waiting for a hot drink and the opportunity to speak with her.

He accepted a cup from the thermos that contained coffee with milk and went through the same spiel about Remy and how he was hoping that the new appeal would lead to justice this time. The woman nodded along vigorously. Her name was Lizzie, and she'd known Max and Remy for years, she said.

"I lived in Jersey for a spell when my husband had a good job there," she explained. "Our house was in the same neighborhood as the Sullivans'. Remy was such a cute kid back then. Blond hair and the biggest blue eyes you ever saw. He used to come to my door for candy, and I always gave in, even though I knew it was bad for his teeth. There's no way he could have done what they said he did to that girl."

"I couldn't agree more, Lizzie." Fat raindrops plopped into Leonard's coffee. "It's terrible how Remy's life has been ruined. The justice system has totally failed him."

"Do you know Remy?" she asked. "Was he a friend of yours before he went to prison?"

Leonard was tempted to point out that Remy didn't have any friends, but that would probably ruin the rapport he was trying to build with the woman.

"I don't know Remy, no, but I know all about his case. Lots of circumstantial evidence and not a lot of proof. Probably some police corruption too."

Those were the lines most often peddled by his supporters.

"Exactly." Lizzie was nodding hard again. Then her eyes narrowed slightly, and she peered at him through the rain. "I don't think I've seen you at any of our meetings or marches before."

Leonard gulped down some lukewarm coffee. "I've been to a few of the protests. You maybe just don't remember me. Even my mom says I don't have a very memorable face."

She smiled. "Oh, I don't know about that. You have a very handsome face."

He craned his neck, as though surveying his surroundings. "I haven't seen Max today." Leonard made a point of using Sullivan's first name, as though he knew the father, if not the son. "Is he still in Jersey?"

"He sure is. He's running their protest today."

"That's what I thought. Has he been in the city much recently?"

"He was at one of the Manhattan meetings in May, I think. Or maybe it was June."

"Not last month? I thought I saw him in town, but he disappeared before I had a chance to say hi."

Lizzie's forehead creased. "I don't think so. He usually goes down to his place in Florida with Sandra in September. Unless it was after they got back. Was he very tan?"

"I don't really remember." Leonard saw one of the unfriendly-looking guys making his way toward them, looking even less friendly now. "Look, it was great to meet you, Lizzie, but I gotta go as I have to work this afternoon. I'll hopefully see you at the next one."

He hurried off in the direction of the Forty-Second Street subway station. Caroline Cooper smiled down at him from a huge, animated billboard ad for *Rise & Shine*. When he glanced over his shoulder, the man was deep in conversation with Lizzie. Leonard quickened his pace.

◆　◆　◆

Once back at his apartment, Leonard peeled off his wet clothes and dumped them into the laundry basket and then had a long, hot shower to try to force some heat back into his bones.

After he'd dried off and changed into sweatpants and a T-shirt, he picked up his cell phone and entered the number Martha had left for him.

"Hello?"

He wondered why she sounded so wary, then remembered she hadn't had his number until now.

"Hi, it's Leonard."

"Oh, hi. I thought you were one of those people phoning about an accident I didn't have or claiming my computer had been hacked. How did you get on at the protest?"

He told her about his conversation with Lizzie and how Max Sullivan was currently in Jersey, but she thought he might have been at his vacation home in Florida last month with his wife, Sandra. If it turned out he was sunning himself on a beach in Key West at the time of Anna Bianco's murder, that gave him an ironclad alibi.

Martha said, "Okay, I'll check it out. I haven't had much luck with my online searches so far. Nothing of real interest on Max yet. He doesn't seem to have any personal social media accounts, only ones attached to the Free Remy Sullivan campaign. I'll look into the Florida angle."

Leonard made a pot of coffee and warmed some soup for a late lunch, the chill from the protest earlier still lingering. He was debating whether to climb into bed for an afternoon nap when his phone shrilled. It was Martha.

"Max is in the clear," she said without preamble.

"That was fast. How?"

"Photographic evidence. I already told you Max doesn't have any personal social media accounts, but his wife, Sandra, does. However, her Instagram account is private, meaning only those who have their follow requests accepted can access her photos."

"So, how were you able to access her photos?"

"Simple. I sent her a follow request, and she accepted straight-away. My own feed is full of cute babies in baskets so no real reason to turn me down. She has a lot of followers, so I suspect she uses the privacy function to weed out the haters and journalists. No offense."

"None taken. I'm guessing she had photos of her and Max in Florida when the murder took place?"

"Sadly, yes. I'll send over some screenshots now. Looks like they were there for about a month, and it was great weather the whole time, the lucky things. So, he's pretty much off our suspects list."

Leonard heard a ping in his ear. He switched to speakerphone and opened his messages, where he found three screenshots from Sandra Sullivan's Instagram account: Max on a white sandy beach in almost indecently short trunks; Max and Sandra having a meal on a terrace with the ocean in the background; Max and Sandra clinking cocktail glasses together as the sun set behind them. It definitely wasn't Jersey. Or Manhattan. At the top of each photo was the location in Florida—Key West, just as Leonard had guessed—and below it was the date. The same date as Anna Bianco's murder.

Leonard said, "Looks like Max Sullivan is in the clear—for the murder anyway. Might be worth keeping him in mind for setting me up at the Fairview Hotel for the time being, though."

"I agree. It's possible we could be looking for two different people."

"What about Walter Shankland?" Leonard asked. "Any luck finding him?"

"None so far," Martha said. "I had a look at some databases for court and prison records but found nothing. I'm not sure how up to date they are anyway, if they'd even contain information about someone incarcerated in the last few months. From what you've told me, it sounds like he had mental health issues, so it's worth bearing in mind that he could be in a psychiatric facility some-where—either voluntarily or otherwise—and I suspect it would be next to impossible to find out that kind of information online."

"Don't worry about it," Leonard said. "I'll check out his moth-er's place this evening. See what I can find out."

The last time Leonard visited the Shankland apartment was five and a half years ago.

He'd wanted a right of reply comment from Walter Shankland before running the story about the continued harassment of Gina Garcia upon his release from prison.

Walter had refused to open the door and give his side of the story. He had cowered behind it crying. Leonard had planned on hanging around outside the building awhile, hoping the man would change his mind. But Walter's mother had screamed from an open window to get off her stoop before she called the police. They both knew there was no way she was getting the cops involved, but Leonard was a reporter, not a vigilante, so he had left. He'd stated in the final paragraph of the article that Walter Shankland had declined to comment. Then the letters started arriving at the *Reporter*'s office.

The apartment was on the second floor of a grubby building in one of the city's rougher neighborhoods. Leonard parked across the street where he had a good view. The blinds in both of the front windows were pulled all the way down. As dusk gave way to a starless night, lights blinked on in the other apartments. The Shankland place remained resolutely dark. There was no sign of either Walter or his mom coming or going through the street entrance. There was no flickering blue light of a TV behind the thin fabric of the blinds or muted glow of a solitary lamp being turned on. Either the apartment was empty, or the Shanklands were trying to seriously cut back on their utility bills.

Leonard decided to go take a closer look. He got out of the car, closed the door, and pocketed the keys. He was already inside the building when he realized he'd forgotten to lock up the Chevy. He worried briefly about leaving his car unlocked in this neighborhood but figured a thief would have to be really desperate to make off with his old rust bucket. If anything, they'd be doing him a favor.

The soles of his sneakers were silent as he made his way upstairs. He heard the faint burbling of televisions in other apartments. His cell phone vibrated in his back pocket, and he removed it to see that he had a text from Martha.

Good luck! Let me know how you get on :)

The building was in an even greater state of disrepair than it had been on his last visit. More rust, graffiti, and flaking paintwork outside. A strong smell of weed, old takeout food, and urine inside.

Leonard pressed a finger to the doorbell and heard a ding-dong echo inside an apartment that felt even emptier now that he was standing right outside. The place gave him the creeps. He bent down and opened the mail slot, and his nose caught a musty smell. He used the flashlight function on his phone to peer inside.

The beam played over dusty furniture and a pile of mail and junk mail on the floor.

He let the mail slot close with a snap and was just about to go knock on a neighbor's door and ask if Walter still lived in the building—a scenario that seemed unlikely judging by all the unopened mail behind the door—but he didn't get the chance. The door across the hall flew open to reveal a woman with an ugly dog straining on a leash. She was skinny under baggy clothes, with a bad yellow dye job and teeth to match. She could have been thirty or sixty.

"What the hell do you think you're doing snooping around outside folks' apartments this time of night?" Her voice was twenty-a-day gravel, her stare sharper than a gangster's blade.

The dog growled at him, saliva dripping from its mouth and pooling on the dirty floor. The mutt was squat and muscular. Leonard didn't know what breed it was, just that it would gladly rip his balls off given half a chance.

"Sorry if I alarmed you," Leonard said. "I'm a friend of Walter's. Thought I'd drop in on him while I was in the neighborhood. A surprise visit."

"A friend of Walter's, huh? Since when did that weirdo have any friends?"

Leonard decided to answer the question with a question of his own. "He hasn't moved, has he? The place appears to be empty."

She sized him up for a long moment, then said, "The mother passed away earlier this year, and the son freaked out and was carted off to the loony bin. He's probably still in a padded cell somewhere. All I know is the apartment hasn't been cleared out or leased by anyone else yet, so who knows?"

Leonard tried not to wince at her crude and unsympathetic words. "That's so sad," he said. He kind of meant it. "I didn't know about Mrs. Shankland or what had happened to Walter."

"Yeah, well, I don't think they had much worth stealing if you were planning on casing the joint."

"Don't worry, I have no intention of burglarizing the Shankland apartment or anyone else's." The dog was still growling, straining, and salivating. It barked suddenly, and the sound was too loud in the small space. Leonard winced. "Thanks for letting me know about Walter. I'll be off now. Let you and your friend here get on with your evening."

"Yeah, you do that."

She made a point of watching him until he disappeared down the stairwell. When he emerged on the street, she was at the front window, curtain pulled to one side. The mutt was there too, paws up on the windowsill, hot breath fogging the glass. It was only when Leonard opened his car door that the curtain fell back into place.

He slid into the driver's seat and slammed the door shut. Fastened his seat belt and was just about to turn the key in the ignition when he became aware of movement in the back seat. Before he could turn around, he felt something pushed against the back of his skull, followed by the unmistakable click of the safety being disengaged on a gun. Leonard's pulse spiked.

"Start the car and drive," a man's voice said.

13

LEONARD

Leonard started the car with shaking hands.

Only five words had been spoken, but he was sure he didn't know the man in the back of his car, didn't recognize his voice. His eyes flicked to the rearview mirror. The nearest streetlight was several yards away. All he could make out was a hooded figure with a scarf pulled right up over the nose, obscuring most of the face. Only the eyes were visible.

Small and set close together.

Unfamiliar.

As he pulled away from the curb, Leonard's brain went into overdrive with questions, his heart rate racing every bit as fast. Who was behind the ambush? Was it a carjacking? He quickly ruled out that possibility. Who would want to carjack a 1998 Chevy Malibu? The answer was no one. A robbery? It was possible. But why not make Leonard empty his pockets right here and then make a quick escape?

He realized he'd be better off trying to think of ways out of his current predicament. That was the priority. The who and the why could wait until later. But any sort of thinking wasn't exactly easy with the cold metal of a gun kissing your skull and the hot breath of a stranger on the back of your neck.

"Take a left here."

Leonard nudged the blinker out of habit and turned left onto an empty street. The knotted leather of the steering wheel was slick with sweat. He had to work hard to stem the rising panic and keep a cool head. He needed to be smart.

Leonard was wearing a seat belt. He didn't think the other guy was because he was sitting right in the middle of the back seat and leaning forward apparently unrestrained.

"Now take a right."

Leonard took the next right.

He could floor the gas, build as much speed as the old car could muster, then slam on the brakes. Hope he'd escape with some whiplash, while the guy in the back went headfirst through the windshield. But what if the guy in the back *was* buckled up? What if the gun went off, and he was hit by a stray bullet? What if the other guy's momentum took Leonard through the windshield with him?

Or he could stop the car, take the guy in the back by surprise, and try to wrestle the weapon from him. But what were the chances of him succeeding? Not great. This was real life, not the movies, and Leonard was no action hero.

Neither scenario was without risk, and neither was a particularly attractive option. In short, he was screwed.

Before he could do any more thinking, the hooded guy said, "Stop here."

Leonard did as he was told, slowed to a halt, and set the parking brake. He peered out the window. It wasn't good news. A patch of wasteland, no apartment buildings, and an unmarked white van with no company branding on the side and its lights on. He was even more screwed than he'd first thought. Suddenly, trying to launch the guy through his windshield didn't seem like it had been such a dumb idea.

The man spoke again. "Get out of the car slowly, Leonard. Don't even think about trying anything. It won't end well for you if you do."

Leonard.

So, not a random robbery. This was personal.

Leonard unclipped the seat belt and risked another look in the rearview mirror. It was even darker here, away from the residential streets. He still couldn't get a good look at the guy's face.

Hood, scarf, beady eyes.

Leonard opened the door and climbed out slowly, as instructed. Behind him, he heard the other man get out of the car too. Before he even had a chance to close the door, a hard and unexpected blow hit him square in the right kidney. Leonard dropped to his knees. Then there was another blow. This time, a kick to the gut. It knocked the wind out of him. He crumpled to the ground and drew himself into the fetal position. Tried desperately to pull the cold night air into his burning lungs.

In among the breathlessness and waves of pain, Leonard became aware of noise and movement: a door opening and closing, boots on concrete, the creak of old hinges, heavy breathing, footsteps getting closer and louder.

Just as his chest pushed out a few ragged breaths, something was thrown over Leonard's head. He felt his wrists being bound tightly together. His ankles were also tied. His restraints felt like they were made of something thin and tight with zero give. He guessed plastic zip ties. Then he was being grappled roughly under his armpits by strong hands. Another pair of hands grabbed his legs. There were two assailants now.

He was dispatched roughly into what he assumed was the back of the van, his shins clattering painfully against metal, his bound hands doing little to break his fall. His left shoulder took the brunt of it, and he gasped at the bolt of pain. He heard the creak of old hinges again, and two thunks as the van doors were slammed shut. Then two more thunks after his captors had presumably climbed into the cab up front.

With his vision obscured, Leonard's other senses kicked up a gear. He felt the vibration of the van's engine beneath him. He heard the rumbling over his overworked heartbeat. He smelled the gas from the engine. More immediate was the stench of burlap jute and damp soil. He guessed a potato sack had been used to blindfold him. His hands were tied to the front, not behind his back, so he could have reached up and pulled it off, but he didn't dare.

Leonard tried to focus on the twists and turns the driver was taking to establish where they were going. But, between the throbbing pain in his back, gut, and shoulder, and the disorientation of having a sack over his head, he very quickly lost his bearings. His focus switched to bracing himself against the side of the fast-moving vehicle with his feet so as not to exacerbate his wounds.

He felt two short vibrations in his back pocket. An incoming text. His captors hadn't taken his cell phone from him. If he could reach it, he could call for help. Or hit the side buttons on the device for one of those emergency calls where you didn't even have to speak. The cops would be able to track his whereabouts, wouldn't they? Leonard writhed and wriggled and twisted and grunted. Sweat broke out and beaded his brow, and he was thrown around like he was in a pinball machine. But the wrist restraints prevented him from reaching into his back pocket.

Eventually, the van stopped. Leonard lay on the floorboard panting and perspiring. He heard the back doors open. Rough hands gripped him by the ankles and pulled him out, his skin burning under his jacket and jeans. He was picked up and carried a short distance and then dumped like a bag of garbage onto hard, uneven ground.

Up until now, he hadn't spoken. Now Leonard said, "Who are you? What do you want with me?"

"We're the ones asking the questions."

A different voice this time. The van driver. Leonard didn't recognize his voice either. What the hell did they want with him?

"What were you doing in Times Square today?" asked the one who'd ambushed him with the gun.

So, this was about Remy Sullivan. Or rather, about Max.

"It was a public protest," Leonard said. "Lots of people were there. Okay, not lots of people at the protest. In fact, hardly anyone at all, but I wasn't the only one there."

"A wise guy, huh?" It was the guy with the gun again. "Think you're smart, asshole?"

Leonard, still blinded by the sack, couldn't see the blow coming, so wasn't prepared for it. When it landed, it knocked the breath out of him once again. Another boot to the belly. His lungs felt like they were on fire. He coughed up phlegm under the sack. At least he hoped it was phlegm. He was in a world of pain and wondered about cracked ribs and internal bleeding.

"You were the only one there asking a lot of questions, though," the driver said.

"What's your interest in Remy and Max Sullivan?" asked the other guy.

Leonard was sure neither man was Max Sullivan. Even so, there was no doubt in his mind that they'd been sent by Remy's father. Leonard guessed one of them was the unfriendly guy he'd spotted speaking to Lizzie at Times Square, just as he'd made a sharp exit.

Leonard didn't say anything. He could hardly tell them the truth, could he? He brought his knees up to his chest in anticipation of more kicks and punches as a result of his silence.

"Maybe my hearing ain't as good as it used to be, but I ain't hearing much of an explanation." It was the guy with the gun again.

He seemed to be in charge, the one doing most of the talking. "What were you doing there?"

Leonard still said nothing. He tried to focus on breathing under the suffocating sack. Tried not to focus on the throbbing agony everywhere. He no longer knew which parts of his body were wounded and which parts weren't. Everything felt sore.

"Maybe he's out cold," said the driver. "Out for the count. Can't answer you."

Leonard was hauled up violently by the lapels of his jacket, sparking a fresh explosion of pain. He groaned and coughed up more phlegm.

"Nope, he's still with us," said the other one. "Okay, why don't I make this real easy for you, Leonard? A question with a yes or no answer. Are you writing those stupid fucking articles about Remy Sullivan for that rag of a newspaper again?"

Seriously? That's what they were worried about? Some bad press for Remy Sullivan? Leonard grabbed onto the explanation being offered.

"Uh, yeah, I'd been thinking about it. Don't think I will now."

"Good idea. We don't want you causing trouble for Remy again with all your nasty lies, do we? Not with the new appeal coming up."

"No, we don't."

"So, we're clear, then? No more stories from you about Remy Sullivan in the paper?"

"Yeah, we're clear."

"Good. Because if you do write anything about him or his appeal, our next chat won't be so friendly. Got it?"

"Got it."

Leonard was thrown onto the ground, causing another involuntary moan, and landed on what felt like concrete and dirt and lumps of rubble. The parting shot was to the face this time. A fist, rather than the toe of a boot. Leonard felt his front teeth pierce his bottom lip and warm liquid trickle down his chin.

Doors slammed shut, followed by an engine starting up. Then the sound of tires spitting gravel as the van drove away. Leonard waited until he was sure they were gone and weren't coming back. Then he pulled the sack off his head.

He lay on his back, chest heaving. Took in huge gulps of air. He was inside an abandoned building. Rain battered what was left of the roof. In the gloom, he could make out graffitied brickwork, decaying steel beams, old pipes, and the shells of a couple of burned-out cars. He guessed it was an old pump station or power plant, long since discarded and dilapidated.

Leonard moved his head gingerly to the side and saw lights twinkling like diamonds in the distance through what had once been a window. The rain was coming down in sheets outside, but he knew what he was looking at.

The Brooklyn Bridge.

After a while, he became aware of a buzzing sound over the thrum of the downpour. It was coming from under a pile of dirt and metal. He turned in the direction of the noise and saw a small rectangle of light in the gloom.

His cell phone.

It must have fallen from his jeans pocket while he was being thrown around by Max Sullivan's heavies. He flipped over onto his belly and half crawled, half dragged himself toward it as fast as the wrist and ankle restraints allowed. He knew he had to reach it before it stopped ringing and was lost to the darkness again. His fingers clawed at the dirt, and sweat got in his eyes and his mouth, as he hauled himself closer.

Finally, he was within touching distance. He could see the name of the caller on the screen now.

It was Martha.

14
LEONARD

"You saved my life," Leonard said. "And how do I repay you? By ruining your upholstery."

They were in Martha's Mini Cooper, the heater on full blast, him shivering under a blanket with his knees almost to his chin in the cramped space, while she expertly navigated the dark, wet streets.

"I don't care how dirty the car is," Martha said. "The car can be cleaned. You can't be fixed so easily." Her eyes flicked momentarily to meet his own. "You know, I'd feel a whole lot better if I was taking you to the emergency room right now."

"No hospital and no doctors. That way, no awkward questions."

They drove on in silence. The only sound was the repetitive squeak of rubber against glass as the windshield wipers battled the rain.

"I'm glad you made that phone call," Leonard said after a while. "Especially after I hadn't answered your messages. A lot of people would've assumed they were being ignored and given the silent treatment right back."

"I've learned to trust my instincts."

Leonard felt like she wanted to say more, so he waited for her to speak again.

Finally, Martha said, "I was in a relationship with a man called David for a long time. Almost ten years. Everything was great, until it wasn't. Suddenly, he wasn't answering my calls and messages, he was working late all the time, he was on his cell phone at strange hours. I was convinced he was having an affair. All the classic signs were there. He told me I was imagining it, that it was all in my head. After a while, I started to believe him. For months, I thought I was losing my mind. Then one day I came home early from work feeling unwell and found him in bed with one of the neighbors."

"Shit, Martha," Leonard said. "I'm so sorry." Now he understood her reaction to his own tale of infidelity.

"Turns out, I wasn't losing my mind. My gut feeling had been correct. That same gut feeling told me something wasn't right when you didn't answer my messages. That's why I decided to call you, even if you did think I was a pain in the butt who wouldn't leave you alone. At least then I'd know you were okay."

Martha slowed to a stop for a red light. An older man, wearing a soaked beige trench coat and a plaid newsboy cap, was attempting to cross the street while the crosswalk sign was lit. He'd clearly had a few alcoholic beverages and was making more progress swaying from side to side than he was putting one foot in front of the other. His arms were outstretched to an imaginary audience as he crooned "One for my Baby." He stopped in front of the Mini and serenaded them for a few seconds before continuing on his way. By the time he'd reached the other side, the red light had changed to green and back to red again.

Martha shook her head with a smile. "Saturday night in New York City, huh?"

Leonard said, "A night like this, he'd have been better off doing a Gene Kelly song rather than Sinatra."

The green light glowed, and Martha drove on. "Do you want to tell me what happened tonight?"

Leonard filled her in on the visit to Walter Shankland's apartment and what he'd learned from the scary neighbor with the only slightly less terrifying dog, his unexpected ride in the back of a van courtesy of Max Sullivan's goons, the beatdown by the Brooklyn waterfront, and the warning not to write anything unflattering about Remy Sullivan.

Martha frowned but didn't say anything. They drove in silence for a while.

Leonard said, "Do you want me to sing some Sinatra too, to fill this uncomfortable silence? Can't promise I'll be any good, though. Especially with this fat lip."

Martha laughed, and the tension evaporated. "I think you'd struggle to beat our friend with the newsboy cap for entertainment value."

"Can't argue with that."

She turned onto Leonard's street and backed into a parking space. Switched off the engine and turned to face him in the gloom of the tiny car. "I'm going to say something, and you're not going to like it."

"You want me to drop the investigation."

"Yes, I do. I get that your life was ruined, and that you want answers. I want answers too. I just think it's too dangerous. Maybe you should destroy the photograph and the film roll. Forget about Anna Bianco. Move on. Reclaim your life."

"Okay, I'll drop the investigation," he said.

"Really?"

"Only for a few days, though. Until I'm feeling better. I'm not much good to anyone in the shape I'm in right now."

She sighed. "Is it worth even trying to change your mind?"

"Nope."

Martha eyed his building, dark and brooding against a deep mauve sky. "Speaking of the shape you're in, let's get you inside and rested up."

The elevator was out of service, meaning it took almost ten minutes for them to reach Leonard's apartment, Martha having to prop him up like he was a Saturday-night drunk as they made slow, sweaty progress to the top floor.

Leonard was about to collapse onto a chair when Martha hit the wall switch in the living room. "Let me have a good look at the damage." She held his chin up to the bright glare of the lightbulb, her grip displaying both tenderness and authority, and assessed his lip. "The cut isn't too deep. I don't think it needs stitches. Should heal in a day or two."

She then instructed Leonard to remove his jacket and pull up his T-shirt. The skin on his back was unmarked where he'd received the initial blow. The front of his torso was a different story. Purple-red bruising was already starting to mottle the skin. Martha gently pressed a hand to his ribs, and he winced through gritted teeth.

She bit her own lip. "I really do think you need to be checked over by a doctor."

"All I need is a warm bath, a couple of painkillers, and a large Scotch or two." He saw the disapproving look on her face. "No arguments. Please."

Martha sighed. She was doing a lot of sighing tonight. "Okay, I'll make us some dinner while you're in the tub. If you're going to be throwing back booze and pills, you're not doing it on an empty stomach. No arguments. Please."

A half hour later, when Leonard emerged from the bathroom, he found Martha in the kitchen. The table had been set. There were two plates heaped with pea-and-ham risotto. A glass of wine had been poured for her, a whisky for him.

"Smells amazing," he said. "You really didn't have to go to so much trouble."

"It's risotto. Hardly a lot of trouble." She flapped a hand dismissively, but he could tell that she was pleased with the compliment. "Now sit and eat."

He did as he was told. Scooped a forkful of rice and peas into his mouth, being careful not to aggravate his busted lip. It tasted amazing too. He realized he was ravenous and quickly cleared the plate. After second helpings for both of them, Leonard took another Scotch into the bedroom with a bottle of painkillers. Then he gingerly maneuvered himself into the bed with Martha's help.

She said, "I googled the symptoms of internal bleeding while you were in the tub."

"Martha . . ."

She held up a hand to silence him. "I'm going to stay over again tonight. Obviously, this time, I'll take the couch. I want you to let me know immediately if you experience any tingling or numbness, severe headache, dizziness, or change in vision or hearing. Okay?"

"Okay, Nurse Weaver."

Leonard's eyelids felt heavy. He had a nice buzz from the booze but none of the symptoms she'd just mentioned. He patted the bed beside him.

"Lie with me for a while."

He felt her hesitation hang in the air, then a slight dip in the mattress as she climbed in next to him. Her warmth and closeness were comforting.

Then he was fast asleep.

◆ ◆ ◆

Over the next few days, Leonard worked on articles that had deadlines looming, and Martha took photos of babies and picture-perfect families.

In the evenings, she brought takeout food or cooked for them both, and then they watched TV together. He had always preferred pulpy detective novels to the screen but was finding himself enjoying her favorite true-crime shows.

Martha had even taken a taxi to where Leonard's car had been dumped to pick it up for him. Some kids, aged around eight or nine, had been playing in it, taking turns each at pretending to be NASCAR drivers, while the others provided the *vroom-vroom-vroom* soundtrack. They'd run off, doing a way better impression of Usain Bolt, when Martha had approached the Chevy Malibu in her nice suit. She figured they'd mistaken her for a cop and was delighted by the thought.

Leonard said, "I still can't believe the Chevy hadn't been torched by then."

"Just as well the kids got to it before the bored teenagers, or it would've been," Martha said.

On Friday, almost a week after the assault, and with the swelling on his lip all but gone and the bruises starting to fade, Leonard paid a visit to his dad.

Arden Blaylock had been in a care home for a couple of years now.

Leonard hadn't even noticed anything was seriously wrong at first. Mainly because they weren't spending as much time together by then, not like the old days, before the business with Red. His dad had always been as sharp as a tack, and even though he seemed to be a little more forgetful and confused at times, Leonard had dismissed it as simply getting older. He hadn't been around enough to realize he should have been a hell of a lot more worried.

Then one Saturday, his dad had gone out for a walk and had become distressed when he couldn't remember how to get back home.

Every time Leonard thought of that day, his face flamed with shame, and guilt twisted his insides. His dad had tried calling him several times, but Leonard, still shutting out the people who cared about him, had turned his cell phone off. He'd been pissed at the persistent disruption while trying to nurse a hangover. Apparently, his dad, in his state of confusion, had then taken a tumble and hit his head on the sidewalk. There had been a lot of blood, someone had called an ambulance, and Arden Blaylock had been taken to the emergency room.

The head wound wasn't serious, just a few stitches were required, but the medical staff knew they were dealing with a far bigger problem and wanted to run some tests. They tried to reach Leonard, but his cell phone was still off, and their voice mails were left unanswered. Later that night, his dad's neighbor showed up at Leonard's door to tell him what had happened. By then, Leonard was back on the booze and in no fit state to visit the hospital. The guy had looked at him as though he were a piece of shit on the sole of his shoe. He was right.

When Leonard went to the hospital the next morning, a nurse had asked if he was Arden's son. He'd nodded. "Mr. Blaylock has been crying out for you all night." The expression on her face was even more disgusted than the neighbor's had been.

The Alzheimer's diagnosis shouldn't have come as a surprise, but it had still floored Leonard. Arden Blaylock's decline had been rapid.

Sometimes when Leonard visited the care home, his dad would stare out the window at the gardens or the weather without saying a word. Leonard would hold his hand and chat to him about anything and everything—articles he was working on, the Mets' last game, good books that he'd read.

Other times, Arden would call his son by the name of Petey or Joe—who Leonard knew had been his dad's best friends as a boy growing up in Greenpoint—or he'd sing songs from his childhood.

Two things never changed—Leonard's tears each time he visited and the way his dad gripped his hand. Somewhere, among the brain fog and the jumbled memories and the confusion, Leonard knew his dad felt a connection between them, even though he no longer recognized his only child.

Today, they sat in front of the window, holding hands, Leonard's cheeks stained with tears. He stared down at the wrinkles and liver spots and blue veins on the older man's skin. An overwhelming sadness engulfed him, and a sob escaped from his lips.

"Don't cry, Petey." His dad patted his sleeve softly with his free hand. "Everything's going to be okay."

But it wasn't going to be okay. Leonard was in the here and now, while the most important person in his life was living sixty-some years in the past. He desperately wished he could go back to his own childhood, to a time not long after his mom had left, when the screaming matches were over, and the tension was gone, and it was just him and his dad. Weekends in the park, comic books and pizza, watching old movies on the TV together.

Then Leonard thought of a more recent time. Right after Red, when he'd ignored calls and texts from his dad. When he had shut down conversations about his downward spiral and had shut out the person who had tried the hardest to help him. Back when Arden Blaylock still bought the paper every morning, and did the crossword, and remembered what he'd gone to the grocery store to buy.

Back when he still remembered his son.

But Leonard had been too consumed by his own misery, too obsessed by a woman he didn't even know, to realize he was missing out on precious time with the people who really mattered.

What he would give now for a phone call or message from his dad . . .

He knew he was in danger of making the same mistakes all over again with Martha. He knew he should take her advice and move on with his life.

But Leonard couldn't let it go. Something had been set in motion, and he had to see it through to the end. He had lost too much to give up now.

15

MARTHA

Friday night.

They'd ordered in Chinese food for dinner, and Leonard had opened a bottle of wine. Martha lit some candles. There was the occasional whoosh of a car going past on the rain-slick street outside. The wind moaned and rattled the old windows.

Inside, it was warm and cozy and comfortable. She was starting to feel at home here in Leonard's apartment, especially now that the stress and anxiety over his assault had begun to ease.

That moment, when he'd finally answered the phone and told her he'd been attacked . . . Martha never wanted to experience anything like it again. She still had no idea how she'd been able to remain calm enough to instruct Leonard to open the map app on his phone, screenshot his location, and send it to her. How she'd managed to keep the speedometer on the right side of the law on what had felt like the longest drive ever but, in reality, had been around half an hour. How she'd stopped herself from bursting into tears when she saw him lying in that abandoned old building, bloodied and bruised.

Then there had been the worry over just how serious his injuries might be after his refusal to seek medical help. She'd barely slept those first few nights for fear that he might vomit or collapse or simply not wake up. Now that Leonard was firmly on the mend, Martha was enjoying taking care of him, spending time with him, and getting to know him better. For the first time in a long time, Martha Weaver was happy.

The only thing spoiling the mood tonight was, well, Leonard.

He'd been quiet since returning from the care home after visiting his dad earlier in the day. Martha didn't know all the details, just that Arden Blaylock was in a bad way with dementia, so she could imagine how hard those visits must be. But it seemed to her that there was more to it than that. Leonard wasn't being moody as such, but there was definitely something on his mind.

They were watching a true-crime show. It was about a former prosecutor and a retired CSI who showed up in small towns to help local police departments solve their cold cases. On the screen, the prime suspects were being added to a whiteboard, along with a list of all the reasons why each one could be the perpetrator. Leonard was a recent convert to the show and seemed to be as addicted as Martha was. But not so much tonight. She knew his attention wasn't on what was happening in Cuero, Texas. Or in his apartment in Hell's Kitchen. He appeared to be miles away, lost in his own thoughts.

"My money is on the boyfriend," she said. "It's usually the spouse or partner."

Leonard nodded absentmindedly.

"And the motive will be sex or money," she went on. "If I ever get married, remind me never to allow my husband to take out a life insurance policy on me."

He nodded again, eyes fixed straight ahead, his bottom lip pushed out in thought.

Martha picked up the remote control and paused the television.

Leonard turned to her in surprise. "What's wrong?"

"I was about to ask you the very same thing. Spill."

"Spill what?"

"Leonard, I could have confessed to being a murderer myself and you wouldn't have noticed. Something's on your mind, so tell me."

He sighed. "I know you want me to drop the investigation. *Our* investigation, I mean. But I can't. I need to know who tricked me, who made me think I'd killed a woman."

"Even if it means another beating? Or even worse next time?"

"It won't come to that."

"You don't know that."

Leonard said nothing.

Now it was Martha's turn to sigh. So much for the perfect evening. "Okay, what exactly have you been brooding over?"

"I think we were on the wrong track with Walter Shankland and Max Sullivan. I'd forgotten just how ramshackle the Shankland place was until I went back there. Walter was unemployed, which is why he had so much time to hang around the store where his stalking victim, Gina Garcia, worked. I don't believe he had the kind of cash needed to pay Red. And I think the whole setup was too sophisticated for Max Sullivan. On the basis of last week's little adventure with his buddies, he appears to prefer a more direct way of getting the message across."

"But he didn't beat you up back then when you were writing about his son for the *Reporter*," Martha pointed out.

"I think he was building up to it. The threatening social media messages, the slashed tires . . . If I hadn't left the paper when I did, if I was still following the Remy Sullivan story, I suspect I'd have been bundled into the back of a van a whole lot sooner."

"Okay. So, who are you planning on looking at next?"

"I think I need to look closer to home this time."

"You mean Bobby?"

Leonard shook his head. "You said it yourself—it's usually the spouse or partner."

Martha arched an eyebrow. "Caroline? I thought you'd dismissed her as a potential suspect?"

"I didn't want to believe it. I still don't." He angled his head toward the television, the frozen image of the whiteboard still on the screen. "But I figure we need to follow the example of those TV investigators and start drawing up reasons why Caroline would have wanted to set me up. Why she'd want to destroy me."

"Well, the two biggest motives in cases like this are—"

Leonard cut her off. "Sex and money."

"Oh, so you *were* listening to me after all."

"Sure, I was."

"I'm assuming sex, rather than money, where you and Caroline are concerned?"

Leonard met her eye. "We need to think about money too."

"Wait. What? You're actually a millionaire, with a secret home in the Bahamas and a hidden fleet of Porsches and Jaguars, but you live in an apartment building with an elevator that never works and drive an old Chevy Malibu because this is your way of keeping it real?"

Leonard laughed, then turned serious. "Right now, we can only speculate about the motive. But I think the money that was paid to Red for her little performance at the Fairview Hotel is how we find out who set me up."

Martha nodded slowly. "Makes sense. And how do we do that?"

"When Caroline and I first got engaged, we opened a joint checking account. It was her idea. She didn't want a long engagement, so we set the date for the following summer. The idea was that we would pool all our money together, and it would go toward the wedding and the honeymoon. Caroline also wanted to set aside some cash for a lease on an apartment, whereas I wanted us to live here, but that's another story."

"How good is your memory?" Martha asked. "Do you remember any unusual payments to private investigators or struggling actresses that were made from that checking account around five years ago?"

"I don't." Leonard grinned. "But I don't have to. I guess you could say I'm kind of a hoarder when it comes to keeping stuff. Or maybe I'm just too lazy to get around to dumping all the junk. Either way, the account statements are right over there."

He pointed to the corner of the living room that housed his study. Above the desk was a shelf filled with magazine files. A vision of Leonard's bottom drawer, with Caroline's clothing, personal effects, and photo, popped into Martha's head. She knew the shared financial paperwork wasn't the only reminder of his ex-fiancée still squatting in Leonard's home.

"Might be time to Marie Kondo the place," she said. "Dump all the crap you don't need anymore—once you've finished raking over the past, that is."

"Are you impressed that I know exactly who Marie Kondo is and don't need to ask?"

"Nope. You'd be a terrible lifestyle writer if you didn't know who she was. Let's take a look at those files."

They relocated to the kitchen, where they'd soon filled the dining table with old checking account statements, notepads, pens, and fluorescent markers.

"You and Caroline got engaged when?" Martha asked.

"In early April of that year. I proposed on the observation deck of the Empire State Building as the sun was setting on a beautiful spring day. The first joint statement would probably have been May."

"Neither of you continued to keep separate accounts?"

"I didn't. I'm pretty sure Caroline didn't either."

"How can you be sure?"

"Her salary was paid into the joint account, same as mine. Don't forget, this was back when Caroline was a reporter for a local radio station. I was by far the bigger earner; she wasn't making a lot of money at the time. I'd be surprised if she had any spare cash to squirrel away."

Martha took a gulp of wine. Her cheeks felt flushed, but she didn't know if it was down to the booze or the exhilaration of trying to solve a mystery. Or being so close to Leonard. She realized, despite the potential dangers, that she was the same as him—she couldn't let it go.

"Could Caroline have borrowed money that you didn't know about? Would her parents have had that kind of cash?"

Leonard said, "Her folks weren't rich as such, but they were well off. Very comfortable. Nice apartment on the Upper West Side, two cars. Her dad had his own plumbing business and a staff of four. He's probably retired now, but they weren't short of money back then, that's for sure."

"So, Caroline could have borrowed the cash from Daddy to pay Red and explained away the loan as what? Wedding expenses?"

Leonard frowned. "I don't think so. Like I said, Adam—that's Caroline's dad—was a business owner. Very meticulous about his finances. He'd offered to pay for the more expensive parts of the wedding, such as the hotel and the cars and the dress, but he'd insisted on receipts for everything. I'd be surprised if he was handing over bundles of cash to Caroline without asking any questions."

"Which means," Martha said, "if Caroline was paying someone to carry out the setup at the hotel, the evidence should be right here in front of us?"

"Exactly."

"You take May through August; I'll take September, October, and November."

They both worked in silence for a while, shoulder to shoulder, making notes, highlighting sections. Leonard refreshed their wineglasses. He assumed Martha would be sleeping over again and wouldn't be driving home. They'd come to a comfortable arrangement where they both slept in his bed, albeit in a purely platonic way.

"Nothing's standing out for the summer months," Leonard said. "More money than usual was spent in August, but Caroline was in the Hamptons on vacation with girlfriends at the time. Most of those payments are to bars and restaurants there. Nothing suspicious. How about you? Anything interesting to report?"

"Yup." Martha's pages had more highlighted sections than Leonard's did. "There were some big transactions made from the account later in the year, which I assume were deposits for wedding stuff. You know, florist, photographer, jeweler, that kind of thing. Then there were two reasonably large cash withdrawals."

"How big?"

"One thousand dollars and fifteen hundred dollars." Martha consulted the relevant statements. "The first was late September, a few days after the deposit for the wedding photographer. The second one was a month later."

Leonard's brows knitted together. "Wait, hold up a second. Caroline didn't hire a wedding photographer. That was supposed to be my job. I said I'd find out if one of the photographers at the *Reporter* could do the gig at a reduced price. I never got around to checking."

"A payment of five hundred dollars was made to Click Photography." She showed Leonard the relevant page. "Did you do one of those engagement shoots that are so popular these days?"

Leonard screwed his face up like he was thinking real hard. "No engagement shoot, but I guess Caroline could have had photos taken for some other reason." Then his features relaxed into something like relief. "Yeah, I remember now. She wanted professional photos taken for her portfolio and website. She was trying to find an agent who could secure her some work outside of the radio station—you know, hosting events and the like. She was desperate to boost her profile, with the ultimate goal of working in television. She felt like the photographs would be a good investment in her career, and I agreed."

"So, a perfectly innocent explanation for Click Photography," Martha said. "Any idea what the two cash withdrawals were for?"

"I don't remember. I'm sure Caroline would have had a good reason for withdrawing such large sums of money at the time. Probably the wedding. The second one was late October, right?"

"Right."

"That one could have been for the spa place in Montauk."

"Wouldn't it be unusual to pay for a hotel stay with cash, though?" Martha said. "Especially a fancy place like a spa resort. You'd think those reservations would be made online and paid for by card. According to the account statements, there were no payments whatsoever to a hotel in Montauk, whether for the room itself or the bar tab or room service."

Leonard shrugged. "Maybe her folks paid for the room, and Caroline took out the cash to cover extras when they got there? Things like champagne and spa treatments."

"It's possible, I guess. How were things between you and Caroline back then? I mean before Red? I'm guessing you weren't a whole lot of fun after the night at the Fairview Hotel."

Leonard gave her a wry smile. "I guess I wasn't the most fun person to be around for a while. The truth is, we weren't getting on so great before the night I met Red either. Snapping at each other, silly arguments about nothing and everything. I put it down to the stress of planning a wedding. A preview of what married life would be like."

"The big question is—did Caroline have a motive? Would she have had any reason to hire a private investigator or a beautiful woman to honeytrap you? If the answer is no, then I think we have to turn our attention to Bobby Khan, who sure did benefit from your breakdown."

Leonard didn't answer her. His cheeks colored, and he puffed out some air and ran his hands down his face.

"What is it?" Martha asked.

"I cheated on Caroline. After we got engaged."

"You mean other than Red?"

"Technically, I didn't cheat with Red. We didn't sleep together, remember?"

"No, you didn't, but it wasn't for the want of trying," Martha snapped. She took a steadying breath. "What you're saying is, you had sex with someone who wasn't Caroline or Red?"

Leonard slumped in his chair. "Yes. And no, I'm not proud of it. I know how you feel about cheaters."

"When did it happen?"

"When Caroline was in the Hamptons with her girlfriends."

"Which would have been in August of that year?"

Leonard nodded, his eyes on the dining table.

Martha snatched up one of the statements and flipped through the pages. "A few weeks after she returned from vacation—and you'd had sex with someone else—Caroline paid a visit to Click Photography. And, just days after that, a mysterious sum of cash was taken out of your joint checking account."

Martha picked up her cell phone.

"What are you doing?" Leonard asked, staring at her.

"What we should have done in the first place—googling Click Photography." She read the information displayed on the small screen, then met Leonard's gaze. "Click is a one-man operation run by a photographer by the name of Ron Kincaid. He provides all the usual photographic services. But that's not all he does."

"Go on."

"He also offers surveillance work for those who suspect their spouses are having an affair."

16
JIM

When Jim returned from yet another morning perfecting his swing on the golf course, he found a black plastic rolling suitcase and a Louis Vuitton duffel bag in the hallway.

Debra was in the kitchen. She was sitting at the island, a large Scotch and soda in front of her, the open bottle next to her as though the double might not be enough.

The time on the wall clock was just past noon.

"A little early, even for you," Jim said.

Debra's response was to pick up the crystal tumbler and take a long drink.

"I couldn't help but notice the bags in the hallway," he said. "Are we going on vacation, and I just forgot?"

Debra carefully set the drink down on the marble counter. She didn't look at him. The ticking of the clock seemed very loud. "I'm leaving you, Jim."

For a split second, he thought his wife had found out about Anna Bianco, and his stomach dropped like he'd hit the fast descent on a roller coaster. Then he remembered this was about the affair. *Her* affair.

Jim spoke calmly, despite the fury bubbling inside him. "Who is he?"

She nodded. "I spoke to Maddie. She told me about your phone call and that you suspected something was going on. She was upset that she'd messed up and let me down."

A couple of days after he'd burned the photos of Anna Bianco, Maddie had called him asking for a loan. It was the only time his youngest daughter made any effort with him, when she was looking for cash. He'd asked how dinner with her mom had been, and there had been a long pause that had set Jim's Spidey sense tingling before she'd hastily told him they'd had a great night.

"That new Thai place, wasn't it? Any good?"

Debra had told him they'd eaten at Mastro's. Steak and cocktails.

"That's right," Maddie had said. "The Thai place. It was okay."

He'd felt bad about tricking his daughter, but not as bad as knowing Debra was likely cheating, while the nearest he got to a good time these days was a better scorecard than McClure on the course. He had assumed she would get it out of her system, and it would fizzle out soon enough. He'd clearly been wrong.

"Does Becca know?"

Becca was their oldest daughter, who lived in London with her boyfriend.

"Not yet. I'll call her later."

"At least I'm not the last to find out. I guess that's something."

"Jim . . ."

"Who is he?" Jim asked again.

Debra sighed and stared into the drink. "Does it matter?" Her manicured finger traced a line of condensation on the glass.

"Someone at work, I'm assuming. The way you've been all dressed up for these 'presentations' lately. Your boss. *Brian.*"

He said the name like it tasted bad.

Her head snapped up, and her mouth formed a little O of surprise before the poker face was back in place—but not fast enough. Confirmation that he'd hit the bull's-eye on the first attempt. The nearest Jim would get to a hole in one.

He said, "It was hardly going to be the intern who picks up the coffee, was it? A handsome young boy toy might be okay for a one-night stand, make an older woman feel good about herself. But to walk out on all of this"—he gestured around him at the fifty-grand kitchen they'd had built just eighteen months ago—"it had to be someone with plenty of bucks in the bank."

"It's got nothing to do with money."

Jim snorted. "You keep telling yourself that, sweetheart. So, where're you going? His place? A little love nest where you can be together now that you don't have to worry about big, bad Jim finding out?"

"I'm going to a hotel."

"A hotel, huh? Don't tell me he's married too?"

Debra pursed her lips.

Jim laughed. "He is, isn't he? What? Hasn't told the wife yet?"

"Not yet," she said stiffly. "But he will."

"Oh, sure. That's what they all say."

"Don't be an asshole, Jim."

"I'm not the one screwing around. I'm not the one breaking up our family."

"Don't you dare try to take the moral high ground," Debra hissed. "Do you seriously think I don't know about all the little tramps you've fooled around with over the years? The reason I always turned a blind eye was to keep this family together."

Jim felt a hot flush creep from his neck all the way up to his receding hairline. He *hadn't* realized she'd known about his flings. He thought he'd been careful. But, the big difference was, that's all they were. Meaningless flings. His embarrassment was quickly replaced by anger again.

"I never walked out on you, though, did I?" he yelled. "I never gave up on our marriage. I never gave up on you. Although God knows why I didn't. I could have traded you in for a younger model years ago. *Model* being the operative word."

Debra gave him a withering look. "Fuck you, Jim."

"No, fuck you," Jim roared. "And get the fuck out of my house."

"But my taxi won't be here for another half hour."

"You can walk for all I care. Now get the hell out!"

Debra slid off the stool and moved past him toward the hallway, where her bags were waiting. She paused in the doorway.

"You know, this is all on you, Jim," she said softly. "This past year, you've changed—and not for the better. I feel like I don't know you anymore. And what's worse is that I don't like you very much either."

Jim heard her move her things outside, and then the door slammed shut behind her. Debra was right. He *had* changed. He'd had to make tough decisions and do things he didn't want to do—and he'd done it all for the sake of his wife and his kids.

And this was how she repaid him.

He strode across the kitchen and picked up the Scotch and soda.

Anna Bianco's face flashed into his mind, and Jim fired the crystal tumbler against the wall, sending booze and ice and broken glass flying everywhere.

17

CAROLINE

Caroline Cooper was in the kitchen, drinking a cup of coffee and wishing it was a glass of wine. She was trying very hard not to scream.

Of course, Harry wouldn't approve of day drinking in the house and especially not when the kids were visiting. The "kids" being a surly sixteen-year-old boy and a catty fourteen-year-old girl, both of whose default settings seemed to be grunts and eye rolls whenever Caroline tried to engage either one of them in conversation. But Harry was at work, as was increasingly the case when his children were here, meaning she was the one who had to spend yet another Saturday afternoon being tortured by *Call of Duty* or *Grand Theft Auto* or whatever other goddamned video game was popular this month. And always at an insufferable volume.

She closed her eyes and gently massaged her temples.

A loud banging at the front door startled her.

It was an insistent knock, like a fist was being used instead of a polite rap of the knuckles. Like the person wasn't going to take no for an answer. Loud enough to be heard over the shrieking gunfire and irritating music being pumped through the surround-sound system in the lounge.

Caroline frowned as she got up from the table and made her way down the hallway. She could see the outline of a tall figure through the frosted-glass panels. She realized that she'd stopped halfway between the kitchen and the front door, her breathing coming in short bursts. Caroline wasn't expecting any visitors, and Harry hadn't mentioned anything about a guest stopping by. He'd occasionally show up with work clients for dinner or drinks, but he always messaged her first to make sure both Caroline and the house were presentable, as though either one of them was ever anything less than perfect. Plus, Harry would have no need to knock on his own front door.

It could be a door-to-door salesperson, Comcast or Avon or whatever, but wasn't that all done online now? Did people really still show up at other peoples' houses trying to sell cable TV or cosmetics these days?

Caroline made a detour to the lounge and was immediately assaulted by crashes and bangs and shouts when she entered the room.

"Would you turn that goddamned noise down, please?" she snapped.

The response was twin eye rolls from Matty and Ava. Neither of them reached for the remote control to reduce the volume. Caroline knew her sharp tone would be reported back to Harry, but she didn't care. They'd been arguing a lot recently. She felt like she was on edge all the time, scared of her own shadow, jumping whenever the phone rang or someone unexpected was at the door.

Like now.

Caroline peered out the window and saw a battered old green Chevy Malibu parked in the driveway next to her dark gray Jeep Grand Cherokee. The rust bucket was exactly the kind of thing a struggling paparazzo or reporter might drive. Had she forgotten about a photo shoot or interview?

She returned to the hallway, closing the lounge door behind her, and started as a fist connected with the front door again. She pressed an eye to the peephole. When she saw who was standing there, she felt like her heart had just stopped. She was right about it being a journalist, but it was also the last person she expected to turn up on her doorstep. The last person she wanted to see.

Leonard Blaylock.

How the hell did he even know her address? Caroline usually stayed in a suite at the Belman Group's Midtown hotel when she was filming weekdays in the city. On weekends and holidays, she and Harry were here at their colonial farmhouse in Bedford. She guessed one of those at-home features they'd done in a Sunday supplement was how Leonard had tracked her down.

He didn't look particularly friendly either. Kind of agitated and pissed. Caroline took a couple of steadying breaths and opened the door with shaking hands.

"Leonard," she said neutrally. "This is a surprise."

"We need to talk," he said bluntly. Then he frowned at her. "Are you going somewhere?"

She should have said yes and gotten rid of him fast, but the truth popped out before the lie was fully formed. "No, I'm home all afternoon. Why?"

"You're all dressed up."

It was true. Caroline wore Louboutin heels, tight black jeans, and a fitted baby-pink cashmere sweater. Her blond hair (or rather, her expensive extensions) was curled, and her makeup was flawless. A subtle spritz of Miss Dior perfume provided the finishing touch. It was how Harry liked her to dress even when she had no plans for the day other than to tolerate his irritating offspring.

Caroline hadn't seen Leonard since the night they broke up, almost five years ago, during that weird anticlimactic period between Christmas and New Year's. By then, she couldn't bear to be in the same room as him, never mind allow him to touch her. He'd become distant and moody, and she'd told him it wasn't working out and that New Year's should be a fresh start for both of them. A fresh start apart. He'd just nodded and mumbled his agreement, and Caroline had walked out of his apartment without a backward glance. She hadn't even returned to collect the stuff that she kept there. Her dad had taken care of all the wedding cancellations, and all she'd had to do was agree to close down the joint checking account she shared with Leonard and split the cash equally between them.

Despite both of them living on a relatively small island, working in the same industry, and knowing the same people, they'd never once bumped into each other after the split. Now Caroline was secretly pleased that she *was* looking so good the first time they laid eyes on each other again, although she had to grudgingly admit that Leonard didn't look too bad either. She'd heard that he'd really let himself go after she dumped him. Long hair, a bushy beard, a beer belly, and scruffy clothing. He definitely had a bit of a middle-aged spread going on under his shirt, but otherwise, he was still reasonably attractive.

He had an old backpack slung over his shoulder that she recognized as the same one he used to carry his laptop, notepads, and voice recorder around in.

"Why are you here, Leonard?" she asked. "If it's for an interview, I don't think that's a good idea. It would be too awkward considering our past."

Leonard snorted out a laugh. "An interview? Ha, that's a good one. No, I don't want an interview, Caroline. I want to ask you a question, and I want you to tell me the truth."

She folded her arms across her chest and tried to appear disinterested, even though her insides were churning. The timing of his unexpected visit bothered her.

"Okay."

"You're not going to invite me in?"

Caroline hesitated. The last thing she wanted was Leonard Blaylock in her house.

He shrugged. "Or we could just stand out here and have a discussion on your doorstep about how you hired someone to spy on me while we were engaged. Hey, maybe we *should* do that interview. It would make a good story for one of those trashy magazines. I can see the headline on the front cover now: 'Paranoid TV starlet paid grubby private dick to snoop on fiancé.' What do you think? Bound to sell a few copies, huh?"

Caroline stared at him for a long moment, then stepped aside to make way for him to enter.

"Go straight through to the kitchen at the end of the hallway," she said stiffly. "The kids are in the lounge, and I don't want them knowing you're here."

Caroline closed the door behind him, her drawn features reflected in the frosted glass.

How much did he know?

Why was he here *now*?

She didn't offer Leonard a drink or even a seat. He sat down at the kitchen table anyway and gazed around admiringly. "I have to say, this is an amazing house. You've done well for yourself, Caroline. No wonder you didn't want to slum it in my old apartment."

"What do you want, Leonard? What's all this crazy talk about a private eye?"

"It's not crazy talk, though, is it?"

Leonard fished in his backpack, pulled out a handful of printed pages, and thrust them at her.

"What's this?" she asked.

"Statements from our joint account from five years ago."

"Why are you showing them to me? Why do you even still have them?"

He ignored her questions. "Those cash withdrawals highlighted in pink—for a grand and fifteen hundred—what was the money for?"

Caroline fixed an expression on her face that she hoped conveyed a mixture of pity and incredulity—and didn't betray her real feelings.

"You're seriously asking me to remember why I took money from the bank five years ago? And who's to say it was even me? We both had access to the account. Maybe you took the cash out yourself."

"I didn't."

"If it was me, it must have been for the wedding. Seeing as I did all the organizing."

"It wasn't for the wedding. The receipts for all the deposits that we did pay back then are in my files. There are no receipts that correspond to those cash withdrawals."

"What? You're accusing me of stealing from you? Is that it? You saw that I've 'done well' for myself as you put it, and now you want a piece of the action?"

Leonard glared at her. "I don't want your money, Caroline. I just want the truth."

"I don't remember anything about the cash, okay? *Nobody* would remember cash withdrawals from five years ago."

"They would if the money was to pay a private investigator. That's not exactly an everyday expense."

Caroline threw her hands up in exasperation. "What private investigator? What is wrong with you, Leonard? Who seriously finds a couple of transactions on an old bank statement and decides the money must have been spent on a private eye? Who even goes trawling through old statements in the first place?"

"Tell me about Ron Kincaid."

Caroline's mouth opened and closed again. "Who?"

"You know, if the TV presenting doesn't work out, don't even think about a career in acting or playing poker. You'd be terrible at both. Ron Kincaid is the private eye."

"Oh, for fuck's sake!" Caroline took a deep breath, then softened her voice. "Look, Leonard, I heard you went through a really tough time after we ended things. Some sort of breakdown. I do feel bad that I didn't reach out to you at the time and make sure you were okay. But all this talk of private eyes and spying, you do realize it sounds crazy, don't you? A load of old, paranoid nonsense."

"So, you don't know anyone by the name of Ron Kincaid?"

She sighed. "No, I don't."

"He's a photographer at Click Photography. A payment of five hundred dollars was paid to his company from our joint account shortly before the two cash withdrawals were made. It's highlighted in blue."

Caroline leafed through the statements and nodded. "Okay, yes, Click Photography does sound familiar. I think I had some photographs done there. I would never have remembered the photographer's name, though. I only used him once."

"Ron Kincaid also offers surveillance work where he spies on people and takes covert photos of them on behalf of suspicious husbands and wives."

"So what? I had some professional photos taken at his studio. That's it. He was kind of a creep, and the photos weren't great, so I never went back."

What Caroline wanted to say was *What reason would I have for hiring a private eye to follow you? Are you finally confessing to being a lousy, cheating bastard?* But it would be too dangerous to go down that route. She wanted Leonard Blaylock out of her house more than she wanted his remorse or an apology for the way he'd treated her.

He said, "How do I know you're not lying about the photos?"

"I'm not lying. They're on my website if you don't believe me."

"They're not. I checked. Your media kit only has more recent shots. No picture credits at all for Click Photography or Ron Kincaid."

"I guess you'll just have to take my word for it."

"You don't have copies of the photographs anywhere? Or the invoice?"

She sighed again. "Probably. I'm not sure where exactly. Maybe in the study upstairs."

Leonard sat back in the chair and crossed his legs. "I'm in no hurry, and you already said you don't have anywhere to be this afternoon. I don't mind waiting."

"If I find the stupid photos, do you promise to leave me the hell alone?"

"Yup. Scout's honor."

"Wait here. And if either of the kids come into the kitchen, tell them you're a journalist who's here to interview me."

Caroline gripped the handrail tightly as she climbed the stairs and not just because the stilettos were completely inappropriate for the thick, plush carpeting. Her legs felt like they might give way at any moment.

Once inside Harry's study, she made a beeline for one of the pink file boxes that contained all her press cuttings and magazine shoots. Despite what she'd told Leonard, Caroline knew exactly where to find the photos taken by Ron Kincaid. She should have destroyed them, gotten rid of any connection to Click, but as Leonard had just pointed out, there was a paper trail leading straight to Caroline Cooper whether she liked it or not. At least the photos might satisfy Leonard's curiosity and stop him from asking any more questions.

She opened the fastening on the box and riffled through the contents until she found a dozen black-and-white prints near the bottom. The young woman in the photos was pretty and appeared happy and confident as she went through a series of poses, but Caroline knew the wide smile was hiding a whole lot of pain and heartbreak that day. She turned one of the prints over and saw the stamp on the back:

© Click/Ron Kincaid

She made her way downstairs with the photographs and found Leonard in front of the kitchen sink with his back to her.

"What do you think you're doing?"

He turned around and held up a glass. "Helping myself to some water if that's okay? Seeing as you didn't offer."

She threw the prints onto the table.

"The photos for my portfolio that were taken by Kincaid," she said. "His company stamp is on the back. There's no date, but my hair is shorter, and I have bangs in the photos, which is as much proof as you're going to get as to when the photo shoot took place. After we broke up, I grew out the bangs and got extensions."

Leonard drank the water, then walked over to the table and picked up the photo on the top of the stack and studied it. He flipped it over and nodded. "Okay, I believe you." He held up the print. "Can I hold on to this?"

"I guess so. Why?"

He shrugged. "For old times' sake." He shoved the photo into his backpack. "In case you were wondering, neither of the kids came in here while you were upstairs, so no need to tell any lies. Seeing as you're so big on the truth."

"I'll see you out, Leonard."

Caroline watched from the doorway as he climbed into the Chevy Malibu, tires crunching on the gravel as the old car trundled past the manicured lawn, the perfectly curated flowerbeds, the water feature, and finally, through the open gates at the end of the driveway.

Leonard had quizzed her about Ron Kincaid, but he hadn't mentioned any other names. She tried to convince herself that he didn't know anything, that he wasn't a threat to her. But the ball of anxiety in the pit of her stomach refused to go away.

Caroline knew she had to protect her career, her marriage, her home, and the life she'd worked so hard to build for herself.

She wouldn't let anyone take it away from her.

No one could ever find out the things that she'd done.

18

CAROLINE

FIVE YEARS AGO

Click Photography's website had claimed it was a "centrally located" business, which Caroline had assumed meant central to Manhattan. She had assumed wrong.

She only realized as much while standing in the middle of a bustling street, getting in the way of busy foot traffic, studying the map on her cell phone. Trying to figure out how to get from where she was to where the little red pin was. She pinched two fingers to expand the map and saw that the little red pin appeared to be in Queens. The street name had been unfamiliar, and she berated herself for not checking the place out properly when she'd first booked, or at least looking up the address last night. But last night she'd had a lot more to worry about than a photo shoot.

Now she felt like she had been duped, even though the fee hadn't been very expensive. That should have been the biggest clue that she wasn't dealing with a high-end operation.

She had the choice of a taxi ride or the subway, but the difference in price between the cab fare and a MetroCard meant it was no choice at all. Despite the longer than anticipated commute, Caroline would still make the appointment on time, but she was pissed at the inconvenience all the same.

She should have canceled anyway. No way was she in the right frame of mind to pose for stupid photographs after the news she'd been given yesterday. But she'd already paid via Click's website, and the $500 had been taken out of her checking account. Tears pricked at her eyes, and Caroline blinked them back. She'd just spent forty minutes at the salon having her makeup done and had no intention of winding up with a face like a Picasso painting in photographs she couldn't even afford, not with the wedding less than a year away.

If there was even going to be a wedding now.

It was a nice day, cool but sunny, not even a hint of rain. The end of summer, before the days got shorter and the cold, dark nights settled in. Still light-jacket weather. As she made her way to the subway station, Caroline thought about the chance encounter with Maggie Maloney the day before.

Maggie Maloney was a middle-aged gossip who'd worked in ad sales at the *Reporter* before being laid off around a year earlier. Caroline had met her a couple of times on nights out with Leonard, including at the mass farewell party. She was one of several who'd lost their jobs in that particular round of layoffs, including a few from editorial, which was the only reason Leonard and Caroline had decided to show up. Maggie had somehow managed to get very drunk on wine coolers and spent most of the evening bitching about her now former coworkers.

Caroline hadn't even recognized Maggie when she'd stopped by her table yesterday afternoon while she was sitting outside a coffee shop with a skinny latte. Now she would always remember her as the woman who'd casually dropped a grenade and exploded her life. Caroline had been shopping in Target for some cheap blouses for the photo shoot. She'd been scrolling through her cell phone when she'd sensed someone hovering.

◆　◆　◆

Maggie: "Caroline Cooper? I thought it was you!"

　Caroline (trying desperately to place the other woman's face and remember her name): "Oh . . . hi there."

　Maggie: "It's me, Maggie Maloney. I used to work with your ex at the Reporter. You were at my farewell party."

　Caroline (vaguely wondering why Maggie referred to Leonard as her ex): "Oh, sure, I remember. How're you doing, Maggie?"

　Maggie: "Not too bad, doll. Not bad at all. Doing some temp work these days. You still at the radio station?"

　Caroline: "I am. Just finished an early shift, in fact. Decided to treat myself to some retail therapy this afternoon."

　Maggie (nose wrinkled at the sight of the Target bags): "Sorry, I don't listen to your station. Too much of that modern music for my liking. Much prefer WCBS-FM for the oldies when I'm in the car. I have to say, you're looking amazing, doll. You been away on vacation?"

　Caroline: "I have, thanks. Spent a couple weeks in the Hamptons last month with some girlfriends. It was fabulous. We were really lucky with the weather. Didn't rain once the whole time."

　Maggie: "The Hamptons, huh? Fancy. And what's this I spy on your left hand? Is that an engagement ring? Wow!"

　Caroline (a little embarrassed now about the increasingly loud conversation with a woman she doesn't really know): "Yes, it is. We're getting married next summer."

　Maggie: "Well, good for you, doll. Must be a keeper, the size of that rock. I'm telling you, you dodged a bullet with Leonard Blaylock. Men like him never change."

　Caroline (confused): "Actually—"

136

Maggie: "You know he slept with one of my friends a few weeks ago? She's still checking her cell phone every ten minutes, thinking he'll message her. He told her he was single but took her number and didn't give out his number. That says it all. Obviously not interested in anything other than a one-nighter. I told her, 'Karen, it ain't gonna happen, doll. Forget him.' He's always been a player, that one."

Caroline: "You must be mistaken, Maggie. I don't think Leonard—"

Maggie: "No mistake, doll. Look, I know he's your ex and all, but it was Leonard Blaylock all right. Karen's had a crush on him forever, ever since she met him at my farewell party. She hasn't stopped talking about him for the last three weeks. Absolutely smitten. Even sent him a friend request on Facebook. Anyway, enough about Leonard Blaylock. Tell me about this new fella you've bagged yourself."

Caroline (pushing past Maggie onto the street): "Sorry, Maggie. I have to go."

◆ ◆ ◆

Caroline took the F train to the Twenty-First Street–Queensbridge station and quickly established that Click Photography wasn't exactly central to Queens either. It was located in an industrial area that was off the beaten track enough to make her clutch her purse that much tighter and walk a little faster.

She could have just asked Leonard straight out last night if he'd cheated on her. But would he have told her the truth? And would Caroline have believed him if he'd denied it?

Instead, she'd waited until he was in the bathroom before going through his phone. His password was the date for the wedding. There were no suspicious messages, but according to Maggie Maloney, Leonard hadn't given out his number. There were no contacts for anyone by the name of Karen either, so he'd deleted her number or saved it under a different name. Caroline had then opened the Facebook app and saw a pending friend request from someone named Karen Sampson. She'd heard the toilet flush and had dropped the phone back onto the coffee table.

Another early shift at the radio station meant Leonard hadn't been expecting her to spend the night, which was just as well. She wouldn't have been able to go to bed with him while all those horrible thoughts and suspicions were living rent-free in her head. Back home in her bedroom at her folks' place, Caroline had looked up Karen Sampson's Facebook page. The privacy settings meant she was restricted to viewing only the woman's profile images. It was enough to tell her that Karen Sampson was an attractive blonde in her early forties.

Caroline found the photography studio in a drab brown brick building that also housed an appliance retailer and a computer-repair place. A chipped plastic sign next to a raised security gate read "Click Photography and Surveillance Services." She vaguely remembered something about surveillance work on the website but hadn't paid too much attention at the time.

The premises were spread over two stories. The entrance led straight into an office space with a worn carpet, a cheap wooden desk, and a stack of old Yellow Pages. A coffeepot and a microwave sat on top of some battered filing cabinets. There was a single door leading off the office that had been left open to reveal a toilet bowl, a dainty sink, and a well-used toilet brush. Caroline could smell the bleach from where she stood in the doorway and figured at least the facilities were clean if she needed to use them.

Behind the desk was a thin man in his late fifties whose clothes appeared to be wearing him. He had thinning gray hair and bad teeth. He wasn't dirty as such but kind of grubby both in his demeanor and the way he was dressed.

A narrow, carpeted staircase led up to the studio, where a camera, tripod, and lighting rigs were set up. There was a curtained stall for outfit changes, and a pile of props in one corner. Again, a single door off the main room. This one was closed. It had a shiny night latch on the front, and no sign to indicate what lay behind it.

The next hour was spent going through the motions, with poses and smiles and different backdrops and words of encouragement from Ron Kincaid. Caroline tried to put on her best game face, but all she could think about was Leonard and Karen Sampson. In bed together. Kissing, laughing, touching each other.

Back downstairs in the office, Kincaid explained that he would email her proof images for review once he was done editing them. The twenty images she selected would be loaded onto a USB stick that would be mailed to her, along with prints of her twelve favorite shots. Caroline thanked him and stood up to leave. Then she sat back down again.

"The sign outside said you also do surveillance work," she said. "What does that mean exactly?"

"It means I follow people to find out if they're cheating on their partners," Kincaid said matter-of-factly. "If they are, I take photos as evidence. Long lens stuff. Very discreet."

"How much do you charge?"

"A grand."

Caroline couldn't hide her surprise. "A thousand dollars? But that's double your fee for a photo shoot."

Kincaid smiled, exposing the nightmarish teeth again. "Yeah, but this kind of work mostly involves unsociable hours. Weekends and late nights. Plus, I also have to pay my honeys for each job I hire them for."

"Your honeys?"

Kincaid said, "This is how I operate—I don't spend weeks or months following the subject around, waiting for them to hit on someone in a bar one night. I don't have the time, and the clients don't usually have that kind of money. So, we set a honeytrap. One of my honeys—these are all attractive young women, with good jobs, who're looking to make a few extra bucks—will approach the subject, engage them in conversation, flirt with them, and, if the subject takes the bait, I'm there to capture it all on film."

Caroline frowned. "It all sounds a bit . . . seedy."

"Let me be clear about one thing, sweetheart—my girls aren't hookers. There is no sex involved. A bit of smooching and canoodling, swapping numbers, incriminating text messages, that kind of thing. The evidence we compile is enough for the client to establish whether their partner is willing to fool around or not. We can also provide a pretty good guess as to whether they've strayed before. My honeys can usually tell straightaway if they're dealing with a first-timer or a serial cheater. You interested?"

"I don't know. A thousand bucks . . . It's a lot of money."

How would she explain that kind of cash to Leonard? Especially if Maggie Maloney was spinning a web of lies, and he was completely innocent.

"Can't do any cheaper, I'm afraid. Not even for a pretty little thing like you."

"I'd need to think about it."

Kincaid's gaze dropped from Caroline's face, lingered on her breasts, and then landed on her diamond engagement ring.

"Yeah, you do that, sweetheart."

19

MARTHA

"She's lying."

Those were the first words Leonard said as Martha slipped into the seat across the table. He had a whisky in front of him and had ordered a red wine for her. He'd texted earlier to suggest they meet in a bar just off Times Square to discuss his visit with Caroline.

"Hello to you too, Leonard."

Martha shrugged out of her leather jacket. The place was busy, even for a Saturday night. It was a sports bar, with a row of flat-screen televisions that could be viewed from the bar stools or the tables. Even though she wasn't a big sports fan, Martha liked the relaxed vibe. Plus, the food at the next table looked good, and there appeared to be a wide selection of reasonably priced drinks.

"Sorry, hello," Leonard said. "How was your day?"

"Fine, apart from a baby who didn't stop screaming for a full fifty-five minutes. He finally tired himself out and fell asleep for the last five minutes of the shoot, so I was able to get some okay shots in the end—thankfully. I don't think a furious six-month-old throwing teddy bears everywhere was the look the parents had in mind."

"Glad that it all worked out." He gestured to her drink. "I ordered you a merlot. Hope that's okay. Maybe I should have waited until you got here and asked what you actually wanted to drink."

Leonard's fingers drummed an annoying beat on top of the table, and she could feel his leg bouncing up and down beneath it. He seemed all hyped up. She wondered if it was a shot of adrenaline from being in Caroline's company again.

Martha took a sip. "No, the wine is fine. This is a nice bar."

"Glad you like it. It's one of my favorites." He sipped some whisky. "Jim Sanders from *Rise & Shine* used to drink here often, along with a few others from the network. Haven't seen him in months, though."

"Others including Caroline?" Martha asked lightly.

Leonard scoffed. "Are you kidding? Not fancy enough for her. Wine bars with overpriced cocktails and influencers taking photos of their drinks and food they have no intention of eating is more her scene."

"Tell me about your visit to her place in Bedford," Martha said. "Why do you think she lied to you?"

"For starters, she looked like she'd seen a ghost when she opened the door and found me standing there."

"To be fair, if my ex showed up on my doorstep, I'd be none too pleased either. And I have nothing to hide."

"She was all jittery too," Leonard said. "The whole time I was there, it was like she was on edge, and that's not like Caroline at all. If you've ever seen her on TV, you'll know she's calm and confident, even when there's a big breaking news story happening live on air. I swear, her hands were shaking when I confronted her about the money."

"What did she say?"

"That she couldn't remember taking it out of the bank or what it was for, but if she had been the one to make those withdrawals, it was probably for the wedding. All very predictable. She denied knowing

Ron Kincaid, but the expression on her face when I mentioned his name told me she knew exactly who he was. She did admit to hiring Click Photography for a photo shoot, although she claimed that she didn't remember the photographer's name." Leonard rummaged in his backpack and pulled out a black-and-white print. "This is her 'proof' that she used their services for photography rather than surveillance work. The company stamp is on the back."

Martha took the photo and studied it. Caroline Cooper wore a striped Breton top and a megawatt smile. Her blond hair was poker straight and fell to her shoulders. Her pale eyes were bright and sparkling under thick bangs. She resembled a younger Kate Hudson.

"But you think otherwise?" she asked.

"I think Kincaid took those photographs and then Caroline went back to Click and hired him to set me up after she somehow found out about Karen Sampson."

"Who's Karen Sampson?" Martha asked.

"The, uh, woman I spent the night with while Caroline was in the Hamptons with her girlfriends."

"Right. Got it." Martha took a long drink. Why was she jealous of a woman she didn't know? Of something that had happened years ago?

"Are you okay?" Leonard asked.

Martha nodded. "What did Caroline say about Red?"

"I didn't ask her about Red."

"Really? Why not?"

"She'd already denied hiring a private eye and initially claimed she had no idea who Ron Kincaid was, so she was hardly going to admit to knowing anything about Red, was she? I didn't want to tip her off as to how much we know."

"Makes sense, I guess. So, we've established a definite connection between Caroline and Click—but we still don't know if Red actually worked for Kincaid. It's highly likely that she did, but he might not be the only guy in New York hiring women to honeytrap men for money. When I first suspected David of cheating on me, I almost hired a private eye based out of Blissville, a guy by the name of Larry something, who also does this kind of surveillance work."

"Exactly. Which is why our next move is to confirm that Red was one of Kincaid's honeys and also find out if anyone else in my world back then—other than Caroline—had any involvement with Click. I'm still not ruling Bobby out just yet."

"How do we do that?"

"I have a three-pronged plan. But I need your help. Are you up for it?"

"Sure," Martha said.

Leonard had finally quit with the finger drumming and leg bouncing, but he still appeared overly animated, his eyes shining as he leaned in close enough for her to smell the Scotch on his breath.

"The first part is the reconnaissance," he said. "The second part is where you'll play a key role. The third part—which involves me—is a bit riskier."

Martha frowned. "Risky in what way?"

"Risky as in highly illegal."

On Sunday, they carried out the reconnaissance of Click's premises, which basically involved Martha poking around outside under the pretense of trying to find the place that sold fireplaces if anyone asked.

They'd traveled across the Ed Koch Queensboro Bridge to Queens, and Martha had noticed Leonard's jaw was clenched as he'd stared out the window at the East River sparkling below them like a dusky jewel in the fall sunshine. She'd wondered if it was the first time he'd made the crossing since the day he'd attended what he thought was Red's funeral.

Leonard waited in the car while Martha went for a closer look at Kincaid's workplace. The anonymous brown brick structure was at the end of a block of mismatched buildings of different heights and colors. Most had peeling paintwork, some had electrical cables running between windows, all of them were shabby and unappealing.

The photography studio was tightly locked up. The graffiti-tagged security gate appeared only to provide access to Click, even though the building housed other businesses too. They apparently had their own separate entrances. From signage in windows that hadn't seen a washrag in years, she ascertained that Ron Kincaid's unit occupied two stories, which were street level and the second floor. The first-floor window had metal bars and dirty venetian blinds. Martha stepped up to the grimy glass and saw a dated office space inside.

She wandered around to the rear of the building where she found parking for those who leased units. There was a single vehicle in the lot at the far end, an old red pickup truck that she didn't think belonged to Ron Kincaid because of where it was parked. She found two windows that she guessed were part of Click's premises. The first-floor one was higher up than the office window at the front, and it was smaller, with pebbled glass but no bars. Probably a bathroom. The upstairs window had what appeared to be a bunch of black trash bags taped over it from the inside. There was an overflowing lidless dumpster under the bathroom window and some garbage bags stacked next to it.

Martha returned to the car and reported her findings to Leonard. She checked her phone and saw that Kincaid had responded to the message she'd submitted via his website's contact form. She'd told him she was interested in his surveillance work and wanted to meet as soon as possible to discuss hiring him. Kincaid's email reported that he had a full shooting schedule the next day, but if she was available for a later-than-usual appointment, say around six p.m., he would be happy to accommodate her and go over the services he provided. Martha replied to confirm that she was, indeed, available for the meeting.

She turned to Leonard. "I'm in. Part one of the plan is complete; part two gets underway tomorrow."

◆　◆　◆

On Monday, Martha picked up Leonard from his apartment after she'd finished her last shoot of the day.

As she drove over the bridge again, they practiced her script ahead of the rendezvous with Kincaid. By the time they reached the industrial area, dusk had set in and the nine-to-five businesses had fallen silent. A blue tarp covering a block of scaffolding flapped in the wind. The after-dark establishments began to come to life. Fluorescent light spilled from Mexican restaurants and fast-food takeout places. Neon signs bathed black sidewalks in reds and blues and greens.

Click's security gate was up, and the lights were still on.

Martha parked in the same spot as the day before. Leonard's expression was tense. His jaw was clenched again, so tightly this time that she could see the little muscles pulsing.

"I'll be fine," she said. "Don't worry."

"You have your cell phone?"

"I do."

"If you feel in any way uncomfortable, get the hell out of there. If you need help, text or call me. I'll be in there in a flash."

"I'll be fine," Martha repeated.

She found Kincaid behind a varnished wood desk that was so flimsy it could be blown away by a sneeze. He stubbed out a cigarette when she entered the office and moved a tin ashtray to the top of a pile of Yellow Pages that were stacked on the floor. His work surface held a green rotary-dial telephone like the one Martha's parents used to own, except theirs was cream; a notepad; a plastic pen holder; a wire basket containing manila files; and a closed laptop covered in stickers.

Kincaid offered her a smile that would have given Steve Buscemi nightmares.

"Mrs. Smith?"

"That's me."

Martha and Leonard knew it was best to leave as little a trail as possible back to them, so she'd set up an email account in the name of Jane Smith before using Click's contact form to make the appointment with Kincaid. It was hardly original, what with it being the most common surname in the country, but Martha figured if it was good enough for Angelina Jolie, it was good enough for her.

"Please, take a seat," Kincaid said.

He gestured to an uncomfortable-looking orange plastic chair, like the kind you'd find at an AA meeting or in a dentist's waiting room. Martha dropped into the chair, clutching her open purse on her lap, one hand feeling for the cell phone inside. She was more skittish than she'd expected to be. Kincaid picked up on her anxiety.

"No need to be nervous, Mrs. Smith. Can I ask, first of all, how you heard about Click?"

"A friend recommended you. She used your services to, uh, confirm that her husband was fooling around behind her back. She'd rather I didn't mention her name, though. She's in a new relationship now."

"Perfectly understandable. That's fantastic that she's got a new man and even better that she was pleased with the work that we did for her. But now you suspect your own husband is cheating on you?"

"I do." Martha didn't need to fabricate this part of the story. "David's behavior has changed over the last year or so. He claims to be working a lot more than usual, but he never seems to be at the office whenever I call. I've noticed him on his cell phone late at night when he thinks I'm not looking. When he comes home after working late, he smells like he's freshly showered."

Kincaid nodded grimly. "Sounds like an affair to me. Have you confronted him about it?"

"Once, about six months ago." Martha twisted the cheap gold-plated "wedding ring" she'd picked up in the mall. "He denied it, said I was imagining things, that I was trying to cause arguments, and that I'd brought distrust into our marriage. I didn't ask again."

Kincaid tutted. "Classic gaslighting techniques."

He went on to explain how the private investigation side of his business worked and how he employed women known as honeys to set honeytraps and snare philandering spouses. He spun around in his swivel chair, produced a folder from one of the filing-cabinet drawers, and handed it to her.

Martha flipped through the pages of the file. It was filled with photographs of attractive women of different ages and body types. She returned it to Kincaid. "They're all brunettes."

"But you're a brunette," he pointed out. "I assumed that was Mr. Smith's type."

"You're a man, Mr. Kincaid. You should know better. If my husband is fooling around, I suspect he wants something different from what he's getting at home. Let's just say David is a big fan of Julianne Moore and Amy Adams."

Kincaid stared at her blankly.

"They're both redheads," Martha clarified.

"Ah, got it!" Kincaid spun around again, pulled open the same drawer, and came up with a different-colored folder this time.

Martha made a show of leafing through it. She knew Red wouldn't be in there, what with the woman being dead and no longer available for hire.

She said, "My friend mentioned a particular honey that she thought would hook David like a big fat trout. But I don't see her in here."

"Oh? Did your friend have a name for the honey? Maybe she changed her hair color and is in one of the other folders."

"It sounded more like a nickname, to be honest. Absolutely gorgeous, apparently. Went by the name of Red."

Martha watched all the color drain from Kincaid's face and knew that she had confirmation of Anna Bianco's connection to Click before the man uttered another word. "I'm afraid Red no longer works here. But I have plenty of other gorgeous redheads to choose from."

"That's disappointing," Martha said. "Did Red move on someplace else? Maybe I should try a few other detective agencies and see if I can find her. My friend really was convinced that David wouldn't be able to resist this woman, and this could all be very useful if we end up in divorce court."

"You're not going to find Red at another agency, Mrs. Smith," Kincaid said quietly. "She's dead."

"Really? That's terrible. What happened, if you don't mind me asking?"

Kincaid squirmed in his chair, and his Adam's apple bobbed up and down. "She, ah, was murdered. The cops still haven't found the guy who did it."

Martha aimed for a mix of shock and horror. "Murdered? That poor woman. Wait—they don't think it had anything to do with the work she did for you, do they?" She frowned so deeply that

Kincaid couldn't miss it. "I guess this honeytrapping business could be quite dangerous if a man who was being set up figured out what was happening."

Kincaid sat up straighter. "I can assure you that what happened to Anna, I mean Red, had absolutely nothing to do with her work here at Click."

"How can you be sure, though?"

"I just can. Trust me. Anyway, like I said, we have lots of other stunning women on our books."

Martha made to get up. "You know what, maybe this wasn't such a good idea. I'd hate to think I was putting someone in danger . . ."

"Please, Mrs. Smith. Sit back down. Look, I shouldn't really say anything, but . . ."

Martha lowered herself back into the chair. "But?"

"The police asked me about some unexplained cash deposits in Red's checking account. The money didn't come from me. They looked into my own accounts, both business and personal, and they were clean as a whistle. Wherever that money came from, it's probably the reason she wound up dead."

Martha eyed him warily. "The money definitely had nothing to do with your business?"

"Cross my heart. If it did, don't you think the cops would have me in a cell by now? I promise you, Mrs. Smith, Click is a completely legit and aboveboard operation. Nothing hinky whatsoever."

She picked up the file with the redheads again and selected one at random. The woman did actually look a bit like Julianne Moore. "I think David would like her. How much do you charge?"

"A grand."

Martha tried not to smile. A thousand dollars. Bull's-eye.

"That sounds reasonable. I just need to move the money from my savings account into my checking account. I'll be in touch in a day or two to make the necessary arrangements."

"Perfect." Kincaid beamed, treating her to another display of his unfortunate teeth.

Martha stood up and headed for the exit. Then she paused. "Actually, you don't have a bathroom I could use, do you?"

"Sure do." He pointed to a door with "WC" on the front. "It's right through there."

Martha locked the door of the tiny bathroom behind her. The plastic toilet seat appeared flimsy, and sure enough, when she pressed a hand to the lid, it left an indent that popped back out again. She raised both the lid and the seat and tried not to retch at the sight of the pale yellow stain underneath. She stepped out of her socks and shoes and placed a bare foot on either side of the porcelain rim, balancing like a gymnast on a beam.

She reached up to the small window with the pebbled glass that she'd spotted at the rear of the building the day before. Unlatched the catch and pushed the window open a crack. A rush of cool air hit her face. She pushed harder, gauging how far the window would open. After some resistance, it opened all the way. She pulled it down again, leaving it open a couple of inches. Hopefully Kincaid wouldn't need to use the bathroom before he left for the night, and if he did, he wouldn't notice the draft.

Martha silently jumped down onto the tiled floor, took her cell phone out of her purse and fired off a text to Leonard.

I'm on my way out. Part two of the plan is complete. You're up next.

20

CAROLINE

FIVE YEARS AGO

Caroline sat in her VW bug, the rain battering the little purple car like a steel drum. She couldn't bring herself to get out and find out what Kincaid had to report back. She knew that what he had to tell her had the potential to change her whole life. To ruin everything.

It could be good news, of course, but Caroline didn't think so. Kincaid's message stated that he wanted her to come into the office so they could go over his findings and the photographs.

The photographs.

Surely, there wouldn't *be* any photographs unless Leonard had taken the bait?

A few days after her photo shoot at Click, Caroline had returned to the dingy building and hired Ron Kincaid to set Leonard up. The man was a creep, but she had to know if she was engaged to an even bigger creep. She had to know if what Maggie Maloney had told her was true.

If Leonard quizzed her about the $1,000 she'd taken out of their joint account, she'd tell him it was for the wedding. Bridesmaid dresses or glitzy shoes or fancy favors. The kind of "girls' stuff" that was guaranteed to make his eyes glaze over and ensure he'd quickly lose interest in the conversation.

Caroline had felt bad for all of ten seconds after taking the cash out of the bank, then decided it was an investment in their future. If Leonard passed the test, she'd be able to enter married life knowing she could fully trust her husband—and that was worth a whole lot more than a thousand bucks.

Kincaid had given her a folder containing photos of blond honeys. Caroline herself was blond. Karen Sampson was a blonde. It was a safe bet to assume that Leonard was a sucker for a blonde. She'd picked out Karlie who was thirty-two, curvy but not overweight, five seven, had blue eyes and almost platinum-blond bobbed hair.

Then Caroline had handed over an envelope filled with tens and twenties. Kincaid hadn't been happy. He'd claimed that cash transactions looked shady and that his accountant insisted all payments go through the website and be fully accounted for. Kincaid had been investigated by the IRS years ago, and it wasn't an experience he was keen on repeating.

She'd pointed out that Leonard would be suspicious of another payment to Click appearing on their bank statement with no photos to show for it this time. Surely his other clients had similar issues?

Kincaid explained that most of his clients had separate checking accounts or, at the very least, their own credit card so that their partner didn't have to find out about the payment to Click. Caroline admitted her own credit card was maxed out, what with her having a wedding to plan. He'd finally relented and stuffed the envelope in a drawer, and they'd picked the night the honeytrap would be set, when Leonard would be out drinking with his buddy Bobby Khan from the *Reporter*.

Caroline had almost called the whole thing off more than once, but she'd known the not knowing would destroy her and, ultimately, destroy their relationship. If Leonard was innocent, no one ever need know what she'd done. If he wasn't, it was best to know now, before going through with the wedding.

After a while, she'd managed to convince herself that everything would be okay; that Leonard would spurn Karlie's advances and tell the woman he was flattered, but he was already taken; that Maggie Maloney would be shown to have made a mistake or, more likely, been guilty of mischief-making after spotting an opportunity to cause trouble between Leonard and Caroline; that the gossipy bitch had tried to pave the way for her friend Karen Sampson to swoop in if Leonard became a free agent again.

Then Ron Kincaid had gone and mentioned photographs, and all of her doubts had bubbled up to the surface again.

Caroline watched the luminous digits of the clock on the dash as they clicked through the minutes. It was raining so hard now, she could have been sitting in a car wash. Through the side window, she could just make out the blurry light of Click's office across the street. She told herself she was waiting for the rain to stop. She knew it was a lie. Her appointment was forty-five minutes ago. As Caroline drummed her fingers on the steering wheel, her engagement ring caught her eye.

Leonard had chosen it at Tiffany's before he'd proposed on that beautiful spring day barely six months ago. *Breakfast at Tiffany's* was one of her all-time favorite movies, and she'd always dreamed of a diamond from the famous store on Fifth Avenue. He'd refused to tell her how much he'd paid for it, but she knew it was a lot. Leonard told her he'd been saving for months and that she was worth it. She had believed him.

Maybe Kincaid's photos would show Leonard walking out of the bar with Bobby after Karlie had already left, having failed to tempt Leonard?

An hour after she was supposed to meet the photographer, Caroline flipped down the sun visor, switched on the dome light, and used the tiny mirror to apply her signature berry-colored lipstick. That's what Audrey Hepburn, as Holly Golightly, had done in the back of a cab in the movie; she had reapplied her lipstick before being given bad news. But Caroline would be receiving good news, not bad. That's what she told herself anyway. She grabbed a golf umbrella from the back seat, pushed open the door, and waited for a break in the traffic before racing across the street, her boots splashing in the puddles.

Caroline was surprised to find a beautiful redhead sitting where she expected Ron Kincaid to be.

The woman wore a sheer blouse and tight jeans and had very long legs. Her feet were on the desk, crossed at the ankles, and she was occupied by a cell phone. When she spotted Caroline, she dropped the phone to the desk and her feet to the floor.

"I'm here to see Ron Kincaid," Caroline announced.

The redhead consulted the sticky label on a file in front of her. "Caroline Cooper?"

"Yes. That's me."

"Take a seat, Caroline. Ron had some business to take care of, so he asked me to hang around awhile in case you showed up. I'm Red, by the way."

Caroline lowered herself into an orange plastic chair. "Sorry I'm late. Are you Ron's secretary?"

Red laughed at that. "I'm one of his honeys, but yeah, I also man the office from time to time, so I suppose I'm kind of like a secretary but without the cute pencil skirts and typing skills."

She pushed the file toward Caroline. Her black nail polish was chipped. She had stopped laughing.

Caroline stared at the folder as though it were a snake about to strike, then looked at Red. "Are these the photos of the honeytrap?"

"That's right."

There was a big box of Kleenex on the desk. Had it been there the last time she'd been in this office? Caroline didn't think so.

She gave a little laugh of her own that sounded like a croak. "Boy, this is even worse than waiting to hear back from a job interview or for the results of a pap test."

Red didn't return the smile.

"It's not good news, is it?" Caroline asked.

Red shook her head. "I'm sorry, Caroline, it's not good news. You seem like a nice woman. You deserve way better."

Caroline swallowed past the lump in her throat and opened the folder. The first sequence of photographs showed Leonard and Karlie sitting in a window booth at a bar, Kincaid having presumably captured the shots with a long lens from outside. At first, they were just chatting. Then they gradually became more tactile. She ran a hand through his hair. He slung an arm casually around her shoulder. She leaned in close and whispered in his ear. He laughed at something she said.

Red said, "There's a full report in the back of the file, with detailed times and places. But basically, his buddy left soon after Karlie approached them and made it clear she was interested in your boyfriend. Karlie then instigated the move over to the window seat where she knew Ron would be able to snap the pics."

"He's my fiancé, not my boyfriend."

"Fiancé. Right. Sorry."

The next couple of photos showed Karlie leading Leonard out of the bar by the hand. He had what could only be described as a stupid, smug grin on his face. The final series of photographs were the ones that broke Caroline's heart. They were even worse than she'd imagined.

Leonard and Karlie were in an alleyway, next to a dumpster. They were kissing passionately. His hands were in her hair and then on her ass and then up her top as though touching her breasts.

Red said, "Ron wanted me to assure you that that's as far as things went. No sexual acts took place. Karlie made her excuses and left after these photos were taken."

The images in front of her blurred as Caroline's eyes filled with tears. She knew Ron's assurances were about protecting the integrity of his business and the women, not about making Caroline feel any better. Looking at those pictures, there was no doubt in her mind that Leonard would have gone all the way had Karlie not put the brakes on.

"As a fellow honey, I can also assure you that Karlie would have gotten no enjoyment out of this interaction." Red gestured to the image of the scene in the alleyway. "Satisfaction at snaring a rat? Yes. Pleasure? No. Most honeys do it for the money because they have kids to feed and clothe, blah blah blah. Others, like me, do it because these bastards deserve to be held accountable for their bad behavior."

Caroline blinked fat tears onto her cheeks, and her lip trembled. She put her head in her hands and cried harder than she had since she was a little kid. Chest heaving, shoulders shaking, loud racking sobs, the works. Finally, when she was done, Red handed her the box of tissues. Caroline wiped her face and blew her nose while the other woman silently watched her without comment, her expression unreadable.

"Is it okay if I use the bathroom to wash my face?" Caroline asked. "I must look a mess right now." Her voice was hoarse, and her face felt as if it were on fire.

"Sure. And don't worry, it's clean. I suppose you could say I'm the cleaner around here, as well as being the secretary and one of the honeys."

Inside the cramped bathroom, Caroline stared at her reflection in the cracked mirror. Her eyes were red and puffy, her face was all blotchy, and her makeup was like something from an Alice Cooper video. She let the faucet run until the water was really cold, then splashed her face. The brown towel hanging from a ragged nail smelled musty as she dried off.

Dozens of thoughts and questions crowded her brain: What would she say to Leonard? Was she going to dump him? Could she forgive him? Did she want to stay with him? What about the wedding? Should she call it off? What about the money they'd lose? Did the money even matter? What would her parents say? Her friends? Her coworkers at the radio station?

Caroline returned to the office and the uncomfortable orange chair. "Sorry about that."

"Don't worry about it," Red said. "Feeling any better?"

"Not really."

Caroline's cell phone pinged in her purse. Then it pinged again. She pulled it out and saw that she had two text messages from Leonard:

Where are you???

Did you forget about dinner with Bobby and Amina? We're all at the restaurant waiting for you and we're starving. Call or text me asap.

Rage exploded inside her suddenly.

"Fucking asshole!"

Caroline hurled the phone across the room and heard the unmistakable crack of the screen shattering as it hit the concrete wall. The plastic case flew off and bounced across the threadbare carpet.

"Was it him?" Red asked.

"He wants to know why I'm late for dinner."

Red's eyes traveled to where the battered iPhone lay. "That's more like it."

"What?"

"He deserves your anger, not your tears."

Caroline nodded. "You're right. And do you know what? I'm fucking furious. How dare he treat me like this."

"What are you going to do about it?"

"I'm sure as hell *not* going to go and sit in a restaurant with him and his friends and pretend like everything's okay. I'll probably get very drunk, destroy all his clothes, and then dump him as publicly and humiliatingly as possible."

"That's it?" Red raised an eyebrow. "That's all you've got after what he's done to you?"

Caroline frowned. "What do you mean?"

"I used to be married," Red said. "And, like you, I found out my man was fooling around with other women. The only difference was, I went through with a wedding first before discovering my husband was a cheating bastard."

"Seriously? But you're gorgeous. Why would anyone cheat on you?"

Red laughed bitterly. "You've heard that tired old saying that delusional women like to spout about their husbands, right? 'Why would he go looking for a hamburger when he has steak at home.' I'll tell you why—because he can. Even the best rump steak gets boring after a while if there's no variety, so why not slum it with a hamburger every now and then? In other words, my husband cheated on me because he could, and your fiancé cheated on you because he could. And it makes absolutely no difference how gorgeous or smart or funny or adventurous in bed we are. Men are just wired differently. They see something, they want it, and they take it."

"What did you do?" Caroline asked. "When you found out about your husband's affairs, I mean."

"All the things you just said you were going to do. And do you know what he did? He laughed in my face. Told me it wouldn't take him long to find a replacement. And it didn't. A month after I moved out, one of his tramps moved in. The only person who suffered as a result of the breakup of our marriage was me."

Caroline had assumed Leonard would be devastated when she confronted him with Ron Kincaid's covert photos. The idea that he might just simply *move on* filled her with horror. Horror and rage.

"What do you suggest I do?"

Red leaned across the desk. Her lips were very red, and her eyes were very blue. "Let me ask you something, Caroline—do you want to make him pay? And I mean really pay?"

"Yes," Caroline replied immediately. She realized she meant it. "Yes, I want him to pay. I want him to suffer."

"I can help make that happen. But it'll cost you."

"How much?"

"Fifteen hundred dollars. In cash."

"Fifteen hundred? Seriously?"

Red smiled. "Trust me, Caroline. It'll be worth every cent."

21
RED

The door opened, and Leonard Blaylock and his buddy entered the bar, bringing with them the cold, damp chill of a November night. They were laughing and joking and talking just a bit too loudly. Drunk but not too drunk.

Red typed out a text message to Caroline Cooper.

They're here. Will let you know when it's done.

Caroline responded with a thumbs-up emoji.

"Do you want to grab a table and I'll go order the drinks?" she heard Blaylock say to the friend, whose name was Bobby Khan, according to the notes she had on her cell phone.

"Sounds good," Bobby responded. "Same again for me, thanks."

Red watched Blaylock as he waited for the drinks, chatting and flirting with the female bartender the whole time. She'd seen the photos of him with Karlie, of course, but this was her first look at him in the flesh. Mid to late thirties, tall, dark wavy hair, too far away to make out the eye color from here but probably hazel or green, in good shape, nicely dressed. Not gorgeous but quite attractive all the same. A solid seven in the looks department, elevated to an eight by his confidence and charisma. If you liked that sort of thing.

She could see Bobby Khan staring at her from the corner of her eye as Blaylock carried the draft beers to their table. Red dropped her eyes to her phone and made a mental note of the time. According to Caroline, there was a good chance of Bobby, a new dad, being ordered home early by his wife. If he wasn't, Red would have no option but to flirt with Blaylock with an audience present. Karlie's honeytrap experience suggested Bobby wouldn't be a barrier to his engaged buddy getting some action if approached by an attractive woman. She would give it twenty minutes before making her move.

A little over five minutes later, Red heard a loud groan coming from where they were sitting. She saw Bobby pick up his cell phone from the table. He didn't look happy as he walked past her on his way to the exit to take the call. The wife, hopefully, with the expected hook. Blaylock glanced over his shoulder and met Red's eye. She smiled at him and he turned away.

Bobby returned to the bar and pulled on his coat, then slapped Blaylock on the back before leaving. Red signaled for the bartender. She'd been nursing the same cocktail for an hour.

"Another Negroni?" the bartender asked.

"No." Red nodded in Blaylock's direction. "Just whatever he's drinking."

The bartender's eyebrows lifted a fraction, but she said nothing, just started working the Rolling Rock tap. Red paid for the drink, then took a deep breath and walked over to Leonard Blaylock and placed the beer in front of him.

When she'd gone over the plan with Caroline, she'd been confident Blaylock would be attracted to her, even though he was, apparently, a fan of blondes. Red knew she was a beautiful woman, and that wasn't just her tooting her own horn. She wouldn't have been stopped in the street by a model scout at the age of sixteen if she wasn't beautiful. Even so, there was still a very small chance that Blaylock would not take the bait being dangled in front of him.

"Mind if I join you?" Red slipped into the empty seat facing him and held his gaze. Sucked her cocktail through the straw in what she hoped was a mildly suggestive manner.

The expression on Blaylock's face told her she'd had nothing to worry about. His eyes drank in every inch of her. "Um, sure. I guess."

Red quickly got the introductions out of the way, leaning in closer to be heard over the music. "Whatcha See Is Whatcha Get" by the Dramatics played on the jukebox. She tried not to smile. The title of the song couldn't be any further from the truth with regards to her little role-playing exercise with Leonard Blaylock.

The next hour or so was spent making small talk and telling lies. Blaylock insisted on buying cocktails and shots, which wasn't ideal. Red could handle her liquor, but she'd need to have her wits about her for what was to come later. There were lots of little details she had to get just right. Blaylock was drunk enough by then that he didn't realize she was only sinking half the booze in the shot glasses before stacking his empties on top of her own. He also didn't seem to notice that she wasn't making her way through the cocktails quite as fast as he was either.

The rain was coming down hard by the time they moved outside. It was freezing too. Red shivered in her short dress and leather jacket as they both sheltered under the doorway awning. He held open his coat for her, and she thought, *Oh, you think you're such a smooth bastard, don't you?* She pressed her body up against his, and their eyes met, and then their lips did the same. He wasn't a great kisser. Too much tongue and saliva. The sloppy kiss of someone who'd had too much booze.

When they finally pulled apart, Blaylock hailed a yellow cab.

"You take this," he said. "I can walk home from here."

She gave him a playful look and climbed into the taxi. She left the door wide open and made sure her already short dress rode up another couple of inches to show off even more leg. Her heart thundered every bit as loudly as the rain on the cab. This was the big test. Would Leonard Blaylock settle for a kiss, or would he want more? If he walked off into the wet New York night, Red would have to return most of the $1,500 to Caroline Cooper and admit that she'd failed.

Blaylock climbed into the taxi.

◆ ◆ ◆

When Red had explained to Caroline that her fee was so expensive because it also covered expenses—such as props and a hotel room—the woman had been horrified.

"A hotel room?" she'd asked. "You're not *actually* going to have sex with Leonard, are you?"

"Of course not," Red had assured her. "He just has to think that I am. I do kissing, but that's it. Kind of the opposite of Julia Roberts's character in *Pretty Woman* when you think about it."

Red just hadn't realized there would be quite so much kissing.

The short taxi ride felt as if it took forever. Blaylock's tongue was in her mouth the whole time, his hands crawling all over her body. At least he offered to pay the fare. Then there was more kissing outside the hotel in the pouring rain. Red getting soaked and annoyed; Blaylock thinking he was Ryan Gosling in *The Notebook*.

And he was *loud* too.

"You are so hot," he practically shouted in the silent street.

Red tried to hide her irritation with a smile. She put a finger to her lips and nodded in the direction of the hotel.

"The hotel doesn't allow its guests to have guests?" he stage-whispered.

"No, it doesn't."

"What are we going to do?" He glanced up at the windows. The dirty-yellow building was five stories high. "I'm not exactly Spider-Man, you know."

Red forced a laugh at his crap joke. "Don't worry. My room is on the first floor, right next to the rear fire door. I'll go in through the front entrance and pick up my key from reception. You go down there." She pointed to a dark alleyway. "I'll meet you at the back of the building and let you in."

"Won't the fire door set off an alarm?" Blaylock asked.

"Nah, it's always being propped open by staff and guests who want to smoke out back."

Red headed inside, while Blaylock staggered off down the alleyway. Once inside the room, she got to work quickly in the darkness. She kicked off her boots, hung up her jacket, and stuffed her bag and cell phone in the safe inside the closet where she'd already hidden the bottles from the minibar.

Caroline was positive that Blaylock would have some coke on him. She said he usually did when it was a boys' night out. He knew she didn't approve of drugs, but she knew he was still using because she'd found the evidence in his pockets more than once after he'd been out drinking.

Red went into the bathroom and checked that all the props she'd need were in her toiletry bag. They were. She returned to the bedroom and felt under each side of the mattress to make sure her emergency items were within easy reach if needed. They were.

She hit the light switch on her way out of the room, made her way to the fire door, and pushed it open. Blaylock was standing there, drenched and shivering and pathetic looking.

"Get your ass in here." She grinned. "Unless you want to stand out there in the rain all night."

After he'd removed his coat and shoes, he dived onto the bed among the cushions and pillows. Red panicked for a second, wondering if the mattress was thick enough or if he'd felt what was concealed beneath it. He hadn't. He only had one thing on his mind.

Poor Caroline.

He pulled Red on top of him, his mouth on hers, his hands on her ass and then tracing the outline of her breasts above the thin fabric of her dress.

It's only acting, remember. Just like you've done dozens of times before.

Only this time there was no one to shout "Cut."

Blaylock was just reaching for the buckle on his belt when she climbed off him and tugged her dress back down.

"What's wrong?" he asked.

"Nothing. There's no rush is there? We've got all night."

"Have you changed your mind?"

"Nope. I just want to take a breath for a moment."

"Is that your way of telling me you've changed your mind about us, uh, you know . . . ?"

Having sex? No, I haven't changed my mind, asshole. I still have no interest in screwing you.

"Having sex?" She laughed. "Of course not. I just thought we could chill. Maybe talk awhile."

Blaylock did not look impressed by that suggestion one little bit.

"Um, okay," he said. "You have a minibar, right? Why don't we have a drink? I'll have a whisky if there's any."

"The minibar is empty."

166

"What? You've drunk it all already?"

"Don't be silly. It was empty when I checked in. I think it's a dry hotel."

Leonard frowned. "Didn't the sign out front say there was an on-site bar?"

Shit.

"Maybe it's a dry room, then. A family room or something. And the hotel bar's shut already. Which is a shame as I guess I'm losing that nice little booze buzz from the bar."

This is your cue, Blaylock. Time to bring out that little bag of coke.

If he didn't, she'd have to ask him straight out if he had any on him. But it would be so much better, so much more devastating for him later, if he was to offer. If he was to *persuade* her to shove some drugs up her nose.

He didn't disappoint.

"Hey, if it's a buzz you're after, I can help with that."

"Oh yeah?"

Blaylock reached into his back pocket and produced a little plastic bag with white powder and grinned at her.

Bingo.

Red raised an eyebrow. "Coke? I didn't realize the eighties were making a comeback. Next you'll be confessing to a love of double denim and offering to make a mixtape for me."

Leonard laughed and held out the drugs to her. "Ladies first."

She hesitated.

Had to play this just right.

"What's wrong?" he asked.

"I guess I don't really do drugs. Except for that one time in college when I smoked weed and then threw up."

Leonard looked incredulous. "You've never done coke before? Seriously, you don't know what you're missing. The rush is amazing."

"I don't know, Leonard . . ."

"Trust me, you'll love it." He reached over and stroked her arm, and she tried not to flinch at his touch. "And sex on coke is incredible."

Uh-huh. Is that right, sleazebag?

Eventually, Red smiled and said, "Okay, why the hell not, huh? But you go first. I insist."

Blaylock produced a credit card and a twenty from his wallet. Rolled the note, cut the coke, leaned down, and hoovered up the powder.

"Do you want to come around this side?" he asked.

"No, I'll manage fine over here."

Blaylock handed her the bag, the rolled twenty, and the credit card. Red turned her back to him, cut a line, dabbed a tiny amount onto the side of her nostril for effect, and swept the rest onto the floor. She didn't do drugs under any circumstances. In that respect, she and Julia Roberts's character in *Pretty Woman* were exactly alike.

When she turned to face him, Blaylock laughed and wiped her nose with his finger and tried to put it in her mouth. She shoved it into his own mouth instead. Then she straddled him and reached over and turned off the lamp.

Again, she had to remind herself that it was only acting as she undid the buttons on his shirt and heard him moan, then felt his fingers press into the flesh of her thighs. He was very hard now, and those grabby little fingers were getting too close to her panties for her liking. She tensed up.

Okay, enough.

"Wait," she said.

"Are you okay?" he whispered.

"I don't suppose you have anything else in that magic pocket of yours?"

"What? More coke?"

"No. You know . . . protection."

Blaylock went quiet for a long moment. Finally, he said, "Sorry, I don't. Do you?"

"Yeah, I think so. In my toiletry bag. I'll go look."

Red jumped off the bed. Made a point of stumbling into the bedside table, as though the coke had hit her hard. Let out a little yelp.

"Whoa, steady there," Blaylock said. "Are you all right?"

"I'm fine. Just a rush of blood to the head." Red made her way unsteadily to the bathroom and switched on the light. She closed the door behind her, praying that he wouldn't follow her inside. Not just yet anyway.

She unzipped the toiletry bag and removed three items—a condom in its wrapper, a small plastic bottle of theatrical blood, and a foaming-mouth-effect capsule. Red had used the fake blood and the capsules many times in her stage and screen work. Both could be purchased online cheaply and easily.

Once she'd squeezed some drops of blood onto the rim of the sink and poured the rest onto the tiled floor, Red wrapped the bottle in a wad of toilet paper and stuffed it into an empty tampon carton inside the step trash can. She tossed the condom wrapper onto the scarlet puddle. Picked up a glass tumbler and lowered herself onto the floor, her hair soaking up the wet mess. She practiced her breathing techniques, and then once she was ready, she smashed the tumbler on the tiles. Popped the capsule into her mouth.

Blaylock immediately called out her name and asked if everything was okay. When he didn't get a response, he shouted louder, the panic in his voice unmistakable. Red heard the creak of the mattress springs as he got up from the bed. She rolled her eyes back and let the foam spill from her mouth, then shook her body as though she were seizing.

His shadow fell over her. Red could sense him getting closer, then heard him backing away again.

She stilled her body.

Held her breath.

Waited.

"Red?" he whispered. *"Red!"*

She hoped that Blaylock would not try to be a hero and perform CPR or call for help. If he attempted to do either of those things, Red would have to make a miraculous recovery and assure him she didn't need medical attention. She would still keep the $1,500 Caroline Cooper had paid her on the basis that she'd put in a hell of a shift and had given Blaylock a hell of a fright.

The sound of sobbing came from the bedroom, and Red risked taking a few deep breaths before she began to feel too light-headed from the lack of oxygen reaching her brain. The crying stopped. There was silence. Then there was the creaking of rusted hinges as the hotel door was opened. Then silence.

Leonard Blaylock had—as expected—fled the scene.

Red continued to lie on the bathroom floor, breathing hard, making sure he really was gone. After a while, she pushed herself up. The first thing she did was lock the hotel room door. Then she cleaned up the mess in the bathroom, stripped out of her soiled clothing and showered.

Once she'd scrubbed her skin clean of theatrical blood and Leonard Blaylock's touch, Red wrapped a white fluffy towel around her body. She removed her bag and phone and the bottles from the closet safe. Tapped out a text to Caroline Cooper.

Two words.

It's done.

Red opened one of the vodka bottles and drank it down in one go. The next step would be the obituary in Blaylock's own newspaper with her photograph. At which point, her work would be done. It would then be up to Caroline to decide how long she wanted to make him suffer before revealing he'd been set up as revenge for his infidelity.

Of course, Leonard Blaylock would never find Anna Bianco. That's why she'd locked her personal belongings in the safe—in case he'd decided to go rooting through her wallet and cell phone to find out her real identity while she'd been "dying" on the bathroom floor.

She drank another Tito's and then removed her emergency items from under the mattress—a knife, a hammer, and two cans of pepper spray—and packed them in her suitcase along with the plastic bag containing her ruined dress and underwear.

Tonight, everything had gone according to plan.

Anna glanced at the weapons again. She knew she might not always be so lucky.

22

LEONARD

Martha met Leonard in the car and filled him in on what she'd discovered during her meeting with Kincaid.

"Red was one of Click's honeys," she said. "Kincaid got all twitchy when I brought up her name. He was questioned by the NYPD about the murder."

"The cops think he's a suspect?"

"I don't know. It sounded more like routine questioning, the way he told it. They asked him about a bunch of unexplained cash deposits in her checking account. He was adamant the money had nothing to do with Click."

"Did you believe him?"

Martha considered this. "I think so. He made a good point that they would probably have traced the money back to him by now if he was the source. Plus, the state of that office, I'd be surprised if he had that kind of money to burn."

"The place could be a front for drugs or money laundering?" Leonard suggested.

"Again, wouldn't the police have figured that out once they'd taken a closer look at Kincaid?"

"Good point," Leonard said. "What were your impressions of him?"

"An old creep with bad teeth."

Leonard laughed. "Do you think he could have had anything to do with Red's murder?"

"Honestly? I have no idea."

"So, we've established a clear link between Click, Caroline, and Red, as well as the fact that Red was receiving money from an unknown source. Good work, Martha."

"Thank you."

"Anything else?"

"I also picked out a lovely redhead by the name of Lola to honeytrap my cheating husband, David Smith. Or should that be 'Jane Smith picked out a lovely redhead'? Damn, I should have gone for John Smith instead of David, shouldn't I?"

"A therapist might have a lot to say about the choice of name," Leonard said. "But I'm saying nothing."

"Wise decision."

Martha then got down to the important business of explaining the situation with regards to Click's bathroom window.

"All sounds good," Leonard said.

"Are you sure about this?" Martha asked.

"Absolutely. You did brilliantly. Now it's my turn."

They watched from across the street as Click's office window went dark, and a few minutes later, Kincaid emerged from the front door.

"You're right," Leonard said. "He does look like a creepy old man."

Kincaid stood on his tiptoes, reached up, and pulled down the security gate with a clatter, then bent down and secured it with a padlock. He made his way to the rear of the building, where his car was presumably parked.

They waited another five minutes before Martha started her own car and went down the side street where Kincaid had disappeared. The building's parking lot was empty. She pulled up next to the lot's entrance.

"Good luck," Martha said. "Message me if you need me. I'll do likewise if Kincaid, or anyone else, makes an unexpected appearance. Just . . . try not to get caught and arrested, okay?"

Leonard chuckled to hide his nerves. He got out of the Mini and followed the lead of Max Sullivan's goons by pulling a hood over his head and a scarf over the bottom half of his face. During their recon, Martha and Leonard had established that there were no security cameras or CCTV on Click's building or the nearby street. At least, none that worked anyway.

He found the dumpster and the pebbled window that Martha had confirmed was Click's bathroom. It was too dark to tell for sure if it was still cracked open, the way Martha had left it, or if Kincaid had closed it before leaving.

Leonard glanced around, then climbed onto the garbage bags, and from there, scrambled onto the heaving dumpster, silently praying the trash bags beneath him wouldn't burst open and that he'd suddenly feel something wet and bad-smelling soak through his sneakers and jeans. He groped around the window frame and felt like punching the air when his fingertips found a two-inch gap. He had to work hard to pry the stiff wooden sash all the way open. His muscles strained, and sweat beads popped out on his forehead.

He then had to decide how best to maneuver his way inside—headfirst or legs first? Leonard opted to lead with the legs. He twisted around on the mountain of trash bags and hooked one leg in, then the other, then wriggled his body through the open window. There was a moment of panic when he thought his shoulders weren't going to fit through the tight space, but after a lot of effort and feeling as if his skin were being ripped from the bones, he was in. His sneakers landed on the top of the tank, knocking something over. He dropped onto the toilet seat, and then clumsily to the floor, and saw he had upended a plastic air freshener. It was doing nothing to disguise the smell of stale piss.

He made his way through to the office space and tried to get his bearings in the gloom. He made a beeline for the filing cabinets and hoped they wouldn't be locked. He hadn't considered that possible hurdle. The cabinets all had little locks on them, but thankfully, they weren't being used.

Leonard rifled through the hanging files, which comprised Kincaid's collection of honeys, his client reports, photographs, and USB sticks from regular shoots to be mailed out to customers. Then he found what he was looking for in the next drawer down—Click's accounts.

He pulled the folders for the last six years. Leonard and Martha had established that Caroline had employed Click's services around the time of the night with Red five years earlier. But he had to cover all bases; make sure someone else he knew didn't have a relationship with Kincaid that stretched back even further.

. Leonard captured every bank statement, invoice, and receipt with the camera on his cell phone, not even taking the time to read through the information first, even though he hadn't received any warning messages from Martha and should be good for time. He was just about to make his exit through the bathroom window when he spotted a staircase leading up to the second floor.

His curiosity got the better of him.

Martha hadn't mentioned seeing the upper floor, and it likely held nothing more interesting than a photography studio and Kincaid's equipment, but Leonard wanted to know for sure that he wasn't missing anything important.

He was halfway up the staircase when he heard the rattle of the security gate. Leonard froze. He told himself it was just a gust of wind. The subsequent clatter of metal against metal, which sounded very much like the security gate being thrown open, suggested otherwise.

Fuck.

Should he run for the bathroom or continue up to the second floor?

The sound of a key scraping in the lock and the sight of the door opening made the decision for him. Leonard raced up the remaining stairs.

As expected, he found the ghostly figures of cameras and tripods and light stands. But what drew his eye was the red glow coming from a door that had been left ever so slightly ajar. Leonard knew what it was immediately.

A dark room.

He could hear someone moving around downstairs. He strode across the studio space and pushed the dark room door fully open and stepped inside. The setup was similar to his own. The usual equipment and trays and shelving filled with chemicals. Photographs attached to a clothesline. Everything washed in an eerie carmine tint. Leonard's attention was distracted by slow, heavy footfalls on the staircase.

Shit.

He pushed the door back to its original position, slightly ajar. He heard footsteps coming closer over the thrumming in his ears. There was nowhere to hide inside the small room. The door began to open, and Leonard squeezed himself flat against the wall behind it.

Then the safelight snapped off, plunging the room from red to black. The door slammed shut. Leonard heard the lock click into place.

Shit.

He pulled out his cell phone and sent a text to Martha: **Someone else is in the building.**

He waited for a response.

What???? Then a follow-up text from Martha: I just walked around front and there's a car parked outside on the street. WHERE ARE YOU??!!

Leonard tapped out a reply. Hiding. I'm locked in a dark room.

A few more minutes passed. Then another message from Martha. It was Kincaid. He's gone now. Can you get out??

Good question.

Leonard turned the safelight back on, bathing the room in red once more. He knew he should leave immediately, but he couldn't resist taking a closer look at the prints that were hanging up to dry. He couldn't help himself.

They all featured young, attractive women. The kind of women, he guessed, who would be found within the pages of Kincaid's files of honeys. The difference with these shots was that the women were naked or wearing nothing but underwear, and none of them appeared to be aware that they were being photographed.

Leonard pulled open the top drawer of a filing cabinet and saw cartons of film and packs of resin-coated paper. He opened another drawer and found more photographs like the ones hanging on the clothesline. He leafed through them.

This time he saw a face he recognized.

It belonged to Anna Bianco.

23

LEONARD

"That was way too close for comfort," Martha said.

"But also kind of wild," Leonard said. "Exhilarating."

He was still feeling pumped after the narrow escape at Click. That moment when Kincaid had entered the dark room and was so close that Leonard could smell his cheap cologne, then being locked inside with all those illicit photos . . . He hadn't taken drugs since the night with Red, but the adrenaline rush had given him a similar, crazy high.

As it turned out, Leonard hadn't really been locked inside the dark room. The night latch—as opposed to a double cylinder lock—meant all he'd had to do was release the latch from the inside. He'd then pulled it fully closed behind him before Martha helped him scramble inelegantly back out the bathroom window.

They were now racing across the bridge again, the Manhattan skyscrapers up ahead glittering against a black sky through the gaps between the cantilever beams. Martha's face was pale, and her knuckles were white as her hands gripped the steering wheel tightly.

"It was all just a bit too exhilarating for me," she said.

"Just wait until you see what I found."

She snapped her head momentarily in his direction. "You went through the accounts already?"

"Nope, but I came across something else. Something *very* interesting."

"What?"

"It's better if I show you rather than tell you. But let's just say, Kincaid might not have been in such a rush to call the cops if he *had* discovered me using his premises for a game of hide-and-seek."

"You're nothing but a big tease, do you know that?" Her words and tone were light, but her face was still heavy with tension.

Back in the Hell's Kitchen apartment, they took up their usual position at the dining table. Leonard produced his phone and pulled up the photos he had snapped in Kincaid's dark room. He handed the phone to Martha.

She glanced at the screen and then stared at him in surprise. "Is that Red?"

Leonard nodded. "It sure is."

Kincaid's photograph of Anna Bianco was very different from the ones they'd seen of her online during their Google search. It was clearly a private, candid moment. She was in an untidy bedroom, a cigarette between her lips, wearing only lace panties. The shot was in profile, the curved outline of her buttocks and naked breasts clearly visible despite the lack of light in the room. A series of horizontal lines across the photograph suggested the camera's lens had been trained on a window with open venetian blinds.

Leonard had been mesmerized for several moments when he'd first seen it. A body he had touched and fantasized about, if only for a very short time, laid (almost) bare for him to see for the first time. It had been like ripping the wrapping off a gift after trying to imagine what was inside—and he was far from disappointed. But he didn't share any of this with Martha.

"It's not the only one," he told her. "Swipe through to see some of the others."

Anger flashed in her eyes, and he knew what she was looking at. A woman asleep in bed on a warm night, the sheets kicked off to reveal a bralette and panties. Another, standing in the doorway of an adjoining bathroom with wet hair and a very short towel wrapped around her body. One, completely naked, applying self-tanner or moisturizer to her skin. Some were very narrow shots, as though taken through a gap where curtains hadn't been fully drawn.

"These are really bad, Leonard. It's pretty clear that these women have no idea that they are being photographed."

"That's what I thought. You were right when you said Kincaid was a creep. But he's even worse than we thought. He's a pervert and a peeper as well."

"They can't all live in first-floor apartments, right? Do you think he goes as far as getting up on fire escapes or something to access some of the bedroom windows?"

"I can hardly throw shade on someone for accessing other folks' windows after what I did earlier, can I?"

"True." Martha grinned.

"Although, in my defense, all I did was some harmless breaking and entering."

"Where did you find these?"

"In Kincaid's dark room. He had some hanging to dry that had recently been developed. The ones I took on my cell phone, including Red, were hidden away in a filing cabinet."

"But why keep them in the workplace?"

Leonard shrugged. "Do you think he's married?"

Martha thought for a moment. "Yes, I'm sure he was wearing a wedding ring when I met with him."

"I guess that's the reason, huh? He doesn't want photographs of that nature at home where Mrs. Kincaid might stumble upon them."

"Someone at work could find them instead," Martha countered. "A client or one of his honeys. You said the dark room was next to the studio, right?"

"Yeah, and I figure that's exactly why he has a lock on the door—to keep prying eyes out. Now I'm wondering if the reason he returned to the office this evening was the realization that he hadn't locked up properly. The door was ajar when I went snooping."

"What if it wasn't the first time he'd accidentally left the dark room unlocked? What if someone else found his private collection of photographs?"

Leonard understood what Martha was getting at. "Someone like Red, you mean?"

"Exactly."

"Do you think she discovered his collection, including images of herself, and confronted him about it? Possibly even blackmailed him? And then he murdered her?"

"It's possible," Martha said. "And it would explain all that extra cash she had."

"But the cops already cleared him as far as the money was concerned."

"That's what he says, anyway. Either way, I definitely think we need to add Ron Kincaid to our theoretical whiteboard of suspects for the murder."

"Hard agree," Leonard said.

"Let's have a look at those accounts, see if they turn up anything interesting."

After ten minutes of pinching and expanding photos of documents on the cell phone's screen, Leonard set it down on the table and rubbed his eyes.

"What's wrong?" asked Martha.

"I've barely gotten through the first six months and already my eyes are stinging, and my head is pounding trying to read the print on that tiny screen. And there's six years to get through."

"Six years? Why not just the last five?"

"I wanted to make sure that we didn't miss anything. A relationship with Kincaid or Click or Red that stretches back even further than that night at the Fairview Hotel. Something to incriminate Bobby Khan or someone else."

"Why don't you send all the photos of the accounts to your iMac, and I'll trawl through them while you think about what to make for dinner? How does that sound?"

"That sounds good. What are you in the mood for?"

"Surprise me."

Leonard sent the photos to his email account, then logged on to his desktop computer and set it up for Martha to use. He returned to the kitchen, while she got to work in the living room. He decided to make chili, which he remembered Martha telling him was one of her favorites. He set about chopping the onions, peppers, and chilies and was just browning the ground beef when he heard the printer rattling and whirring in the other room, followed by the sound of paper being spat out by the machine. Leonard wondered what Martha had discovered that was worth having a hard copy of. By the time the chili was simmering in the pot, the printer had been used five times.

He joined Martha in the living room, flopping down onto the couch while she spun the desk chair around to face him.

"Chili? Smells great."

"Should be ready in around twenty minutes. Sounds like you've been busy too."

Her eyes shone with excitement. "I sure have—and so has Caroline Cooper."

"Oh yeah?"

"First of all, I didn't find anything of note in the accounts for the year preceding the night you met Red. No mention of Caroline or Bobby or any other names you've spoken about. Of course, you may want to go through those yourself in case there's someone familiar to you that I don't know of. But I don't think you have to. It only starts to get interesting in the couple months before the events at the Fairview Hotel."

Martha held up two printed sheets of paper, which Leonard couldn't read from where he was sitting. All he could tell was that she'd gotten the fluorescent markers out again. Both pages were streaked with luminous orange.

"What are those?"

"Click's bank statement showing the five-hundred-dollar payment from the joint account you shared with Caroline, as well as Kincaid's copy of a customer receipt. The receipt specifies the fee was for a photography shoot. Caroline was telling the truth about her professional photographs, but we kind of knew that already."

Next, Martha showed Leonard a printout with bright green highlighted sections.

"Click's copy of another customer receipt. This one is a lot more interesting. It's for a cash payment of one thousand dollars. The name of the customer is C. Cooper, and the description of services rendered is surveillance work. The receipt is dated less than a week after the five hundred dollars that went through Click's books—and the date is a match for the thousand-dollar cash withdrawal on your own statement."

"Shit." Leonard dropped his head into his hands and ran his fingers through his hair. He looked up at Martha. "So, Caroline really did hire Kincaid to spy on me? The woman I thought I was going to marry?"

"I'm sorry, Leonard. But, yes, it seems pretty certain that she did." Martha hesitated. "It still doesn't completely make sense to me, though. There are some things that just don't add up."

"Like what?"

"Caroline hired Click for surveillance work in late September, but the stuff with Red didn't happen until early November. Why the delay? And why was the night at the Fairview Hotel so . . . *extreme*? You said it yourself—what happened to you was a lot more than a simple honeytrap. When I met with Kincaid, it seemed like that was all he was offering. There was certainly no hint of anything more adventurous that involved his honeys faking their own death or suchlike. Then there's the unexplained fifteen-hundred-dollar withdrawal from your joint bank account . . ."

"There was no match for that in Click's accounts?"

"No, and that's my point. There is no corresponding payment or invoice or customer receipt. Absolutely zilch."

"Maybe it genuinely *was* for wedding stuff," Leonard suggested.

"Maybe—but it was also right before you were targeted by Red."

"The Montauk spa resort, then. Cash for booze and facials."

"Maybe," she said again.

"You're not convinced?"

"It's the complete lack of activity for an entire month that bothers me. That and the idea that we're supposed to believe that Kincaid took some covert photographs of you and Red getting all hot and heavy at the Fairview Hotel—and what? Red decided to indulge in some amateur dramatics just for the hell of it and get some practice in for her next movie role? Sorry, but I'm just not buying it."

Realization hit Leonard like a punch to the face. His head started to pound again, and this time, it had nothing to do with staring at a cell phone screen for too long.

"Fuck," he whispered.

"What?"

He puffed up his cheeks and slowly let the air out. "Something did happen in that month with no activity. At least, I think it would have been around then."

"Something like what?"

Leonard couldn't meet her eye. "I met a woman in a bar one night. We got talking, she was real flirty, we had a couple drinks together, and . . ."

"And what?" Martha's tone was pure ice.

"Well, nothing. Not really. We had a kiss in an alleyway behind the bar, that's all."

"That's all? And you didn't think to mention this earlier when you told me about Karen Sampson?"

"Karen Sampson was different. This was just a harmless kiss. It wasn't really—"

Martha glared at him. "If you tell me it wasn't really cheating, I swear to God, I'll give you another fat lip. Let me be really clear—if you are in a relationship with someone and you have sex with someone else or kiss someone else or exchange sexy photos or texts with someone else, it's cheating. It's disrespecting your partner. Okay?"

"Okay."

The timer on the stove buzzed in the kitchen.

"Chili's ready," Leonard said weakly. "I'd better go prepare the rice."

"You do that."

He retreated to the safety of the kitchen, where he stuck two packets of rice into the microwave and stirred the chili in the pot. It smelled great, but he didn't have much of an appetite anymore.

Martha came into the kitchen and sat at the table just as the microwave pinged.

"Perfect timing." He spooned the food into two bowls and placed one in front of her.

"Thanks," she mumbled, her eyes on a couple of printouts she'd brought with her.

"Are you still mad at me?"

She sighed. "I'm not mad at you, just disappointed. I don't get it, that's all. If you truly love someone, why isn't that person enough? Why would you even *want* to be with anyone else?"

Leonard sat down facing her. "I could say that maybe I didn't really love Caroline, that she wasn't the one for me and part of me knew it and didn't want to admit it, but that's crap. Another sad excuse. The truth is I was a selfish asshole back then. I was thirty-seven years old and hadn't grown up yet. I'd like to think that I wouldn't behave the same way now."

"Glad to hear it."

Leonard began eating his food. Martha made no move to pick up her own spoon.

She said, "Now that you've come clean about everything, it all makes much more sense."

"It does?"

"I think Caroline either found out about Karen Sampson or suspected you were cheating, learned about Kincaid's private-eye sideline after hiring him for her photo shoot, and paid him a thousand bucks to set you up with the woman you kissed in the alleyway. When Caroline was presented with the evidence, she got mad and somehow crossed paths with Red, and they came up with the plan at the Fairview Hotel. Maybe that's what the mysterious fifteen hundred dollars was for. A job that Kincaid didn't even know about."

"Wow. It makes sense, but . . ." He put down his spoon. "I can't believe Caroline hated me that much. That she'd deliberately set out to ruin my life like that . . ."

"It's not all she did." Martha indicated the two sheets of paper on the table next to her. "Caroline hired Kincaid a second time for surveillance work. This was long after the Fairview Hotel, though, so I doubt it had anything to do with you. It's right there on Click's bank statement and their copy of the customer receipt."

"Really? Do you think she suspected old Harry Belman of fooling around with other women?"

Martha shrugged and finally began to dig into her chili. "I guess."

"When did this take place?"

"Earlier this year. Eight months ago."

They both ate in silence for a while. Then Leonard stopped chewing. "Wait. Eight months ago?"

Martha nodded. "That's right. Why?"

Leonard said, "That was around the same time Caroline replaced Jim Sanders on *Rise & Shine* after his surprise departure."

24
MARTHA

Central Park had ten thousand benches, with more than seven thousand of those having been "adopted" by someone willing to pay the not-insubstantial sum of $10,000 to have a personalized plaque added to the seat back that would stay there forever.

Many of them commemorated births or deaths, others were romantic gestures or even marriage proposals, while some were love letters to New York City itself. The most interesting ones featured a cryptic message, its meaning known only to the donor and perhaps a chosen few who shared in the secret.

Martha often enjoyed long walks there, reading the various inscriptions on those benches, sitting awhile on one to read a book or eat a sandwich. However, her visit to the park today was purely for business, not pleasure.

It was a convenient place to meet a stranger.

She and Leonard had deliberated between choosing a quiet spot away from the crowds or somewhere more bustling, and they had both agreed that hiding in plain sight was the better option. So, she'd arranged for the meet to take place on a bench in Strawberry Fields, located near Central Park West between Seventy-First and

Seventy-Fourth Streets, facing the black-and-white *Imagine* mosaic memorial dedicated to John Lennon.

The day was cold and bright. The trees above her were a canopy of blazing reds and oranges and yellows, and the ground beneath her boots was a thick carpet of fallen leaves. Martha felt the chill air seep into her bones despite her wool coat, beanie hat, and big red scarf.

She should be warm and working in her studio on the Lower East Side instead of enduring dropping temperatures and a mounting sense of apprehension. She had fallen behind with her workload and had a backlog of photographs that needed to be worked on, as well as a mountain of paperwork that required her attention. Martha wondered, not for the first time, why she was allowing herself to be sucked so deeply into this Anna Bianco business. Not only was it having an impact on her working life, it was potentially dangerous. But she already knew the answer:

Leonard.

He'd been worried about her going to the park. He thought it wasn't safe and it should be him instead of her. But it had to be Martha; they both knew that. To involve Leonard in this part of the plan would, at best, unnecessarily complicate matters and, at worst, potentially result in the meeting not taking place at all. They'd agreed that he would wait in a nearby coffee shop and try to work on some articles while Martha played hooky from her own workplace.

She spotted a row of green World's Fair benches up ahead and found one that was unoccupied. Martha sat on the frigid wood and checked her watch. She was five minutes early. She pulled the scarf up to her ears. The brightly colored accessory was how the man would recognize her, but she was grateful for the extra warmth it provided too. Her nose was cold and wet like a dog's. She plunged her hands deep into her pockets and was glad she'd worn gloves.

After forty minutes had passed, Martha started to think about leaving. He wasn't going to show.

Then Jim Sanders sat down next to her on the bench.

He stared straight ahead for several seconds. Tourists snapped photographs, kids shrieked and threw handfuls of leaves up in the air, young lovers walked arm in arm, joggers huffed past flushed and sweating. Sanders's breath was visible in front of him. Martha's own breathing was faster than usual.

Finally, Sanders said, "You're the person who wrote me?"

The voice had the same rich tone that she recognized from watching him on TV, but there was an edge there too—a hint of menace—that would have been unfamiliar to his adoring viewers.

"I am."

"Are you also the one who blackmailed me?"

Martha turned to face him. The last time she'd seen him on screen, his hair had been dark brown. Now it was salt and pepper. He appeared to be thicker around the middle. Without the heavy studio makeup, his face was ruddy, which could have been down to the nip in the air or too much alcohol or a combination of both.

She said, "So, you *were* being blackmailed?"

After going through Click's accounts and discovering the most recent transaction between the company and Caroline Cooper from earlier this year, Leonard and Martha had speculated that Caroline had paid Kincaid to honeytrap Sanders in order to land his job. His public image as a happily married and devoted family man was one of the reasons he was so popular with the show's mostly older, female audience. He was handsome and funny and affable and stood for family values. Except, Leonard said, it was all a lie. It was an open secret within Manhattan's media circles that Sanders had an eye for the ladies.

Another cheat, Martha thought sadly.

Leonard had met Sanders a few times through work in the past, and Sanders no doubt knew of Leonard's short-lived engagement to Caroline, which is why they'd decided it had to be Martha who met with the former TV anchor. Better that it be a complete stranger. That way, there was no reason for him to suspect an ulterior motive when she revealed who had blackmailed him.

So, they'd typed up an anonymous letter to Sanders, suggesting the meet in Central Park, which promised to shed light on his departure from *Rise & Shine*. They didn't know his home address, of course, but Leonard remembered reading a feature in one of the weekend supplements about Sanders developing a green thumb since his retirement. Leonard had spent a few days staking out the community garden mentioned in the article and, when Sanders finally showed, had followed him home. Then they'd mailed the letter.

There was a chance that Leonard and Martha had gotten it all wrong; that Caroline's most recent interaction with Click had nothing to do with her one-time coworker and had, in fact, been a honeytrap to snare her husband, Harry Belman. That the timing had been nothing but a coincidence. In which case, Sanders likely wouldn't show, would assume the letter was from a crank and trash it.

But he had shown—and he'd immediately confirmed their suspicions.

"Yes, I was blackmailed," Sanders said. "But you knew that already. Your letter said so."

"We didn't know for sure, but we suspected as much."

"Who are you? And who is this 'we' you're referring to?"

"That doesn't matter. Tell me what happened."

"Why should I?" Sanders asked aggressively. "You could be a reporter for all I know. Maybe it's best I leave."

"I'm not a reporter. And you're not going to leave because you want to know who did this to you; otherwise you wouldn't be here. You clearly don't know who was behind the blackmail plot. But I do."

Sanders was silent. He stared straight ahead. A gust of wind shook the tree branches, and the leaves seemed to whisper. Martha waited.

Eventually he said, "I was in a bar one night and was approached by a beautiful, young woman. That's not as unusual as you might think, by the way, not when you're on TV. We got talking, and she claimed to have no idea who I was. That's not unusual either. Some are blatant groupies, others like to think they're being coy. She asked what I did for work and so on. I decided to play along. Told her I was a doctor and was on a night out with other staff from the hospital. That part was true. Sort of. I'd been drinking with a couple of the production guys, who'd taken the hint and moved to the other side of the bar when the redhead started to get friendly."

The redhead.

Anna Bianco.

Bull's-eye.

Sanders went on. "We had a few drinks together, and then we shared a drunken kiss at the end of the night."

"In the bar?" Martha asked, surprised.

"No, not in the bar. I'm not that dumb. Or at least I thought I wasn't. I knew I could be recognized, so we hid in the doorway of an office block down the street that was shut up for the night. I didn't think anyone would spot us in there. Clearly, I was wrong. Like I said, it was just a kiss, then we went our separate ways. Nothing else happened, we didn't swap numbers or anything, and I forgot all about it. Until the photographs showed up in my mail at the TV studio, that is. They showed me and the woman leaving the bar together, then the two of us kissing, then both of us coming out of the doorway together. It was clear as day that it was me in those photographs. It seemed to me to be a professional job. Not some amateur playing around with a camera on a cell phone. There was also a note with the photos."

"The blackmail demand," Martha said.

Sanders nodded.

"What did they ask for?"

"Not money, which was a surprise. I kept expecting a follow-up letter demanding cash, but it never arrived. All it said was that I had to quit *Rise & Shine* and leave the network completely. If I didn't, copies of the photographs would be mailed to my wife, as well as the newspapers."

"So, you took early retirement?"

"I had no choice, did I?" he snapped. "If I didn't do as they asked, my marriage would have been over, and my reputation would have been damaged beyond repair." Sanders laughed bitterly. "The irony is that the whole business killed my marriage anyway."

"Your wife found out?"

"No, but she found someone else. Let's just say being black-mailed isn't a whole lot of fun—and neither was I. It changed me and not in a good way. It all took a toll in the end."

"Once you knew your marriage was over, why didn't you go to the network, or the cops, and tell them about the blackmail? Surely, the photographs would have been a lot less damaging if you were separated by then? Effectively, a free agent?"

"I had my reasons."

Martha figured those reasons included "the beautiful redhead" winding up dead and Sanders's reluctance to be implicated in a homicide investigation. He did, after all, have a strong motive.

"Did you ever think about why the blackmailer wanted you gone from both *Rise & Shine* and the network?"

"Sure, I thought about it. Figured it was someone who hated me enough to want to ruin my career. When you're a high-profile TV personality like I was, you don't just get the fans, you attract the haters and the crazies too. And, like I said, I assumed it was just the first step, and then the cash demands would follow."

"Why did they replace you with Caroline Cooper?"

"What?" Sanders stared at her, surprised. "What does that have to do with anything?"

"Humor me. Was it you who recommended her?"

"No, I didn't recommend her. I don't know for sure why she got the job, but I can take a pretty good guess."

"Go on."

Sanders hesitated, then said, "Shortly before the blackmail, there was another . . . incident. A reporter contacted my producer on the show to ask about allegations of sexual harassment that had been made against me. It was all garbage. There hadn't been any allegations. The newspaper had nothing on me, and they never ran with the story, but I think it was enough to cause some concern with the big bosses at the network in the wake of all that #MeToo stuff.

"When I decided to take early retirement so unexpectedly—and so soon after that reporter had been sniffing around—they probably thought the story was about to come back and bite them on the ass and that I was getting out first before the shit hit the fan. I'm guessing someone then decided it would be a good look for the network to have a young woman take over my high-profile role. Show them to be an equal opportunity employer who valued their female workforce."

"Who was the reporter?"

"A guy by the name of Bobby Khan from the *New York Reporter*."

Martha felt her pulse quicken. Was Leonard's one-time best buddy involved in all of this too? Or had he simply been a pawn used by Caroline Cooper to throw some dirt Sanders's way?

Sanders gave her a hard stare. "I've told you everything. Now it's your turn."

Martha took her cell phone from her purse and pulled up a photo of Red. She showed it to Sanders. "Is this the woman you met in the bar? The one in the blackmail photos?"

Sanders nodded. "That's her."

Martha went on. "She worked as a honey for a photographer, who has a sideline as a private eye. His clients hire him to set honeytraps to snare their cheating partners."

Sanders said, "You're telling me Debra set me up?"

"Who's Debra?"

"My wife. Or soon to be ex-wife."

"No, it wasn't your wife."

Sanders had given Martha enough information to fill in some of the blanks, so it was only right that she kept up her end of the deal, even if she didn't particularly like the man. She produced an envelope from her purse and handed it to him. It contained a copy of Caroline Cooper's customer receipt from Click dated eight months earlier.

She walked away, leaving Sanders sitting on the bench staring at the envelope.

She'd already known that Caroline had used Kincaid to honeytrap Leonard. Martha now had confirmation of a link between Caroline and Anna Bianco. She also knew the lengths Caroline was willing to go to in order to get what she wanted.

As she reached the park's exit and headed for her car, Martha checked her cell phone for messages. She had one unread text from Leonard. She opened it.

I'm back at the apartment. It's been ransacked.

25
CAROLINE

Caroline Cooper watched Click's office from across the street.

The last time she'd sat outside this shithole, her wheels had been a tiny, thirdhand VW bug, and she'd been too scared to get out of the car and face the truth about her relationship with Leonard Blaylock. Now her butt was being warmed by the Jeep's heated leather seat, and she had plenty of legroom to stretch out while she waited. Better still, she wasn't about to have her life devastated by a bunch of photographs, like the ones that showed her then fiancé cheating on her with a blonde in a back alley. This time, she would be the one in control of the situation, the one calling the shots.

She'd been in position for a half hour and hadn't seen Ron Kincaid enter or exit the building.

Caroline had been calling Click's landline from a burner phone all week, and each time Kincaid answered, she'd disconnected the call without saying a word. Today, finally, Red had picked up. Again, Caroline had hung up. That had been just over an hour ago. She hit the redial button on the untraceable flip phone now and heard it ring.

"Click Photography."

Again, the voice on the end of the line belonged to Red. Caroline had to assume that Kincaid wasn't on the premises. She snapped the burner shut, checked her makeup in the sun visor's mirror, and got out of the car into a stiff February wind.

Thankfully, there was no sign of Kincaid inside the office, just as she'd guessed. The room hadn't changed at all since the last time Caroline had visited more than four years earlier. Same filthy carpet, old green phone, and stack of Yellow Pages in the corner.

Red hadn't changed much either. Her hair was colored a subtler shade now, more like a natural redhead instead of crimson, and it was slightly shorter too, but the woman was still gorgeous. She wore tight fake leather pants and a top with the shoulders cut out, and she had a light tan even though the weather had been freezing for months.

"You've changed your cell phone number," Caroline said.

Red stared at her blankly. "Sorry, do I know you?" Then she narrowed her eyes. "Hey, you do look kind of familiar actually. You're on TV, right?"

"I'm also one of your clients. Or at least, I was."

Red shrugged. "Ron has lots of clients."

"I meant I was *your* client. You did what you referred to as a 'special' job for me a few years ago?" Caroline sighed at the other woman's lack of recognition. "You lured my fiancé to a hotel in Chelsea and then made him think he'd killed you with a drug overdose."

"Sure! I remember now. That was fun. He really fell for it, huh? I guess all those acting classes weren't a complete waste of time. What's your name again?"

"Caroline Cooper."

"Caroline . . . that's right. It's coming back to me now. You seem different somehow." Red eyed her up and down, taking in the DKNY dress, navy Burberry trench, and Chanel purse. "A lot more glamorous, but a lot more confident too. I like it."

"Like I said, you've changed your number, and I want to hire you for another job."

"I change my number all the time. Makes it harder for people to track me down. In any case, the office number has been the same since the eighties, and it's in the book. We're not hard to find."

"It's you I want to hire, not Kincaid. I need another one of your 'special' jobs. I don't want Kincaid to know anything about it."

Red's eyes went to Caroline's matching platinum engagement and wedding rings. "Oh shit. You didn't actually marry a cheater this time, did you?"

"No," Caroline said. "It's not my husband I want to honeytrap; it's a coworker."

"Okay. So far, so straightforward. What makes this one so special?"

Caroline could have chosen to target Darnell Morgan or Sal Speirs instead of Jim Sanders. She'd worked as the network's entertainment reporter for long enough to hear the gossip and know that everyone had something to hide that they didn't want splashed across *Page Six*. Sal would have been the sensible option, what with the network being more likely to replace a woman with a woman, rather than a man with a woman.

But ending Jim Sanders's career would be a hell of a lot more satisfying.

Her tip-off to Bobby Khan at the *Reporter*—in the strictest confidence, of course—about a culture of sexual harassment, led by Sanders, should hopefully be enough to worry the network's shareholders. Make them realize it was the right time to weed out the lecherous dinosaurs. And Jim Sanders *was* a lech. Caroline knew that from personal experience. She'd be doing every female reporter and staff member a favor, not just herself.

Back when she'd worked in local radio, she'd looked up to the man, saw him as a kind of mentor. Whenever they'd found themselves in each other's company at press conferences or social events, Sanders had always had encouraging words and a ton of advice for her. He'd been the one who'd told her about the network hiring an entertainment reporter after inviting her out for a drink—then he'd told her he could guarantee she got the job if she was "nice" to him. If she hadn't got the inference from his words, the sweaty hand on her thigh under the table had left her in no doubt as to what he expected in return. Caroline had made her excuses and left.

She got the job anyway, and apparently, she also got herself a reputation.

It didn't matter that she didn't have sex with Jim Sanders; that's what he told his buddies anyway. The rumors had never really gone away, no matter how competent and professional she was. Even after she married Harry, men still hit on her on the basis that she was "willing to sleep her way to the top." Sanders had even had the nerve to hit on her a second time, at a Christmas lunch, when he'd moved his place setting next to hers among knowing glances from everyone else in the room.

No, if there was anyone who deserved to have his career and his life left in tatters, it was Jim Sanders.

Caroline told Red what she had in mind.

"This one has to go through the books," Red said. "We need Kincaid on board."

"Absolutely not. I don't want Kincaid, or anyone else, knowing about this."

"He doesn't have to know about the blackmail. I'll take care of that. But we need him for the photographs."

"I could take them," Caroline suggested.

"Not if you want this Sanders guy to take you seriously. If you're going to blackmail someone with incriminating photographs, you need professional photography. If you were to take covert images yourself on a cell phone camera from a distance, they'd be so blurry I could be making out with anyone from Hugh Jackman to Hugh Grant for all the good they'd be."

"But won't Kincaid want to know why I'm paying him to honeytrap a coworker, who just happens to be a famous face on TV?" Caroline asked.

"Kincaid won't care who's being honeytrapped as long as he gets the money. And I guarantee, he'll have no idea who Sanders is anyway. He mostly just watches old Westerns on his ancient VCR."

Caroline considered. "Okay, we get Kincaid to take the photos, but he can't know about the blackmail. That has to be down to you and you alone."

"That I can handle, no problem. Now, let's talk money. It'll be a grand for Kincaid's fee and fifteen hundred for mine."

"You seriously want fifteen hundred dollars?" Caroline asked incredulously. "But this is way more straightforward than the last job you did for me. All you have to do for the extra cash on top of what you'll get from Kincaid for the honeytrap is to type up a letter and mail it. Maybe follow up with a couple phone calls if Sanders doesn't bite at first."

"It's also a lot more illegal than playing a prank on a guy in a hotel room." Red gave Caroline the once-over. "And it's not like you can't afford it. That purse alone would've cost more than my fee and Ron's combined."

Caroline sighed. "Okay, fine."

She gave Red the details she'd need—Sanders's home address, the name of the bar on West Forty-Seventh Street where he liked to drink, and what nights he was usually there with the production guys from work. She paid the two fees—one official, one unofficial—and stuffed her copy of the receipt from Click for $1,000 into her purse. She stood to leave.

"Hey, Caroline," Red said. "Maybe you could interview me for *Rise & Shine*? It sure would give my acting career a boost."

"I don't think that would be a good idea."

As Caroline left the building and crossed the street to her car, she realized she had been wrong. She wasn't the one who was in control and calling the shots.

Red was.

And Caroline had a hell of a lot more to lose now than she ever had before.

26
LEONARD

Leonard buzzed Martha into his building and waited for her on the doorstep of his apartment.

The elevator was out of service again, and he heard her footsteps echo on the stairs as she ran up them fast, slowing just before turning the corner onto his floor. As though panic had suddenly been replaced by trepidation. When he saw her, her eyes were filled with fear and worry.

"It's okay," he said. "Whoever did this is long gone."

"What happened? Are you okay?"

"I'm fine, just a bit shaken." Leonard gestured to the busted lock and splintered wood of the doorframe. "Looks like they used a crowbar to jimmy the door rather than kicking it in. Probably why none of the neighbors were alerted. Still very ballsy to do it in broad daylight, though."

"How'd they even get past the secure entry downstairs?"

"One or two of the neighbors have a bad habit of buzzing everyone inside without even asking who they are. Charity collectors, religious groups, salespeople—I've had them all show up on my doorstep."

"No one heard or saw anything?"

Leonard lowered his voice. "I don't think so. No one's mentioned anything. And I didn't want to go knocking on any doors to ask in case someone got spooked and called the cops. There are some older folks who live on their own, and I don't want to frighten them and have them worried that their apartment might be next."

"But they could be targeted too," Martha pointed out. "You have to tell the cops what happened."

Leonard gestured her inside and closed the door behind them. "This wasn't a normal burglary, Martha. It doesn't look as though anything was taken. I have some cash that I keep in a drawer, an expensive gold watch that belongs to my father, and the usual electronics and devices. They weren't touched. I think whoever broke in wasn't a thief—I think they were looking for something."

"You think the break-in had something to do with your investigation into Anna Bianco?"

"I think so."

"What do you think they were looking for?"

"Who knows? The photograph of Red's murder? The film roll it was on? Maybe they just wanted to know what we know?"

Martha said, "Did you do what I suggested with the photo of Red and the film?"

"I did."

When Leonard had decided against destroying the print and the roll of film after they'd started digging deeper into Anna Bianco, Martha had suggested he get a safe-deposit box to store both items. That way they could still access the photo for reference, but there was no danger of it falling into the wrong hands.

"Where's the key?" Martha asked.

"In my wallet. I keep it with me at all times."

"What about our paperwork? The bank statements and customer receipts from Click and so on?"

"Everything was in my backpack when the apartment was ransacked. Whoever did this didn't find anything useful."

They moved into the living room, where Martha saw for herself some of the destruction. The drawers had been yanked out of the desk and emptied. Paperwork from magazine files was strewn across the floor. Paperbacks that had been housed in a bookcase had been leafed through and dumped on the floor. The collection of vintage cameras had been swiped off the shelf, Leonard's favorite now lying in pieces.

"Oh, Leonard. Your Rolleiflex camera. Why would anyone do a thing like that?"

He shrugged. "Because they're a nasty, horrible bastard? Or maybe they were checking that the film wasn't hidden inside one of the old cameras. The bedroom is much the same. The dark room too."

"What are you going to do?"

"Clean up this mess while I wait for the locksmith. Not much else I can do."

Several hours later, the apartment was tidy, the broken items were in the trash, and a new lock had been fitted. Leonard had paid extra to have a pair of deadbolts installed too so he'd feel safer when he was inside his home.

"Thanks for helping with the big cleanup," he said.

"Happy to help," Martha said. "You'd never know anyone had broken in, looking at the place now."

"Yeah, except . . ."

"What?"

"Someone *has* been in here. It just feels creepy, the thought of an intruder—whether a complete stranger or someone I know—going through my stuff."

Martha touched his arm softly. "I can imagine. It must be horrible. Like being violated in a way. I feel terrible leaving you like this, but I really need to head on home now. Call me if you need anything, okay?"

Now that Leonard had almost fully recovered from his beating, Martha had gone back to spending most nights at her own apartment again. It made sense. She often had early shoots at her studio downtown, and the extra-early starts and additional travel through rush-hour traffic each time she stayed with Leonard wasn't fair to her. Still, he missed having her next to him in those dark hours right before dawn. He'd been sleeping a whole lot better since Martha Weaver came into his life, that was for sure.

Leonard walked her to the door. As she hugged him goodbye, he found himself holding on to her more tightly and for longer than usual. When she finally, gently, pulled away, she asked, "Are you sure you're okay?"

"Not really. I don't think I want to be alone tonight." He saw her eyes go to the new lock and double deadbolt. "But I understand if the thought of spending the night here makes you feel uneasy after what's happened."

"I'm not going to lie, Leonard. It does make me feel uneasy. I doubt I'd sleep at all for worrying, and I've got a full-on day at work tomorrow. But I hate the thought of leaving you here on your own and letting you down."

"I could stay at your place? Just for tonight?"

Martha hesitated. Leonard had never visited her apartment before, which now struck him as odd considering how much time they'd been spending together. He realized she'd never once invited him to her home.

"It's, uh, really untidy," she said, still looking uncertain.

Leonard smiled wryly. "This place is hardly a palace. But I wouldn't want to impose if it makes you feel uncomfortable."

"No, no. Don't be silly. Of course it's fine."

"Fantastic." He beamed, kissing her on the cheek. "Let me go grab some things."

She didn't return the smile.

◆ ◆ ◆

Martha drove. It was fully dark by the time they reached Hester Street.

Another realization hit Leonard as they pulled up outside—until now, he hadn't known her address. Yes, he'd known she lived on the Lower East Side, but that was all. Guilt washed over him like the rain outside the car. He'd been so wrapped up in himself and what had happened with Anna Bianco and Caroline that he hadn't bothered to find out anything, really, about this woman who had been his rock. Not until it had suited his own needs, that is.

Martha's apartment was on the second floor of a tenement-style building, above a pharmacy. The secure entry system was busted, judging by the way she pushed the door open without the need for a key. Leonard noticed that her apartment door also appeared to be far from robust. Like someone could easily use a pry bar on it, just as they'd done to his own.

"Do you mind waiting out here for a couple minutes?" Martha asked. "Just so I can tidy up real quick?"

Leonard grinned. "You make it sound like there's dirty underwear, old pizza boxes, and empty wine bottles lying around everywhere."

She rolled her eyes and gently closed the door on him. He pulled out his cell phone and checked his emails and browsed eBay for mystery film. He hadn't bought, or developed, anything since the photo of Red. He was starting to feel that familiar itch again. After around five minutes, the door opened again, and Martha beckoned him inside.

Her home was bright and spacious and airy. Gray laminate flooring, white walls, and big windows that he imagined let in lots of sunlight during daylight hours. The furniture was all glossy white and spotlessly clean, and the gray sofa was a perfect color match for the curtains.

In many ways, it was the opposite of his own place, which was dark and gloomy and a little old fashioned. The only similarity as far as their respective tastes in decor went appeared to be photography adorning the walls, albeit his was his DIY gallery taped straight onto the exposed brickwork, and hers were works by famous names like Annie Leibovitz and Richard Avedon, as well as local photographers like the late Tony Shaw, that appeared to be professionally framed. There was no dust on the frames or anywhere else. He noticed she'd also lit a few candles that filled the living room with the scent of cedarwood, sandalwood, and lemon.

He had no idea why she'd been so nervous about inviting him over. Not unless she'd literally left a few dirty plates in the kitchen sink or a damp towel on the bathroom floor that would have embarrassed her. The place was neat, tidy, stylish, and comfortable. In short, it was very Martha.

Martha cooked them a quick dinner of pan-fried salmon with long-stem broccoli and asparagus, and then they settled down to watch a movie together. Once the end credits were rolling, Leonard turned to face her to have the conversation that he knew he couldn't put off any longer.

"I think we should drop the whole Anna Bianco thing."

Martha muted the TV. "Because of what happened tonight?"

"Yes. I think we're getting too close to the truth. It's too dangerous."

"You really think you can just let it go? You said before that you couldn't, that you had to know the truth."

"That was then," Leonard said. "Things have changed. I'm now as sure as I can be that it was Caroline who was behind the events at the Fairview Hotel—and I have a pretty good idea why she did what she did. As for what happened to Anna Bianco? Why should I care who killed her? All that matters is that she was still alive when I walked out of that hotel room five years ago. Maybe me winding up with that camera film *was* just a crazy coincidence. Fate's way of letting me off the hook and telling me it's time to start living again." He swallowed hard. "With you."

Then Leonard did what he'd been wanting to do for weeks. He leaned over and took Martha's face gently in his hands, and he kissed her. His mind flashed back to when he'd messaged her to suggest meeting for the first time and feared he'd misread the signals. Part of him had the same concerns again right now. That she'd reject him. That she'd throw him out. That she'd tell him he'd gotten it all wrong and had ruined everything.

Martha did none of those things. She kissed him right back. Then she stood and took him by the hand and led him to the bedroom.

◆ ◆ ◆

When Leonard's bladder woke him, it took a few seconds for him to figure out where he was. The unfamiliar green digits of the alarm clock on the bedside table next to him showed 2:55.

Then he remembered: Martha.

He smiled in the darkness and enjoyed the memory of what had happened a few hours earlier. The way she'd softly kissed his now yellowing bruises, how she'd climbed gently on top of him, the shape of her body in the glow of the moonlight, the way they had moved together.

It was the first time Leonard had been with a woman since the night with Anna Bianco at the Fairview Hotel. As his life had spiraled, and their relationship had deteriorated, neither he nor Caroline had attempted to initiate sex in the weeks leading up to their split.

With Martha, there had been no lies or guilt or betrayal. It had just felt . . . right.

He heard her soft snores and was tempted to wake her and make love to her again, but he remembered she'd said she had a busy day ahead at the studio, and he knew he should let her sleep. He leaned over and kissed her softly on the back of the neck, then threw off the bedsheet. Found his boxers and silently made his way out into the hallway.

Leonard groped around in the darkness and felt the door handle for the bathroom and pushed it open, his hand fumbling for the light switch inside. He blinked in the unexpected wash of red and realized he wasn't in the bathroom; he was in a dark room. Martha no doubt had one in her studio, but he'd had no idea she had one at home too. Again, something else he didn't know about her.

It was a similar size to his own. The setup was much the same too. Trays, bottles of chemicals, a clothesline with photographs drying on it. They were clearly her most recent mystery-film prints—a kid with a dog on a beach, a group of teenagers at a music festival, a family huddled together on a pink chenille couch. Then he spotted something he definitely didn't have in his own dark room. A small metal floor safe with a combination lock. Intrigued, he bent down and tried the handle. It was locked.

Why would Martha have a safe in her dark room?

Then he answered his own question. The thing was old and ugly and wouldn't fit with the rest of the apartment's pretty decor, so she probably kept it out of sight in here to store important stuff like her passport and birth certificate and any valuable jewelry.

He was just about to leave and finally go empty his bladder when he spotted a stack of prints on the workbench. There was something familiar about the one sticking out halfway down the pile, and he slid it out. Again, he blinked in the strange bloodred gloom. It was the entrance to his own building that had caught his eye. And there, walking out of it, was Leonard. Back when he had the Robinson Crusoe hair and beard and wore unflattering plaid shirts and old jeans.

Completely oblivious to the fact that his photograph was being taken.

Before he'd ever met Martha Weaver.

27

LEONARD

There had been more than just one photograph of Leonard.

Six in total. Two of him leaving his building, two close-ups where his features were scarily clear despite the distance they must have been taken from, one of him standing on the street checking his cell phone, and one of him getting into his car.

All taken on the same day, one right after the other, as part of a sequence. Although what day it was, he couldn't say for sure. He wasn't wearing a jacket, but it wasn't T-shirt weather either, so it could have been late spring, or it could have been a few weeks before he and Martha met for the first time. Or it could have been any other damn time. Clearly, Leonard wasn't quite as adept as Martha was at reading the clues in photos, even when he, himself, was the subject.

He remembered the thoughts that had raced through his mind as they'd undressed each other just hours earlier, as hands had explored skin, and they had gone from being friends to lovers.

No lies or guilt or betrayal.

He didn't know if Martha felt guilty about stalking him, but Leonard sure as hell felt like he'd been lied to and betrayed.

The sick feeling in his gut was quickly replaced by a burning anger, and he returned to the bedroom with the intention of waking her and confronting her. Then he pushed open the door and saw her lying there, vulnerable and naked and trusting, her hair fanned out on the pillow like a dark halo. He decided to let her sleep.

After finally relieving himself in the bathroom, Leonard climbed back into bed beside her, but sleep, as had so often been the case in recent times, refused to come to him and provide some solace. He lay on his back and watched the lights from the occasional passing car reflect on the ceiling. Heard the burst of a police siren break the silence of the night. Some voices down below on the sidewalk. After what felt like a long time, the digits on the alarm clock blinked to 6:00, and he got up and got dressed.

Awake, but exhausted, he went in search of coffee. Martha didn't appear to have any of the normal kind that came in a jar, just one of those fancy machines that were loaded with pods. He spent around ten minutes trying to figure out how to use the damn thing before it finally spurted out something vaguely resembling a caramel latte. He took a couple of sips and left the rest to go cold in the cup. A thin layer of milky scum soon settled on top of the liquid. The prints were scattered across the kitchen table. His head hurt from the lack of sleep and the conversation that was to come.

Finally, he heard movement elsewhere in the apartment. A door creaking open, another one closing, the sound of humming, a toilet flushing. Then Martha breezed into the kitchen wearing a navy satin dressing gown and a big grin.

"There you are! I see you figured out how to use the coffee machine. You want some breakfast?"

As she went to wrap her arms around him, her gaze fell on the photos on the table, and the smile slipped from her face. She froze.

"Leonard . . . I can . . . It's . . . uh . . ." She didn't finish the sentence, just let the words hang in the air between them.

"What? You can explain? It's not what it looks like? Is that what you were going to say? What the fuck, Martha."

She dropped into the chair facing him and wrapped her arms around her body. She couldn't meet his eyes. "It's exactly what it looks like," she said quietly. "I found out where you lived and waited outside your apartment, and then I took photos of you. Obviously, this was before we met."

"But why?"

"I already told you how I enjoy playing detective? That finding the people in my mystery film gives me a buzz? Well, I guess I did the same with you. Only I used 'the clues' in our online chats to find out who you were, rather than photographs."

"You also told me that you didn't stalk the people in your mystery film." He gestured to the prints. "This looks a lot like stalking."

"I know it looks bad. But you were different."

"Why was I different?"

Now Martha did meet his eye. "We'd been chatting online for months. I knew I was falling for you, but I hardly knew a thing about you—if you were married, if you had kids, where you worked, even what you looked like. Those feelings scared me. Especially after what happened with David. I did hint about us meeting up. That way I would've had the answers to those questions, but you never seemed interested until you came across the photograph of Anna Bianco. I couldn't help myself. I had to know who you were, who I was dealing with. It was my way of trying to protect myself."

"Are those the only photos? How many times did you watch me?"

"That was the only time, I swear. There are no more photos."

"When did you take them?"

"A couple months ago, I think."

Leonard scooped the prints up, ripped them in half, went over to the trash, and silently dumped the pieces inside.

"I'm so sorry, Leonard." Martha's face was wet with tears. "I've ruined everything, haven't I?"

Leonard felt like he had too many emotions waging a war inside him. "I need to get out of here," he said. "I need time to think."

◆ ◆ ◆

He was out on the street, lungs shocked by the cold morning air, when he remembered he didn't have a car.

They'd left his Chevy behind and taken Martha's Mini when they'd fled the scene of the crime in Hell's Kitchen the night before.

Leonard didn't really know this part of the city, having always lived and worked around Midtown. He started walking aimlessly, witnessing the day coming to life as traffic grew busier, bus stops filled with commuters, and harried workers rushed down sidewalks dressed for a day at the office, clutching travel mugs.

He should be working himself. Settled in front of his desk, writing stories that he'd already pushed back deadlines on, his mind focused on the words on the screen instead of being consumed by thoughts of Martha. The euphoria of the intimacy they'd shared now battled with the horror of seeing those photos of himself.

He wandered through streets with Chinese hair salons and internet cafés and fast-food places. Eventually, he came across a coffee shop named Café Grumpy that caught his eye as a result of the appropriate name and his need for caffeine. The interior was modern, the place hip and trendy, with exposed-brick walls, a colorful tile floor, and neon signs. Leonard knew the lack of food, as well as next to no sleep, was making his headache worse, so he ordered a granola bar along with a latte and found a window seat with a view of the rain-slick street outside.

A half hour later, Leonard felt much better thanks to the snack, coffee, and having reached a decision about Martha. He retraced his steps back to Hester Street but got no answer when he banged on the door of her apartment. Back outside, he saw that her Mini was gone and assumed she must be at her studio already.

He realized he didn't know the address of her workplace or even the name of her business. Shame flamed the back of his neck, despite a persistent cold drizzle that had soaked his hair and dampened his clothes. So much of the time they had spent together had been focused on Leonard and Red and how she'd ruined his life. Martha had never once complained. The only time she'd asked him to drop the investigation had been out of concern for Leonard. Nothing else. He pulled up a Google search page on his phone and typed the words *Martha Weaver Photographer New York City* and found a hit for Dream Weaver Photography. Leonard smiled at the name. The "About" section of the company's website confirmed that it was, indeed, where he would find Martha.

Bowery was a ten-minute walk by foot. The premises were a shopfront situated beneath an apartment building and next to a bridal boutique and a dental practice. It was painted a cheerful bright blue, and the picture window housed framed prints and canvases of babies and families. Martha's car was parked outside.

A sign on the door with the operating hours indicated the studio should be open for business, but another one stating "Shooting in Progress" suggested he wasn't going to gain entry. Leonard tried the door handle anyway. Sure enough, it was locked. He pressed his face up against the glass and peeked inside where he saw a small stylish office space with a white desk, a black leather couch, and a vase with fresh blooms in autumnal colors on a glass coffee table. The walls were adorned with lots more photos and canvases.

Despite being brightly lit, the office was empty, Martha presumably in her studio out back.

He could go find another coffee someplace, but Leonard didn't want to miss the slot between one client leaving and the next one arriving, so he decided to wait outside.

Finally, after twenty-five minutes and some openly suspicious glaring from two elderly ladies, he heard voices inside the building. An old-fashioned bell tinkled as the door opened and a couple emerged. A toddler wearing a bow tie and a bad-tempered expression squirmed in the woman's arms.

The bell tinkled again as Leonard stepped inside. Martha was sitting behind the desk, and she looked up from her laptop in surprise, clearly not expecting her next client so soon. And definitely not expecting to see him standing there.

"Leonard . . ."

"Can we talk? Do you have time?"

"Sure. My next shoot isn't for another half hour." She got up, went over to the door, and locked it. "So that we won't be disturbed. Lindy from the bridal store next door sometimes visits for a chat or a coffee. Do you want to sit?"

Leonard nodded and followed her to the leather couch. It was big enough to hold three people, and they perched awkwardly at either end, leaving a big gap between them.

"How did you know where to find me?" she asked.

"You're not the only one who knows how to find people."

"I guess I deserved that. Are you here to tell me you don't want to see me again?"

"No, that's not why I'm here. Even though I'm still mad as hell about what you did. Remember when we spoke about feeling violated after my apartment was broken into? That's how I felt when I saw those photographs—only much worse because I thought I could trust you."

"I really am sorry, Leonard."

He held up a hand. "Please, let me finish, Martha. What you did was wrong, not to mention creepy as fuck, but I kind of understand why you did it. The curiosity factor, the fact that you'd been badly hurt before." He smiled. "Did you mean what you said about falling for me?"

"I did."

"And now?"

"Even more so now that I've gotten to know you."

"I feel the same way. These last few weeks with you? I can't remember the last time I felt so happy."

It was only when Leonard said the words out loud that he realized just how much he meant them. He wasn't talking about love, it was way too soon for anything like that, but he knew that what they had was worth holding on to. It was worth another shot.

"Does this mean we're good?" Martha asked.

He took her hand and pulled her toward him, closing the gap between them to nothing. He kissed her softly, then whispered in her ear, "Yeah, I think we're good. But no more secrets and no more hiding stuff, huh?"

Martha pulled away from him. "Okay. In that case, there's something I should probably tell you."

"What?"

She chewed on her bottom lip. "I know you wanted to drop the whole Anna Bianco thing—and I do think we should—but . . ."

"But?" Leonard prompted.

Martha went over to the desk and picked up her cell phone. "When all of this started, I had a Google alert set up in Anna Bianco's name. I got an alert this morning."

"What was the alert?"

"Bobby Khan has an exclusive in the *Reporter*. There's been a development in the case."

28

JACKIE

Detective Jackie Rossi stared out the window of the Tenth Precinct, even though there wasn't a whole lot to see this time of night.

It was a habit she had when she was thinking, and tonight she had a lot to think about.

In daylight hours, the street below bustled with foot traffic, cars honking, folks yelling, people going about their business. Now, at just past ten p.m., there was nothing but the occasional bum staggering down the sidewalk under the streetlights.

Her own reflection stared back at her from the glass, illuminated by the light of the single desk lamp. Jackie looked tired. She felt it too. The Anna Bianco case was taking a toll. A month in and no arrests and no real suspects meant she was feeling the heat from both the top brass and the media. But nobody was harder on Jackie than she was on herself.

She drained the last of her coffee and dumped the plastic cup in the wastebasket along with the three other empties from earlier. What was left of the bean burrito she'd picked up from the nearby

Taco Bell for dinner lay cold and globby in the cardboard box on her desk. It was a reminder of another meal missed with her husband, Doug, which added guilt to the indigestion. And it stunk to high hell.

Jackie sat at the desk, pushed the takeout carton to one side, and opened the Bianco file. She spread all the witness statements, reports, and crime-scene photos across the surface. Every word and every image were locked into her memory now, as though seared there by a white-hot stamp, but it was always worth another look.

Jackie badly needed a break in the case.

First, she scrutinized the crime-scene photos again. She'd been on the job almost thirty years and had seen a lot in that time—men involved in drug wars who were dropped from the windows of tower blocks, gangland figures gunned down on their own doorsteps, bar brawls that went too far, and too many people of both sexes killed in their own homes at the hands of their partners. It was the kind of stuff that kept her awake at night, thinking about the violence and hatred that one human being could inflict upon another, wondering why she put herself through this shit every day.

But what had happened to Anna Bianco was something else altogether. It was Jack the Ripper territory. Stabbed thirty-nine times in what appeared to be a frenzied attack.

Frenzied but planned.

The murder weapon had most likely been a standard kitchen knife, one that you could buy at Bloomingdale's or IKEA as part of a six-piece set. The kind of thing you didn't find in a hotel room. Something you brought with you with the intention of doing some serious damage.

Frenzied but planned but sloppy too.

The killer had made mistakes, had left evidence behind at the scene. Most likely a first-timer. Probably not a serial killer. God knows, New York had had its fair share of those—Son of Sam, the

Long Island serial killer, Joel Rifkin, Joseph Christopher—but this felt personal to Jackie.

The ex-husband had, naturally, been the first person they'd interviewed after speaking to Bianco's distraught parents and other hotel guests. He had been their first person of interest.

Jackie had disliked Bryce Hawkins immediately and intensely. He reminded her of the young guys on *The Bachelorette*, a dating show that she sometimes watched with her daughter that revolved around women trying to find potential husbands from a pool of impossibly attractive men in an impossibly glamorous setting. Like them, Hawkins had a deep tan, bleached white teeth, a tattoo sleeve, and a six-pack that you couldn't buy at a liquor store. The difference was that most of the young men on the reality series were in their late twenties or early thirties, and Hawkins was over forty and had the attitude of a sixteen-year-old.

The marriage of Hawkins and Bianco had been stormy and short lived. According to him, she'd been paranoid and jealous and had eventually trashed all his belongings after accusing him of having multiple affairs. He claimed he hadn't seen or spoken to her since their acrimonious split several years earlier. Hawkins also claimed to have an alibi for the night of the murder. Jackie would have loved nothing more than to slap the cuffs on the egotistical asshole and secure a quick result, but he'd been in Connecticut for the whole week with his new girlfriend, and the security cameras at his hotel had backed him up.

When Bianco's checking account details had landed on Jackie's desk, and she'd established that the victim had been earning a regular paycheck from Click Photography, Ron Kincaid had moved front and center in the investigation. A grubby little man with teeth like a row of broken tombstones, he'd been quick to cough up the details of his surveillance work and equally as quick to insist there was nothing untoward going on behind the scenes at his business.

The place was the perfect front for money laundering—and the Criminal Enterprise Investigative Section still had him on their radar—but Jackie didn't think Kincaid was her guy.

She'd turned her focus to the so-called victims of Kincaid's honeytrap operation, specifically those who'd been played by Anna Bianco. It was an extensive list. Jackie's team hadn't even been halfway through those interviews when the DNA results from the scene at the Fairview Hotel finally came back from the lab and appeared to be a game changer.

The results indicated what she'd suspected all along—a first-timer. Or, at least, someone who'd never been caught. There had been no hits on the system. Even if they had gotten a match, it wouldn't have been enough on its own to secure a conviction. A good defense attorney would destroy the validity of the evidence, and how it had ended up at the scene, quicker than a juror could say "reasonable doubt."

No, Jackie needed more. She needed the murder weapon.

The usual searches had been carried out in and around the hotel. Toilet tanks and loose floorboards. Drains and bushes. Nothing. The blade could be at the bottom of the Hudson River by now or scrubbed clean and hidden in plain sight on someone's kitchen block.

Finding that knife was her best chance of finding the killer. If the perp hadn't gotten rid of it already, she had to force them to act, try to flush them out.

Jackie picked up the phone on her desk. The dial tone was loud as she held the receiver to her ear. She hesitated, just for a moment, then punched in the digits for a number she knew by heart. After a half-dozen rings, the call was answered.

"Bobby Khan."

"Bobby, it's Jackie Rossi. I have something for you about the Anna Bianco case, but my name can't be anywhere near it. Okay?"

"Shit, Jackie. Do you know how close we are to deadline for the final edition?"

"Do you want the story or not? I can give it to the *Times* or the *Post* instead if you're not interested."

"No, no. It's fine. What you got?"

Jackie told him they'd recovered DNA from the scene—found on the victim—that could belong to the murderer. But she made sure to hold back on the key details. She didn't tell him what it was or where exactly it had been found.

And she didn't tell him that the DNA profile was female.

29

MARTHA

The rest of the day passed by in a blur.

Martha and Leonard both had work commitments to take care of, so they had arranged to meet later that evening for dinner and drinks. It would be their first official date as a couple.

She would no doubt perk up by then, but right now, Martha was mentally exhausted. She'd been through a whole gamut of emotions in a short period of time—the joy of her relationship with Leonard moving from friendship to something more, which had quickly been followed by the sorrow of thinking she'd lost him.

There was no point having any regrets about the photographs. Martha knew it was simply who she was, and that she wasn't going to change. If she was going to open herself up to someone, she had to know everything she could about that person. It hadn't been a lie when she'd told Leonard she was only trying to protect herself.

To Martha, it was no different from those women who trawled through the social media accounts of potential lovers, and no one ever thought they were weird stalkers, did they? It was something girlfriends did together over a bottle of wine. Completely normal. Check out the exes, the friends, where they hung out, moon over their cute photos. Leonard was no longer on Twitter or Facebook or Instagram—he'd apparently deleted them all in the wake of his ill-fated night with Anna Bianco—which meant Martha had had to get creative.

While chatting online, he'd mentioned his favorite bar near Times Square, so she'd guessed he resided in or close to Midtown. Then he'd spoken of Hell's Kitchen restaurants close to his apartment building and a liquor store down the street. The biggest clue had been the reference to his old green Chevy Malibu. From there, it hadn't been too difficult to track down Leonard Blaylock.

Martha had enjoyed looking at the photos she'd captured from her Mini across the street from his building. Again, was that really any different from checking out a guy's Insta feed? No, it wasn't. But leaving those images lying around where Leonard could find them? That had been beyond stupid.

She knew they were on her coffee table in the living room when Leonard had unexpectedly suggested spending the night at her place. That's why she'd asked for a few minutes to "tidy up" when they'd arrived at her apartment. She really did have to tidy up too, quickly running a duster over the furniture, changing the towels in the bathroom to laundry-fresh ones, smoothing over the bedsheets in the hope that the bedroom was where Leonard would be sleeping with her.

She'd assumed that hiding the photographs of Leonard in among the rest of the prints in her dark room would suffice. He hadn't even known she had a dark room, so he'd had no need to go in there and have a look around. In hindsight, Martha should have stored them in her safe, but the combination lock on the old thing was unpredictable, and the last thing she wanted was to find herself in a position where she'd opened it and then couldn't secure it properly again.

When she'd seen those prints spread across her kitchen table this morning, and the thunderous expression on Leonard's face, Martha had felt as if her world were falling apart. Everything she'd worked for, had dreamed about, shattered in an instant. In the end, it had been a good thing because it had forced them both to open up about their true feelings for each other. No tiptoeing around after their night of passion, no wondering if it'd been a mistake or a one-off, if they'd go back to being just friends or friends with occasional benefits.

Martha Weaver already knew she was in love with Leonard. Of course she was. Those feelings had already been tested to the full, hadn't they? And she'd decided he was the one she wanted anyway. She doubted he felt quite as strongly about her, not yet, but she was confident that he would in time.

Her last shoot of the day had been photographing a six-week-old baby boy. Oliver Tate was teeny and gorgeous and had stared up at her with big blue eyes and had gripped her thumb in his tiny fist. That unique baby smell, the feel of the soft fuzz of hair on his head, the ridiculously small chinos and shirt his parents had picked out for him to wear . . . it was impossible not to have her insides turn to mush being around perfection like that. Impossible not to want what the Tates had for herself.

From what Leonard had told her about his engagement to Caroline, it sounded like he'd expected them to have kids once they got married, that having a family had very much been part of his plans. There was no reason to believe that his desire to be a dad had diminished. Did Martha even dare to hope that babies might be a part of their future together?

After locking up the studio, she got into the Mini for the short journey home. Martha smiled to herself as she passed by the DL. The restaurant and lounge on the corner of Delancey and Ludlow was one of her favorite spots in the Lower East Side, and it was where she'd be dining with Leonard this evening. Having spent so much time at his place over the last few weeks, she'd decided it was time to introduce him to her stomping ground. Martha's mouth was already watering at the prospect of the steak she'd order later.

As she carried on toward Hester Street, she hoped that today would prove to be the turning point in her and Leonard's relationship. Sure, the whole business with Anna Bianco had brought them together, but Martha would love nothing more than to leave it all behind now. Focus on the future instead. Leonard had confirmation (or as close as he was going to get to it) that Caroline Cooper was the one who'd set him up at the Fairview Hotel. It was time to let it go now.

As she turned onto her street, she cussed when she saw a car parked in her usual spot outside her building. As Martha craned her neck to see if there were any spaces farther along, the car—a big gray boxy thing—suddenly pulled out into the road far too fast, tires squealing and engine revving, before taking off at high speed.

"Asshole," she muttered.

Her eyes instinctively went to the license plate on the rear bumper, but it appeared to be partially obscured by mud.

After backing into the newly vacated space, Martha headed inside her building, making a mental note yet again to chase down the super about the broken lock on the secure entry. She noticed the scent of a woman's perfume that she didn't recognize as something any of her neighbors wore.

She climbed the stairs—and then stopped dead.

The wood on her door and the frame surrounding the lock was chipped and scarred as though someone had tried to pry it open. Tentatively, she took a few steps forward and felt the toe of her boot connect with something, which she heard skitter across the concrete floor before coming to a stop against the wall. Martha reached down, picked up the object, and frowned. She slid it into the pocket of her leather jacket and gently pushed against the door. It didn't give. Whoever had attempted to jimmy it open had failed.

Martha unlocked the door, went inside, and immediately called Leonard. The call went straight to voice mail, and she remembered he had an interview lined up for a magazine article and had told her he might not be contactable for an hour or so. She left a message, then locked the door behind her, went into the kitchen, and poured a glass of wine.

She didn't call the police. There was little doubt in Martha's mind that whoever had attempted to break in to her apartment was the same person who'd trashed Leonard's place. Twenty minutes later, her phone buzzed. It was Leonard returning her call.

"Are you okay?" he asked. "What's wrong? You sounded upset in the voice mail you left me."

Martha told him what had happened.

"I'll be right over. Keep the door locked and don't open it to anyone."

Leonard was there in less than fifteen minutes. He assessed the damage and then asked if she'd seen anything—or anyone—suspicious. Martha told him about the vehicle that had been parked outside when she returned home and how it had taken off quickly.

"Can you describe the car?"

"It was one of those big SUV-type things. I'm not sure of the make. Dark colored. I'm pretty sure it was gray. I didn't see the license number."

Leonard's jaw tensed. "Could it have been a Jeep?"

"It could have been, but I'm not great with car makes and models." Martha reached into her pocket and pulled out the object she'd found. "This was right outside my door."

She handed the lipstick to Leonard. He removed the top from the gold-colored case and twisted until the lipstick itself was showing. It was a deep berry shade. The tension in his face turned to anger. He squinted at the tiny sticker on the base and swore.

"What's wrong?" Martha asked. "Do you recognize it?"

Leonard nodded. "This is the same brand and color of lipstick that Caroline used to wear when we were together. I know for sure because I bought it for her for birthdays and Christmases. It's the same one she still wears now, or at least, it looks like it. And there's something else too."

"What?"

"That day I visited her place in Bedford to confront her about Click Photography? There was a dark gray Jeep in the driveway. I think it was Caroline who tried to break in to your home."

30

LEONARD

Despite the attempted break-in, they both agreed to keep the reservation at the restaurant, deciding that there was no point moping around Martha's apartment for the rest of the evening.

Even so, Leonard told Martha he was reluctant to leave her on her own after the bungled burglary attempt, so he didn't go home to get changed. He was already fairly smartly dressed and was also wearing his new Hugo Boss overcoat. He'd do.

When Martha emerged from the bedroom, it was fair to say she'd more than do. She looked—and smelled—beautiful. She wore a little more makeup than usual and had teased her brown hair into loose curls. Her dress fell just below the knee and hugged her gorgeous curves in all the right places.

Leonard was glad, yet again, that he hadn't allowed her covert photos of him to wreck their fledgling romance. In fact, he could probably count himself lucky that she hadn't dumped his ass for going through her private belongings. He'd been so consumed by his own anger and sense of betrayal that it had only just occurred to him that he'd been in the wrong too. How would he feel if he found Martha rooting through his stuff?

He thought of the items he'd kept in the drawer of his bedside table. No, that wouldn't be good at all. But Martha, being the sweet woman that she was, hadn't called Leonard out for being a nosy bastard. She really did deserve to be treated better, and he was determined not to fuck things up this time.

For the most part, their first real date was amazing.

The menu was simple comfort food served up in elegant surroundings at Dinner on Ludlow on the first floor of the DL. Martha ordered the steak with peppercorn sauce, and Leonard opted for a burger and fries. The food was delicious. They touched fingertips across the table, drank good wine, and chatted about nothing important. The flickering candlelight, crystal chandeliers, dark wood, and ornate filigree set the perfect romantic tone.

But as they waited for their desserts to arrive, he knew they would finally have to address the big, fat elephant sitting right there at the table with them, like a hanger-on, a spare part, an unwanted third wheel.

It was time to discuss Leonard's ex-fiancée.

He said, "If Caroline attempted to break in to your apartment, then I have to assume that she was the one who also ransacked my home. But why? And what was she looking for?"

They silently pondered those questions while the waitress placed their desserts in front of them and topped off their wineglasses.

Once they were alone again, they started thinking out loud.

Leonard said, "It's possible that I spooked Caroline by showing up at her house unexpectedly like that. Maybe that was a mistake. Maybe that's what set these recent events in motion?"

"But you only asked about Kincaid and whether she'd hired him to spy on you," Martha pointed out. "All you had to confront her with was a payment she'd made to Click Photography. You never mentioned Red. Caroline had no way of knowing that we also had a copy of a customer receipt in her name for surveillance work. What does it really prove anyway? Nothing. It's not like you could take it to Bobby Khan—or some other reporter—for a big exposé on Caroline Cooper the TV star, is it? You ask me, getting caught breaking in to someone's property is a lot more likely to end someone's career than hiring a private eye. But she didn't just do it once; she tried it twice. So, we're back to the same question: Why?"

"You're right. It makes no sense. Unless . . ."

"Unless the break-ins were about the murder and not the setup with you and Red at the Fairview Hotel," Martha finished for him.

They were both silent while they ate their desserts. Once their plates had been cleared and replaced with coffee and mints, Leonard said, "Let's say Caroline did murder Red. What was her motive?"

"Not sex," Martha said immediately. "So, probably money."

"Blackmail," Leonard said.

"You think this is about Jim Sanders?"

"I think it's possible. Caroline used Red to blackmail Sanders and steal his job. Her career since then has been pretty impressive. She's already being touted for much bigger things. And we know that Red was willing to go to fairly extreme lengths to get her hands on some cash."

"So, Red tried to blackmail Caroline after witnessing her lucrative rise?" Martha said. "She knew how damaging the truth about Jim Sanders's exit from *Rise & Shine* could be for Caroline if the story got out and tried to capitalize on it?"

"It all makes sense," Leonard said.

"It does," Martha agreed. "And the break-ins?"

"Maybe the burglary was always part of the plan. Maybe you were right all along when you said the crime-scene photo of Red was to frame me for her murder. How about this for a scenario? Caroline killed Red, took the photos of her dead body, and planted the film on me, having found out about my interest in mystery film. Then, once I'd had enough time to develop the roll, she attempted to steal the photos with my fingerprints all over them with the intention of anonymously sending them to the cops, along with my name. Suddenly, I'm the prime suspect. When she didn't find any photos or the roll of film at my place, she then tried your apartment."

"How would she even know about me?"

"We've been spending a lot of time together. Caroline has probably been tailing me for days, if not weeks. I'm guessing she knows exactly who you are. Don't forget, she's way sharper than people give her credit for. You wrote her off yourself as being ditzy and silly, but I already told you she's smart. She's good at digging, finding stuff out about people. She's a hell of a journalist, and she's one hundred percent capable of masterminding everything that's happened if it means protecting herself and her career."

The waitress returned with the check. Leonard paid, and they headed outside. He wrapped his arms around Martha, and they shared a long, slow kiss until some passing teenagers on skateboards made loud kissing noises, and they laughed as they reluctantly pulled apart. The night was cold but dry, and they decided to take a leisurely stroll back to Martha's apartment.

They were partway along Ludlow when she said, "What if our theory about Caroline is right? What do we do about it? Do we even do anything?"

"We need to end this thing once and for all. Coming after me is one thing. Coming after you? That's unacceptable. I think Bobby's latest story is the key."

Martha stopped and turned to face him. "How do you mean?"

"We turn the tables on Caroline. The police have the killer's DNA on file, right? So, we give them her name, and if it's a match, it's over. Case closed."

Martha didn't appear convinced. "And if it's not a match?"

"Then we've got it all wrong," Leonard said. "But I don't think we do. I think it'll be a match."

She considered for a moment, then said, "Okay, how do we do it? Get our information to the police, I mean."

"I have no idea," Leonard admitted. "Jackie Rossi knows me. She was one of my main sources when I worked the crime beat at the *Reporter*. And she knows I'm Caroline's ex. I can't exactly walk into the station and point a finger at her. It's more likely they'd throw me out or arrest me for wasting police time than thank me for solving their case. Even worse, they might start looking too closely at me and discover I also have a connection to Anna Bianco. That I also have a motive."

They started walking again. A moon as bright as a stage-show spotlight lit the way as they carried on past silent apartment buildings and shuttered storefronts.

Martha said, "I have a plan."

31

MARTHA

Martha spent her lunch break in Target picking out the kind of items she'd never usually wear. A navy zipped hooded top from the menswear floor that was too big for her, a pink sweater in her size, a pair of wool gloves, and a camouflage-patterned ball cap.

It was everything she'd need, and all for less than thirty dollars, which was just as well because she wouldn't be getting much wear out of any of them, seeing as they would all be disposed of soon enough.

In the days after their dinner, while traveling between client appointments, Martha had kept an eye out for the perfect place to execute the plan she'd discussed with Leonard. She needed a pay phone that was still operational and located in a neighborhood that wasn't too busy but also wasn't downright rough or dangerous. There had been one that seemed promising until she noticed the receiver was off the hook right next to a bottle of wine in a stained paper bag. No real surprise that there had been no dial tone. At least two others smelled so bad that she didn't even get close enough to check whether they were still working.

Most of the city's public pay phones were in the process of being disconnected and yanked from their booths following complaints that they were an eyesore and no longer of any real use. They were set to be replaced with the LinkNYC system, but Martha discovered there were still four old-school-style pay phone booths on West End Avenue. She did recon on all of them and decided the one on the corner of Ninetieth Street was the least exposed.

Martha returned to the intersection on the Upper West Side later that evening. She'd changed from her work clothes into black skinny jeans, boots, and the pink sweater, with the oversized navy hoodie on top.

Leonard drove. It made sense not to take her own car, seeing as she'd be the one trying to avoid being identified. Plus, he wanted to be nearby in case she needed help or felt unsafe. His concern was sweet but unnecessary. Martha didn't expect to be in any danger. The nerves that she did have, which grew more intense the closer they got to their destination, were down to her fear of messing up and ruining everything for him.

Leonard parked on Riverside under some trees and turned off the engine. Martha pulled up her hood and swung open the passenger-side door.

"Wish me luck," she said.

"Be careful," Leonard said, giving her a quick kiss on the lips and her hand a squeeze.

Martha had four items shoved into the front and back pockets of her jeans—the ball cap, a packet of antibacterial wipes, some loose change, and a plastic shopping bag.

She thrust her gloved hands into the hoodie's pockets and tucked her chin into her chest to keep out the bitter chill. It wasn't even eight p.m. and already it was pitch-black.

Her destination was a residential area, the pay phone overlooked by prewar co-ops and low-rise walk-ups. Martha hadn't seen any CCTV cameras nearby when she'd been here during daylight hours, but that didn't mean there weren't any.

The booth was a modern replica of the old ones that used to be found all over the city. A full-height, enclosed silver box like the kind Superman might've used. It was free of graffiti, vandalism, and the stench of urine or any other bodily fluids. Kind of what you'd expect on the Upper West Side.

She assured herself it didn't matter if she was spotted. Okay, the sight of someone using a pay phone might be unusual in an age where everyone had smartphones, but it was hardly a crime. For all a curious passerby knew, she could have run out of juice or lost her cell and had to make a call. In any case, the possibility of cameras that she had missed, or unexpected witnesses, was the reason why she'd taken precautions with her attire. Martha was confident she wouldn't be identified after the call had been made.

It was why she'd decided to use a pay phone, rather than a burner. The issue had been discussed at length with Leonard, both of them weighing the pros and cons. It seemed likely that the police would be able to trace a batch number from a burner and thus find out where it had been purchased and possibly pull security footage from the store or pharmacy's own closed-circuit cameras.

So, old-school communication had won out over modern technology.

Martha lifted the receiver and wiped it down with an antibacterial wipe before placing it to her ear. Breathed out a big sigh of relief when she heard a dial tone. Martha had no idea if calls to nonemergency police numbers were free or not, so she dropped some coins into the slot in case they weren't. Then she punched in the tip-line number that had appeared in the newspaper articles about Anna Bianco's murder. She heard ringing on the other end of the line. Martha swallowed down her nerves. She peered out from under the hood to see if anyone was watching from the street or a window. Saw nothing that gave her cause for concern.

When the call was answered, Martha spoke over the voice of the female operator who'd picked up. Her words came out in a rush. It was the spiel she'd practiced with Leonard.

"I have information about a homicide. I'm not going to give you my name, so don't ask. This information is for the attention of Detective Jackie Rossi."

Martha told the operator which case she was calling about and the date the murder had taken place.

She went on. "I saw someone coming out of the Fairview Hotel that night. She was covered in blood. I didn't know who she was at the time, which is why I didn't say anything before now. But I just saw her again today. She was on TV. Her name is Caroline Cooper. This isn't a prank call. You have the killer's DNA. Check out Caroline Cooper. I think you'll find you have a match."

Martha could still hear the operator babbling away as she replaced the handset in the cradle. Somewhere in the distance, a siren shrieked, and she held her breath until the noise faded without any cop cars skidding to a halt in front of her and she could breathe easy again.

There was construction scaffolding in front of the building next to the booth, and Martha stepped underneath it. She followed the covered scaffolding around the corner onto Ninetieth Street, where she unzipped the hoodie and stuffed it into the plastic bag, along with the gloves. She tucked her hair under the ball cap and fitted it onto her head. Waited awhile until a small cluster of people made their way along the street before tagging along behind them as though she were part of their group. Martha casually dropped the plastic bag into a trash receptacle and kept her head down as she walked.

By the time she reached Riverside, she had also trashed the ball cap and the pink sweater and was shivering in a long-sleeve T-shirt as she climbed into Leonard's car. Her precautions had no doubt been over the top. Then again, Martha had no idea the lengths the cops might go to in order to track down a potential witness in a high-profile homicide case.

"Done?" Leonard asked, starting the car.

"Done," Martha said. "Now we wait and see what happens."

SIX MONTHS LATER

32

CAROLINE

The clerk stood and addressed the jury foreman. "Have you reached a verdict upon which you are all agreed?" he asked.

"We have," said the foreman.

"Do you find the defendant guilty or not guilty?"

A hush fell over the courtroom, so silent you could hear a heartbeat. Caroline Cooper closed her eyes and clenched her fists. Willed the chubby man with the thick glasses and goatee beard to say those two little words.

Not guilty.

"Guilty."

There were gasps from the public gallery. Cheers from Anna Bianco's family. Caroline tried to say the word "No," but it came out as a pathetic little yelp. This couldn't be happening. Her legs went weak, and she felt like she was going to faint.

Caroline had spent months dreaming of the moment she would stand outside the courthouse a free woman. All she wanted was to sleep in her own bed. To shut out the rest of the world for a while. Try to make sense of what had happened to her.

In her fantasies, she was surrounded by camera crews and photographers and former coworkers, flashes popping, questions being yelled, everyone jostling for the best position, while Caroline stood serenely in a smart suit and calmly read out a prepared statement.

She would tell them she was innocent, that she had been set up, and that she was determined to fully clear her name by urging the police to continue with their investigation and find the real killer. It was no less than what she, and Anna Bianco, deserved.

The reality couldn't have been any more different.

Caroline left the courthouse still handcuffed to a police officer and wearing an ill-fitting suit because she'd said she was a size six but had dropped two dress sizes while awaiting trial.

Being denied bail had been the first shock. The brutality of the crime and being branded a flight risk—what with Harry's millions meaning they could charter a private jet anyplace in the world without too many questions being asked—were the reasons for that decision.

But the guilty verdict . . . ?

There were plenty of reporters and cameras waiting for her outside the courthouse, but there were also dozens of hecklers who swore and shouted and shoved and spat at her.

Her lawyer had urged Caroline to take a plea deal. It would mean being out of prison when she was still a young woman. Her whole life ahead of her. A conviction for murder would mean a life sentence.

Maybe she'd been naïve, but Caroline couldn't get her head around the idea of confessing to something that she didn't do. Even now, she didn't regret her decision.

Caroline Cooper did not murder Anna Bianco.

So, why would she say that she did?

The defense lawyer had been hired and paid for by Harry. Vivian Stoll was a fearsome woman with an excellent track record of acquittals. She was nicknamed the Terrier because she was small, fearless, tenacious, and her bite was worse than her bark. She'd been pissed when Caroline had insisted on sticking with a not guilty plea, hadn't wanted to blot her track record with a bad result.

"Cards on the table, Caroline," Vivian had said. "I don't see how we can win this one. Not with the evidence they have against you."

The lawyer had been right.

The prison van's engine thrummed beneath her now, swallowing up the interstate miles on the journey back to Bedford Hills Correctional Facility for women. Caroline could smell her own sweat. There was a stench of fear too. She tried not to think about what the future held for her now. Rules and regulations. A tiny cell. Suicide risk assessments. Rehabilitation and therapy sessions. Desperate survival. Maybe the opportunity to work in the prison canteen or hairdressing salon with the other lifers if she was lucky.

Caroline was so, so tired. She closed her eyes and was immediately transported back to that night at the Fairview Hotel.

When she'd first received the text message demanding the cash, she'd assumed Ron Kincaid was behind the blackmail. Caroline had had misgivings about involving him in the Jim Sanders scam from the outset, and the text had been sent from an unfamiliar number.

The next message had been signed "Red," but Caroline had still suspected Kincaid—until the Fairview Hotel had been suggested as the drop-off point. The message from Red was loud and clear. This wasn't just about Jim Sanders—it was about Leonard Blaylock too.

Caroline had been vibrating with anger as she'd opened the hotel room's door, her purse heavy with the bundle of cash. Fifteen grand. As far as she was concerned, it was the last payment Red would ever receive from her. If the woman demanded more, she'd call her bluff, tell her to go to the newspapers with the story. She wouldn't be getting another cent out of Caroline Cooper, that was for sure.

If Caroline thought the bottom had dropped out of her world when she'd received the blackmail text, it was nothing compared to seeing Anna Bianco's dead body on that hotel bed. There had been so much blood.

At first, she'd thought it was another setup, Red playing dead again. Caroline had stepped farther into the room, had gotten right up close to the woman, and had seen torn skin and flesh and glimpses of bone, and she had known there was no makeup artist in the world who could recreate such realistic wounds.

Then there was the smell too.

She had run from that hotel room as fast as she could.

If she had called the cops and waited for them to arrive, would it have made any difference?

Caroline had had more than six months to mull it over, and the answer was no. It wouldn't have made any difference at all.

The jobs she'd hired Red to carry out in the past, the texts, the blackmail, the $15,000, her discovery of the body—it all looked bad. It meant she had the means and she definitely had the motive.

But none of it made her a killer.

Caroline had reported on lots of criminal cases, so she knew that her hair being found at the scene was far from conclusive in terms of her guilt. Especially once she'd admitted to being in the hotel room after Red was already dead. But not when it was found in a dead woman's clenched fist.

However, the fatal blow had been the murder weapon.

Found in her home, swaddled in one of her old T-shirts that had her own DNA all over it, as well as Anna Bianco's dried blood.

Even the Terrier couldn't explain that to a jury.

It made no sense to Caroline.

The hair.

The knife.

The T-shirt.

Someone had set her up. Someone who had hated her enough to frame her for Anna Bianco's murder. Someone who had been able to pull the whole thing off.

Caroline's eyes snapped open.

There was only one person it could be.

33

JACKIE

When Jackie Rossi returned from the courthouse, the celebrations were already well underway.

Whisky and wine and even a few party hats. Cops and secretaries and the top brass all reveling in a job well done. There was lots of backslapping and a couple of renditions of "For She's a Jolly Good Fellow." Jackie accepted a plastic cup filled with lukewarm white wine and indulged her team's congratulations and good-natured bantering for a while before escaping to the relative quiet of her desk on the other side of the squad room.

Anna Bianco's case file was still sitting there. It could officially be moved from "Open" to "Solved." What had started with an anonymous tip-off had finally resulted in today's guilty verdict.

Jackie knew she should be feeling relief, satisfaction, elation. But she wasn't experiencing any of those emotions. Just a kind of sadness at the sheer waste of two young women's lives. One dead, the other facing a very long time in prison. There was a lingering uneasiness too, a sense that something wasn't quite right, even though she knew it was a solid conviction.

She opened the case file and flipped through the crime-scene photos. Bianco lay on her back on the bed. Her left hand was hanging off the edge, her right was outstretched on the bedsheet. Her head was turned to the side, eyes wide and unseeing. The wounds that pierced skin and flesh and even exposed chipped bone were stark and shocking.

All the evidence pointed to Caroline Cooper being Anna Bianco's killer.

Jackie had given Bobby Khan the story about the DNA in the hopes of flushing out the murderer, making them panic, making them act rashly. That hadn't happened, but the article in the *Reporter* had resulted in a witness coming forward.

The phone call naming Cooper had set everything in motion—and it was the first thing that bothered Jackie.

She'd never been able to track down the woman who'd made the call from a pay phone on the Upper West Side, despite scouring CCTV footage from nearby streets. It seemed like the witness had gone to some lengths to make sure she wouldn't be identified.

If it wasn't for the information that Jackie and her team already had by then, the caller would likely have been written off as a crank. A TV personality spotted at the scene of a murder? Seriously? It wasn't a million miles away from the crazies who wasted police time with their claims that crimes in the city were being carried out by Elvis Presley or Marilyn Monroe.

But there was no way the witness could have known about the DNA profile being female or that it was extracted from two strands of long blond hair gripped in Bianco's fist or that the hotel's night manager had seen a blond woman outside the Fairview Hotel around the time of the murder.

Jerry Morris had witnessed a lot of comings and goings on the night in question—guests checking in, others heading out for the evening, some enjoying a drink in the hotel bar. His sighting of the blond woman hadn't been particularly significant until the DNA results had landed on Jackie's desk.

Morris had noticed the blonde loitering around the hotel's entrance. Her hair was long around her shoulders, and she wore dark clothing. Possibly jeans and a black or navy trench coat, but he couldn't say for sure. She had seemed familiar somehow, but he couldn't put his finger on why. The woman had consulted the phone she held in her hand and had then walked away. She hadn't entered the hotel. Or, at least, not through the main reception area. Morris had assumed that she'd been searching for someplace else, but later conceded it was possible she'd gained access to the building via a rear fire door that was next to Bianco's room.

Following the anonymous phone call, Jackie had brought Morris back in to take a look at a six-pack of photos to see if he could identify the mystery blonde. The pack contained images of five random fair-haired women and one image of Caroline Cooper.

Morris had immediately pointed to Cooper's photograph.

Jackie's team had requested access to Cooper's bank accounts and cell phone records, and the case had quickly escalated from very circumstantial to extremely incriminating.

Jackie's reverie was interrupted by Tommy DeLuca's butt being parked on her desk.

"You okay, Rossi?" he asked with a wink. "You do know this is your show, right? You should be center of attention, milking it for all it's worth, not hiding away over here on your own."

DeLuca was a great cop who had a terrible track record with women. His nose was still off-center from the time he'd been punched by the young private eye he was dating after she found out about Mrs. DeLuca.

Jackie smiled. "I'm fine, Tommy. Just tired is all."

"A bunch of us are heading to the bar. You coming?"

"I'll meet you down there. I have a couple things to take care of here first."

"Sure thing, Rossi."

"Oh, and DeLuca? Make mine a large Rioja, huh? This white wine is revolting."

DeLuca grinned. "You got it. See you down there."

He walked off, and Jackie went back to the file and to her thoughts.

Caroline Cooper's bank statement revealed that a cash withdrawal of $15,000 had been made on the day of Bianco's murder. Such a large sum of money had meant she'd had to pay a visit to her local branch with proof of identity. CCTV from the bank showed it was, indeed, Cooper who'd made the withdrawal herself.

Her phone records revealed several text messages to and from an unknown number in the days leading up to the crime and on the night of. When Rossi had accessed those deleted texts from Cooper's cell phone, they'd indicated Cooper was being blackmailed over another blackmail plot she had instigated herself. Jim Sanders's name had been mentioned in those texts.

Jackie had hauled Sanders in for questioning, and he had admitted that, yes, he had been the victim of blackmail. Bianco had hit on him in a bar, he'd been drunk and dumb enough to make out with her on the street, and an unknown person had later mailed incriminating photographs to him at the studio, with a demand to step down from his role at *Rise & Shine*.

"Why the hell didn't you come to me with this at the time?" Rossi had asked, exasperated. "We've known each other for years, Jim. Why didn't you trust me?"

"It was nothing personal, Jackie," he'd replied defensively. "The way I saw it, I could lose my career, or I could lose my family. My wife and kids won."

"And when Bianco turned up dead in a hotel room? You didn't think to come forward then and, you know, assist in a homicide investigation?"

Sanders had scoffed at the suggestion. "I might as well have held out my wrists and begged you to throw a pair of handcuffs on them. We both know I would've been a prime suspect, even though I never touched her."

He'd then told Jackie about his meeting in Central Park with an unknown woman, who'd given him information suggesting Caroline Cooper had been behind his blackmail.

"Again, you didn't think this information might be worth sharing?" Jackie had fumed, shaking her head.

Sanders had shrugged and tried to give her an endearing smile.

"And you can wipe that stupid grin off your face, Jim. I should arrest you right now for obstruction of justice."

Jackie hadn't arrested him. He'd agreed to appear as a witness for the prosecution, even though the useless bastard had destroyed the photos, blackmail note, and the customer receipt from Click Photography in Cooper's name that had been passed to him by the woman in the park.

The brunette who'd set up the meet in Central Park was another thing that made Jackie uneasy. Two female witnesses, both of whom didn't want to be identified, and who'd both had key information about Caroline Cooper.

Or was it the same woman?

But how would an eyewitness at the scene of Bianco's murder also have information about a blackmail plot involving Jim Sanders? It made absolutely no sense to Jackie.

Cooper's DNA sample was a match for the strands of hair found on Bianco. Her fingerprints were a match for those found on the hotel room's door handle, both inside and out. And the knife that had been used to stab Bianco thirty-nine times was found behind a cupboard in the laundry room at Cooper's home in Bedford following a search of the property.

The case was a slam dunk.

Jackie swallowed down the rest of the wine. It really was vile.

The final aspect of the case that bothered her was Cooper's insistence that she was innocent. Right up until today's guilty verdict, she had never once wavered. Had point-blank refused a plea deal from day one.

And the reason it gnawed at Jackie was that she didn't believe Cooper went to the Fairview Hotel with the intention of killing Anna Bianco.

Cooper had already withdrawn the $15,000 from the bank. She'd admitted she had gone there with the intention of handing over the cash, but claimed Bianco was already dead when she arrived. It seemed to Jackie like something had gone badly wrong during the handoff between the two women.

Before the DNA results had changed the direction of the investigation, a bunch of sleazy men who had been honeytrapped by Bianco had been interviewed. One in particular, a guy by the name of Al Parker, stood out because his experience had been very different from the others.

While those "victims" had been photographed kissing Bianco in alleyways and outside bars, Parker said he had gone to a hotel with her so that they could have sex. It was while she was using the bathroom that he claimed to have found weapons hidden under the mattress. Cans of pepper spray, a hammer, a knife. He'd fled immediately, fearing that she was going to "bump him off," as he'd put it. By which he meant he feared Bianco was planning on murdering him.

Jackie had wondered if Al Parker was a fantasist when he'd made the statement, if all the talk of sex and weaponry and his life being in danger wasn't his way of trying to get some attention for himself. Then, after Caroline Cooper's arrest, she'd started to wonder if he was telling the truth. That the knife used to murder Anna Bianco had been her own, that she had taken it to the Fairview Hotel herself for protection or for some other purpose.

At that point, Jackie no longer believed the murder was premeditated.

Cooper could have agreed to a plea bargain, saved the city a lot of money on a trial, and guaranteed herself a much shorter sentence than the one she was facing now. But she hadn't, despite the mountain of evidence against her. Why hadn't she?

Jackie sighed and closed the file. "Enough, Rossi," she said out loud. "It's done. No more thinking."

She dropped the folder into a drawer in a file cabinet labeled "Closed Cases." But, even as she did so, Jackie wondered how long it would stay in there. How many times she would pluck the file back out again, and go over the details once more, and ponder if there was something she'd missed.

She picked up her cell phone and opened the Uber app. She was dog tired and should really go home and spend some time with Doug. Instead, she typed in the bar's address as the destination. The app reported the taxi was six minutes away.

Jackie scrunched up the plastic cup and fired it into the wastebasket under the desk. She needed a real drink, but it didn't feel much like a celebration.

34

JIM

"Which one?"

Jim Sanders held up three neckties—a pink-and-purple paisley-patterned one, a blue-and-silver striped one, and a plain red one.

Debra lay on their bed, wearing a black satin slip. She peered over the top of her Chanel reading glasses at the options, then said, "The patterned one."

"You don't think it's too loud?"

"No, you want to make a statement, not fade into the background. You want everyone who's watching tomorrow morning to know that Jim Sanders is back."

He nodded. Debra was right. As usual.

Jim Sanders *was* back.

Or he would be within a matter of hours. Back on the *Rise & Shine* couch where he belonged.

Debra was back too.

Back in their home. Back in their marital bed.

She'd reached out to him after the story broke about Caroline Cooper's arrest for murder and the allegations that she'd also blackmailed Jim to land his job.

"No wonder you'd changed, Jim," his wife had said when she'd come over that first time to talk things over. "The strain must have been terrible. I should have known something was wrong and tried to help instead of walking away."

She'd told him she'd only realized just how much Jim loved her and the girls when it emerged that he'd quit his beloved job to protect his family and prevent details of his liaison with Anna Bianco from being made public.

Jim and Debra had ended up in bed together, and the sex had been incredible—better than it had been in years. It was like they were discovering each other for the first time all over again, rather than simply going through the motions, which is what it had been like for way too long.

Afterward, she'd confessed that things hadn't worked out with her lover, Brian. Jim had been right. Her boss had no intention of leaving his wife and had been horrified when Debra told him she'd left Jim after revealing the affair. She had joined a rival PR firm and was renting a one-bedroom apartment not far from her new office.

She wanted to come home, and she wanted Jim back.

There had been a few dalliances with young women after his wife walked out on him. Jim had needed something to get the blood pumping after spending all day on the golf course or at the community garden. And there was no doubt those nights had been fun, that he'd enjoyed the feel of firm flesh and exploring new territory so to speak. But the truth was, he missed Debra like mad. He still loved her. He just didn't function right without her.

Even so, he'd been reluctant to rush into a reconciliation. Did Debra really want him back? Or was it a return to the fancy house and the luxury lifestyle that was the true motivation behind her wanting to give their marriage another shot?

Then his old producer had gotten in touch to ask Jim to meet him for dinner. Over lobster thermidor and chilled martinis at one of the best restaurants in town, they'd discussed Jim's possible return to *Rise & Shine*—*if* the jury delivered the right verdict when Caroline Cooper's case went to trial.

From that moment on, Jim had set about preparing for his return to the small screen. He'd ditched the golf and the gardening, much to the disappointment of the community garden group. He didn't care. He had no intention of spending a minute longer with those old-timers. Not when he had another shot at the big time. He'd renewed his membership at the gym, pounding the treadmill every morning and lifting weights every other day.

And then he'd told Debra he wanted her back.

Jim figured he had a much better chance of earning the forgiveness of the nation for his extramarital shenanigans with Anna Bianco if his wife had already forgiven him.

Jim and Debra would be providing a united front in a sit-down interview with a Sunday newspaper this week—for a nice, juicy fee, of course—where they would open up about their marriage and pose for happy, smiley photographs together.

Before then, though, was his big return to the couch. There, Jim would be expected to reveal all about how he'd become embroiled in a tale of lust, blackmail, and ultimately, murder.

"Which shirt?" he asked. He liked how comfortable this all felt. Him, standing there in his boxers and T-shirt asking for sartorial advice. His wife, taking charge like she'd always done.

Debra sat up and surveyed the row of pristine, pressed shirts hanging on the rail in the closet behind him.

"Definitely plain white. Not the pale lilac. The image you want is 'bags of confidence' not 'children's entertainer.' Plus, the white will look good with the tan, which has come out great by the way."

He'd treated himself to a spray tan, a facial, a men's manicure, and a haircut.

Jim Sanders was back all right.

He knew what questions to expect from his cohosts, Darnell Morgan and Sal Speirs, and was already mentally preparing the answers.

Darnell/Sal: How did you feel about the death of Anna Bianco?

Jim: I obviously only knew her for a short time, a matter of hours, but it's desperately sad. Such a promising, young life snuffed out so soon. My heart breaks for her parents . . .

What were the parents' names again? Don and Theresa? Dan and Tricia? He'd better check.

Jim decided he'd also throw some compliments in Jackie Rossi's direction. He suspected she was still pissed at him for not reporting the blackmail. He knew she'd been bluffing when she'd threatened to arrest him—they went way back after all, and she'd always had a bit of a thing for him—but he'd have to work his way back into her good graces as soon as possible now that he was back on the job and might need her for a story one day.

Then there was the toughest question of all.

Darnell/Sal: Why do you think Caroline Cooper targeted you?

Jim: Honestly, guys, I have no idea. It could have been any one of us. I'm just glad it was me and that you were both spared the ordeal that I had to go through.

But Jim had a pretty good idea why Caroline had set out to destroy him. She'd spent months flirting with him whenever they found themselves in each other's company. A squeeze of the arm here, a flutter of the eyelashes there. Then, when she got what she wanted, when Jim had thrown her name into the mix for the entertainment reporter's gig at the network, she was suddenly colder than a snowball in Alaska.

They'd been seen together, drinking in a bar, the night she'd turned him down. When Jim had been asked about it later, he'd given the impression that the night had been a lot more successful than it was. It had seemed harmless at the time. Then the rumor mill had gone into overdrive, and there was nothing he could do other than accept the knowing nudges and winks with a sly grin.

Once Caroline was part of the team, Jim had tried to smooth things over at a Christmas lunch. He'd switched the place settings so he'd be next to her for the meal and have a chance to talk to her and to explain. But she'd ignored him completely. Humiliated him.

Back then, Caroline Cooper had been gorgeous. Sexy, vibrant, smart, funny. The woman he'd seen in court these past weeks had been none of those things. She'd always been slim, but now she was just plain skinny, and her clothes hung on her like they belonged to someone else. Her hair was lank with black roots. The dark circles under her eyes suggested she hadn't slept properly in months. She appeared to have aged a decade.

Jim should have felt sorry for her. But he didn't. There was only fear.

Anna Bianco had been stabbed thirty-nine times.

Jim Sanders knew it could easily have been him in those crime-scene photos instead of her.

35

BOBBY

Bobby Khan's fingers trembled as they struck the keyboard.

Shock and excitement.

He was still stunned by today's verdict, that Caroline Cooper had really been sent down for murder.

Shocked but not surprised.

Not after listening to the evidence every day from the public gallery. He'd watched the lawyers on both sides go through the necessary theatrics, had studied the faces of the twelve jurors, and he had known there was no way Caroline was walking out of that courthouse a free woman.

When the jury foreman delivered the guilty verdict, she'd let out a little cry of surprise. Or maybe it was pain, like a wounded animal. Then she'd kind of crumpled.

Bobby had watched her diminish in front of his eyes as the trial had unfolded. In the end, she didn't look capable of killing a spider she'd found in her bathtub, never mind another human being.

But that's exactly what Caroline Cooper was—a cold-blooded murderer.

When Bobby had first been tipped off about her arrest, he'd assumed it was for some minor offense. A traffic infraction or fudging her taxes or a domestic dispute with that old husband of hers. It would still make a good story, though, especially if he could get his hands on a copy of her mug shot.

He'd tried Jackie Rossi, and she hadn't picked up. Another of his sources within the NYPD couldn't be reached either. His calls had gone unanswered all day, and that's when he'd started to suspect something big was going down. He'd wondered if there had been a break in the Anna Bianco case. But he hadn't anticipated that the "something big" would turn out to be Caroline Cooper being accused of murder. Blackmail too.

When Bobby first started covering the Bianco homicide and saw a photo of the victim, he was convinced he knew her from someplace. But where? He'd racked his brain, trying to come up with the answer.

A beautiful redhead. The kind of woman who made an impact.

Then he'd remembered—or he thought he had. One night, years earlier, when he'd been out drinking with Leonard Blaylock. Back in the days when his old pal was still good fun and before he'd completely lost his marbles after being dumped by Caroline.

Bobby had pointed out a gorgeous woman, who he was sure had the hots for Lenny, but Lenny had denied hooking up with her or even speaking to her. Could it have been Anna Bianco? Bobby had been drunk and hadn't spent much time in the bar, so he couldn't say for sure. He'd almost called Lenny to ask him if it was the same woman, but what did it matter if it was?

"I once had a beer in the same bar as a murder victim."

It was hardly a story, was it?

There was also a chance that Bobby had seen one of her crappy movies and that's where he knew her face from.

How odd, though, that it turned out to be Lenny's ex, Caroline, who'd actually known Bianco?

Bobby *had* gotten in touch with his old buddy to try to sign him up for a series of exclusives that the *Reporter* would run if Caroline was found guilty. He figured Lenny would show a bit of loyalty toward Bobby and his former employers. He could already picture the headlines:

My lover, the killer

My life with a murderer

Murderer's ex tells all: It could have been me

But Leonard hadn't been interested. He was in a new relationship, he was very happy with the woman, he had moved on with his life, and he didn't want to dwell on the past. He had no comment to make about Caroline Cooper's conviction to the *Reporter* or to anyone else.

The snub had stung, but at least Bobby wouldn't be trumped by a rival media outlet if Leonard wasn't talking at all.

There had been no point in pursuing Jim Sanders. He'd apparently been signed up by a Sunday newspaper with a bigger budget than the *Reporter* and would be spilling his guts on the *Rise & Shine* couch in any case. Plus, there was the small matter of Bobby contacting the network about sexual-harassment allegations against the man, which had turned out to be completely unfounded. Bobby's face burned as he thought about how he'd been played by Caroline as part of her dirty little blackmail plot.

Bobby had delivered some great front pages throughout the Bianco investigation, and his big fear was missing out on a scoop when everything finally came to a head. He'd known he would need something big to run with once the verdict was announced.

The one trump card he had was his previous friendship with the accused. Bobby and Amina had often gone on double dates with Leonard and Caroline, and the foursome had even vacationed together down in Florida the summer before Bobby's oldest kid was born.

My friend, the murderer

It wasn't bad, and Bobby liked the idea of having a starring role in the story himself, but it wasn't great. His editor had given the first-person piece the green light. It would make a double-page story but probably not the front page. It was missing that extra oomph that would set it apart from similar stories by every other reporter who'd known Caroline Cooper.

Then he'd been sitting in court one day, following the trial as usual, when the jury had been shown the item of clothing the knife had been wrapped in when it had been recovered during a search of the defendant's house.

Bobby's pencil had frozen above his notepad. His heart had thundered in his chest. He'd leaned forward in his seat for a better look. Yes, he was sure of it.

He'd seen that item of clothing before.

Caroline's social media accounts had all been deactivated following her arrest. Leonard didn't have any social media profiles anymore either. Bobby was prolific on Twitter but had never had any interest in Facebook or Instagram.

But Amina had an Instagram account.

Bobby had left the courthouse immediately and driven home, where he'd asked his wife to hand over her phone. He'd frantically scrolled through dozens of photos on her Instagram feed, while she'd watched with a bemused smile on her face.

Eventually, he'd found what he was looking for.

"Yes!" he'd shouted, waking his baby daughter, who'd been having an afternoon nap. "You fucking beauty."

He'd planted a big smacker on Amina's lips before taking a screenshot of the image. Her account was set to private, but Bobby was taking no chances. He had told Amina to temporarily deactivate it until the trial was over. He didn't want anyone else getting their hands on that photograph.

Bobby read over his copy now, then leaned back in his chair, satisfied. He opened the file containing the photo that he had sent to the picture desk an hour earlier.

The photograph that would be splashed across the front page of tomorrow's *Reporter* alongside the words *Picture Exclusive*.

His hands were still shaking. Mostly excitement now.

The photo showed four people huddled together on the terrace of a beach bar in Miami. Holding cocktails and beers, the sun blazing bright behind them. Amina was on the far left, and Leonard was on the far right. In the middle were Bobby and Caroline.

Caroline was wearing a pink T-shirt with a faded Disney print on the front.

It was the same T-shirt that had been held up in the courthouse that day. Stained with Anna Bianco's blood. Used to conceal a murder weapon.

36

LEONARD

Leonard Blaylock wasn't a photographer. He never took any of the photos in his collection himself.

Except for the night he photographed the dead body of Anna Bianco after he murdered her.

Five years earlier, his life had fallen apart when he thought he'd accidentally killed the woman he'd known as Red. In the days, weeks, and months that followed, he'd seen her everywhere he went—in the grocery store when he was buying bread and milk, on the street laughing with friends, drinking an orange-red cocktail in one of his favorite bars.

Except, on that occasion, it wasn't his guilty conscience playing tricks on him.

Red had been sitting at the bar, flirting with a man Leonard recognized. He'd met Jim Sanders, the charismatic host of *Rise & Shine*, a handful of times over the years while covering the crime beat, and he had seen him drinking in the bar near Times Square often. The redhead wasn't wearing a red dress. She'd been dressed in tight leather pants and a low-cut blouse, and her hair had been a slightly different color than what he'd remembered.

Leonard had gotten right up close to her to make sure it really was Red.

It was.

She'd stared straight at him—then turned her attention back to Sanders. Leonard had a beard and longer hair, and he was a bit heavier around the middle; but the woman had ruined his life, and she hadn't even recognized him.

Leonard had driven to the bar straight from an interview and had planned on walking home after a few drinks, picking up his car the following day. He'd barely touched his first beer. He was okay to drive. So, he'd waited outside in his Chevy Malibu.

An hour or so later, Red had left with Sanders. He appeared to be a lot more drunk than she did. Leonard had an involuntary shiver of déjà vu. They had walked down the street and huddled in the entrance to an office building where they had shared a long, lingering kiss. Then they'd both hailed separate taxis.

Leonard had followed the one Red got into.

It dropped her at a modest apartment building in Queens. He watched a light go on in a window soon after. Leonard studied the apartment numbers on the panel outside the doorway and guessed Red's was 3A. He had no idea if she lived alone. He made a note of the street name and the apartment number.

He was back early the next morning. It was a Saturday. He had a long wait. She didn't emerge until past noon and climbed into a heap-of-junk car parked on the street. Again, he tailed her, all the way back to Manhattan and Central Park. She left her car on a side street and headed into the park on foot, making her way to the Loeb Boathouse. Then she stood on the path looking out at the water as though she were simply enjoying the view.

But Red hadn't been there for the view. She'd been meeting someone.

That someone was Caroline Cooper.

When Leonard saw his ex-fiancée, parts of a puzzle finally began to fall into place.

He'd spent the previous night lying awake, his brain busy with questions and possibilities. It was clear that he'd been set up to believe that Red had died in that hotel room. What wasn't clear, while he'd tossed and turned, tangled in damp bedsheets, was who was behind it.

In that moment in the park, he had known exactly who it was.

A brown envelope had changed hands between the two women, and then days later, Leonard had watched as Jim Sanders stunned viewers by quitting *Rise & Shine* and Caroline Cooper was announced as his replacement on the couch.

Leonard's skills as an investigative reporter were rusty, but it didn't take him too long to figure out what exactly had happened. Red occasionally worked out of a grubby photography studio in Queens that also offered surveillance work. Click's website clarified that "surveillance work" meant honeytrapping people on behalf of their suspicious spouses and partners. Caroline had presumably found out about his romantic indiscretions and had hired Red. Except it had gone way beyond a simple honeytrap. Caroline had set out to destroy Leonard—and she'd almost succeeded.

She had then paid the same woman to help plot the downfall of Jim Sanders so she could steal his job.

When Leonard thought about everything he'd lost—his job, his dad, his sanity—he had wanted to scream and shout and smash stuff. He'd wanted to punch someone, hurt them, make them suffer. More than anything, he had wanted revenge.

A plan had begun to form in his mind.

It would take time. Months to get it right. But it would be worth it.

Caroline had, as expected, changed her cell phone number after the split with Leonard and since becoming a minor celebrity.

But he had a good idea where he'd be able to find her new digits. He still had a security pass for the *Reporter's* office, his former employers having agreed to allow him continued access to the library for his freelance work. He mostly kept his visits nocturnal, to avoid running into former coworkers during regular hours. Leonard preferred the quiet of the night shift.

On this occasion, he had made a point of swiping into the library before heading upstairs to the newsroom floor, where he'd helped himself to a coffee in the kitchen and had then taken his "research" to one of the empty desks.

Bobby Khan's desk.

Like a lot of reporters, Bobby kept a physical contacts book, as well as storing important numbers on his phone. He was also careless when it came to other folks' personal information. Sure enough, his desk drawer was unlocked, and his contacts book was stuffed inside along with steno pads, pens, spare batteries, and assorted stationery items. Leonard had flicked to the section labeled "C" and snapped the entry with Caroline Cooper's details with the camera on his phone.

He then made another visit to Red's apartment building, this time around the back where the trash cans were located. He removed two garbage bags, stuffed them into the trunk of his car, and then dumped their contents onto his dining table and meticulously sifted through the garbage. A cell phone number was on a discarded invoice for a cosmetics company order for apartment 3A. So was her real name—Anna Bianco.

Leonard had purchased two burner phones. He sent a text from one to Caroline demanding $15,000, or details of the Sanders blackmail would be made public. When she didn't respond, he followed up with another message instructing Caroline to drop off the cash at the Fairview Hotel. The room was to be accessed via the fire door at the rear of the building. He had signed that one "Red."

Leonard had then used the other burner to send a message to Red from "Caroline Cooper's new cell phone" to arrange a meeting at the Fairview Hotel about another job. The text from "Caroline" asked Red to make a reservation and pay for her usual room on the first floor so she could access it discreetly via the fire door at the rear of the building—which would be propped open by Red. Caroline was a celebrity, married to a hotelier, and couldn't be seen reserving a room in a hotel that wasn't part of the exclusive Belman chain. Red was assured that "Caroline" would remunerate her for the cost of the room, as well as pay her handsomely for the new gig.

When Leonard followed a pale-faced Caroline to the local branch of her bank, he had known the game was in play. What he didn't know, for sure, was whether he would be able to kill someone in cold blood.

As it turned out, he had nothing to worry about.

When he walked into the hotel room—the same one he'd stumbled into, drunk and horny, years earlier—Red still hadn't remembered him. Not really. There had been surprise and more than a little trepidation at finding a stranger in front of her and maybe just a hint of recognition as she'd frowned at him.

"Who the hell are you?" she'd asked, backing away from him. "Do I know you?"

"My name is Leonard Blaylock. I'm the guy whose life you ruined."

Finally, the full realization of who he was dawned on her.

Then she'd *laughed* at him.

"Get the hell out of my hotel room, you loser. I'm expecting someone."

Something inside of Leonard snapped just then. He took his hands out of his pockets, and that's when Red noticed the knife and the latex gloves.

She begged for her life. She told him Caroline was supposed to reveal the truth to him after a few days. She claimed to have no idea about the devastating effect that her "prank" had had on his life.

He didn't care what she had to say. It was too late for apologies and explanations. One minute, Anna Bianco was crying and pleading. The next, she was dead on the bed, Leonard standing over her, soaked in her blood. The attack had been carried out in a frenzy, but somehow, he had then managed to clear his head enough to carry out the work that still needed to be done.

First, the photos.

He'd brought with him a duffel bag from which he removed a camera. Leonard framed the shot—capturing the body, the blood, the knife—then pressed the shutter button over and over again.

Click. Click. Click.

When he was done, he returned the camera to the bag and removed a small tin. Inside the tin was a pair of tweezers and several strands of long blond hair. They'd been plucked from the hairbrush Caroline had left in his bedside table along with her other junk. He'd read somewhere that DNA could only be extracted from hair that still had the root attached, so he'd carefully selected two suitable strands with the tweezers and placed them inside Anna Bianco's fist. He'd then removed the gloves and the bloodied hoodie and sweatpants he was wearing and swapped them for clean clothing. The soiled items, the knife, and Red's cell phone went into the duffel bag, which he took with him as he left by the open fire door.

Leonard had then watched from the shadows as Caroline made her way to the rear of the hotel and entered through the open fire door. Her hands were all over that door, leaving behind lots of nice fresh prints. He guessed the door handle to Anna Bianco's hotel room would be the same. He held his breath, waiting to see if she would do the right thing and call the police. Seconds later, he breathed out a sigh of relief. As expected, she'd reacted exactly the same way Leonard had almost five years earlier.

Caroline Cooper had fled the scene.

The next phase of his plan was to recruit an ally. Someone who could help with his "investigation," garner information from Ron Kincaid, alert Jim Sanders to Caroline's role in his blackmail plot, and eventually, tip off the cops about Caroline Cooper being at the Fairview Hotel the night Anna Bianco was murdered. Leonard was familiar to Sanders and especially to Jackie Rossi, his old contact at the NYPD. It had to be someone with no known connection to himself.

Someone like his online buddy at the Found Film forum.

The "mystery film" that showed the murder of a young woman would be the hook to reel in WVR-16. Leonard had sat on the film for a month after the murder, waiting for the right moment. Then she'd tipped him off about a potential haul at Chelsea Flea, and it'd been the perfect opportunity.

Mostly, it had all worked out beautifully. Caroline was in prison, convicted of the murder of Anna Bianco. Two women who had wronged him. One dead, one locked up. Both paying for what they'd done to him.

There had been a few unexpected developments along the way, though.

Firstly, the names of Remy Sullivan and Walter Shankland had only been thrown into the mix to add a veneer of authenticity to Leonard's "investigation" for Martha's benefit. There had to be other suspects; he didn't want to point the finger at Caroline straightaway. Sure, as his ex-partner, she was always the most likely culprit. But Leonard figured Martha would feel a lot more comfortable about giving Caroline's name to the cops if they'd ruled out everyone else by then. A severe beating at the hands of Max Sullivan's buddies hadn't been part of the script.

He'd only gone through with the charade of asking about Sullivan at the Times Square protest because he'd known Martha would be expecting answers. He'd told her to stick to online sleuthing to keep her away from Sullivan's mob, then realized she might actually come up with some answers herself about Max's whereabouts around the time of the murder. If Leonard lied and gave her bogus information that didn't match up with what she found out online, she would have been suspicious. He figured it would be simpler just to go to the protest and ask some questions rather than risk being caught in a lie. Ditto Shankland. Plus, Leonard wanted to know if the man was still stalking women. If he was, there might've been a story there for the papers.

Then, after he'd ransacked his own apartment, Leonard had realized he couldn't bring himself to do the same to Martha's place. It'd been painful enough smashing up his favorite camera in order to make his break-in look convincing without destroying her stuff too. So, he had settled for an attempted burglary instead.

It had taken a lot of online searching to find a car rental company with a dark gray Jeep he could hire for the day so that he could drive away from Martha's street at high speed just as she returned home from work. It wasn't the exact same model he'd spotted in Caroline's driveway, but it was close enough. The lipstick case that he'd dropped outside Martha's door and the perfume he'd spritzed in her lobby had both been found in the drawer in his bedroom containing his ex's belongings.

Ditto the Disney T-shirt that had once belonged to Caroline, which he'd wrapped the murder weapon in before stashing it in her laundry room the day he'd visited her house in Bedford to confront her about Click Photography. The same day Caroline had admitted to knowing about his breakdown, yet she had done nothing to end his misery at the time, despite being fully aware that his belief that he had killed Red was the real cause of his mental anguish. In that moment, he'd known for sure that she deserved to have her life destroyed just like his had been. That she deserved to lose everything—and everyone—who was important to her. Just like him.

It was almost poetic.

By far the biggest unexpected development in Leonard's plan had been WVR-16. His mystery-film buddy. His coinvestigator. His friend. His lover.

The last thing Leonard had expected was to fall in love.

But he had. Completely and utterly. It was like nothing he'd ever experienced before. He finally had closure. He was finally happy.

Sliding doors.

Leonard Blaylock had a reason to live again—and her name was Martha Weaver.

37

MARTHA

Martha Weaver loved to play detective.

She'd been a fan of mysteries since she was a little girl: Nancy Drew books from her local library, old episodes of *Murder, She Wrote* on TV.

The first time she heard about mystery film was while sourcing cheap camera film online for a photography hobby that would soon become her career. The idea intrigued her. The name even more so. Mystery film. There was nothing Martha enjoyed more than a good mystery.

Like other enthusiasts, she got a thrill out of not knowing what those used rolls of film would reveal. Would the resulting photos be spoiled? Would they be boring? Would they provide an insight into the lives of complete strangers?

It was the little details that really got her blood pumping. A car license plate. An advertisement billboard in the background. A restaurant sign. A street name. A style of haircut or outfit that had long since gone out of fashion.

They were all little clues about the lives of the people who were captured in those photos or who had been behind the camera. And social media and Google searches made it possible to track those strangers down.

Her first success story had given Martha one of the biggest buzzes of her life. She didn't drink a lot, and she'd never even so much as tried drugs, but that rush of adrenaline had been intoxicating.

The roll of film had featured a series of photos taken at a Bon Jovi concert. The audience appeared to be at an outdoor venue. The attire of the concertgoers suggested a warm summer night. The decade was probably the nineties. There were three teenage girls in the photos who appeared to be around sixteen or seventeen years old.

By picking out small details in the images, Martha was able to ascertain that the concert in question had taken place at Jones Beach Theater in Wantagh in July 1995 and had been part of the band's These Days tour. Better still, she'd eventually tracked down one of the girls on Facebook. Her name was Laura Silvester, and, at the time of Martha's discovery, she was in her late thirties and married with two kids. She still had the same long red curly hair and slender figure from that night decades earlier.

Martha had taped the before and after pics of Laura Silvester into a photo album. That had been the start of it.

When she began sharing lots of private messages with another Found Film forum member—who called himself LAB123—she couldn't resist keeping a note of the clues he let slip about himself.

After a while, Martha started to wonder if she was falling for LAB123. By then, she was single, having endured a traumatic breakup with David following his affair with one of their neighbors. She'd occasionally catch a glimpse of David's car from her living room window and knew he was still involved with his mistress, who was now presumably his girlfriend. Martha would then see them together when she'd show up at the same restaurant they were dining in or the same bar where they were enjoying a drink. David called it stalking; Martha called it not hiding away as though she were the guilty party, rather than them. Eventually, they'd moved away. Deleted all their social media accounts.

Martha wondered if she was simply lonely. Maybe she didn't really have feelings for the man on the forum. How could she? She didn't even know him, had never met him, knew next to nothing about him and his life. But what she did know was that he was witty and attentive and smart, and she enjoyed spending time with him, even if it was only in front of a computer screen.

After a while, her notepad contained enough information about LAB123 to find out who he really was. She felt sweaty and excited and guilty at the prospect. Probably how an addict felt when they knew they were about to give in to their desire for a fix.

That day, sitting in her car, her Nikon raised, lens focused on the denim-and-plaid-clad figure emerging from the Hell's Kitchen building, Martha couldn't deny it any longer. She was in love with the man she now knew as Leonard Blaylock.

When Leonard had discovered those very same photos weeks later in her dark room, he had asked if she had any more photographs of him, and she'd told him no; there were no others. Her covert surveillance of him had been a one-off.

Martha had lied.

She had followed Leonard Blaylock many more times. Saw him eating on his own in a restaurant and wished she could join him. Helping an elderly lady with her shopping. Interviewing someone in a coffee shop for one of his features. Holding a door open for a harried young mom holding a toddler by the hand and with a baby in a stroller. On each occasion, her love for him grew stronger.

She'd also followed him the night he'd parked his car on a quiet street in Chelsea, before setting off on foot.

Martha had followed him to an old dirty-yellow building that housed the Fairview Hotel. He was carrying a duffel bag, as though he was going to check in for an overnight stay. Instead, Leonard had made his way to the rear of the building and entered via a fire door that was propped open by half a brick. Then a tall shadow had moved across a first-floor window.

Leonard.

Martha had experienced a whole cocktail of emotions—and none of them good. Jealousy, anger, betrayal. Leonard—*her* Leonard—was clearly meeting another woman for an illicit tryst. A night of lust and maybe even love. It didn't matter that Leonard had no idea who Martha was. She was devastated all the same.

She'd found herself walking toward the window. Tears dampened her cheeks. She had to see for herself. As she got closer, she heard two voices. One male, one female. Her heart broke in two. Martha aimed the camera at a gap where the curtain hadn't been pulled all the way across the barred glass. When the focus of the lens sharpened, the scene inside the hotel room was not what Martha had expected to see.

A struggle. A knife. And lots and lots of blood. Martha had pressed down on the shutter button again and again.

She was horrified and numbed and shocked.

But she was also relieved.

Leonard hadn't betrayed her with another woman.

In the weeks that followed, Martha told herself that he must have had good reason to do what he did in that hotel room. She'd gotten to know him online; she'd watched him for months. She knew he was a good person, didn't she? A good person who had done a bad thing. Then he'd messaged her to ask for her help, and she'd known there was no way she was going to turn down the opportunity to find out why he had killed the woman in the hotel room.

Now she knew, and her opinion of Leonard Blaylock hadn't changed.

A good man who had done a bad thing.

She still loved him. Even more so now that she'd gotten to know him properly.

But Martha had also known she had to protect herself.

Now she had someone else to protect too.

Martha thought of the test she'd been carrying around in her purse for the last couple of days. Two lines in the tiny window. After all these years of photographing picture-perfect families every single day, she'd finally have what she always wanted for herself. She would break the news to Leonard tonight. It would be a double celebration following Caroline Cooper's conviction for the murder of Anna Bianco.

Sure, Martha knew Leonard had lied to her, pretending he didn't know who had killed Red. But she liked that he'd picked her to be his ally, that he'd gone to so much trouble with his fake investigation for her benefit. There had been a few worrying moments along the way, though. Leonard being beaten up. Finding her photos of him in her dark room. The revelation that the police had the killer's DNA on file—but Leonard had been so sure it would be a match for Caroline that Martha knew he must have planted evidence at the scene.

Martha was sure Leonard would never cheat on her the way he did with Caroline, that he would never treat her so badly. Especially not now that two would soon become three. A proper family.

But it didn't hurt to have a little insurance policy.

Photos of Leonard Blaylock, in a hotel room, covered in a dead woman's blood. Locked away in the safe in her dark room where he'd never find them.

Just in case.

THE END

ACKNOWLEDGEMENTS

I first had the idea for this book back in 2019 after reading a newspaper article about a rather unusual hobby—people who develop the lost camera film of complete strangers. I was intrigued by the prospect of delving into other peoples' lives and what those photographs might reveal. It seemed like an interesting premise for a novel. Of course, my being a crime writer, that would mean my protagonist discovering something really bad on a roll of "mystery film"—and a photo depicting a murder scene is pretty much as bad as it gets! From there, *The Dark Room* was born.

It's hard to believe that *The Dark Room* is my fifth book. It's also my very first standalone, so if you're a new reader of mine, thank you for giving it a go. If you're already a fan of my series, I hope you enjoyed it as much as the Jessica Shaw thrillers.

Now for the thanks. To my fantastic agent, Phil Patterson, and all the team at Marjacq for everything that you do for me. To my amazing editor, Victoria Haslam, and everyone at Thomas & Mercer for doing such a brilliant job with my books. A special shout-out to developmental editor, Ian Pindar, for making this one so much better.

Big thanks to all the bloggers and reviewers for helping to spread the word and to my crime-writing pals for their friendship and support—you know who you are. *The Dark Room* is dedicated to my best friend, Lorraine Reis—here's another book for your and Darren's conservatory library! Thanks also to Danny Stewart for being my book-festival buddy and for letting me waffle on about my writing for hours at a time.

A special mention for my family. Mum, Scott, Alison, Ben, Sam, and Cody—you mean the world to me, and your love and support is invaluable. I couldn't do this without you. And to my dad, whom I think about every single day.

Last but not least, a massive thank-you to my readers. I get to do my dream job every day because of you. PS—this book contains three Easter eggs relating to the Jessica Shaw series. Did you find them all? Send me an email and let me know!

ABOUT THE AUTHOR

Lisa Gray is an Amazon #1, *Washington Post*, and *Wall Street Journal* bestselling author. She previously worked as the chief Scottish soccer writer at the Press Association and the books editor at the *Daily Record* Saturday Magazine. She is also the author of *Thin Air*, *Bad Memory*, *Dark Highway*, and *Lonely Hearts*. Lisa now writes full-time. Learn more at www.lisagraywriter.com and connect with Lisa on social media @lisagraywriter.